MW00881141

A neverending night exists beneath the veil of day,
giving life to shadows who still cling to yesterday.
We cannot put to rest that which refuses to expire.
Darkness comes alive, alight within the vale of fire.

Vale of Fire

By

Nicoline Evans

Vale of Fire copyright © 2019

Author: Nicoline Evans – www.nicolineevans.com
Editor: Max Dobson – www.polished-pen.com
Cover Design: Dan Elijah Fajardo –
www.behance.net/dandingeroz

To my beta readers and everyone else who has offered support (in all ways, shapes, and sizes) during this entire process—thank you!

All rights reserved. Without limiting the rights under copyright reserved above, no part of this publication may be reproduced, stored in or introduced into a retrieval system (excluding initial purchase), or transmitted, in any form, or by any means (electronic, mechanical, photocopying, recording, or otherwise) without the prior written permission of the above author of this book.

This is a work of fiction. Names, characters, places, brands, media, institutions, and incidents are either the product of the author's imagination or are used fictitiously. The author acknowledges the trademarked status and trademark owners of various products referenced in this work of fiction, which have been used without permission. The publication/use of these trademarks is not authorized, associated with, or sponsored by the trademark owners.

A waltz with the neverending night

Prologue

Juniper hobbled as fast as she could toward Roscoe's vined cocoon. His fate depended on her.

::*You are not well*,:: Rooney sensed as he trotted beside her.

::*I will be far worse if Roscoe dies. I need to get to him so I can heal him*.::

The little red fox said no more but followed Juniper closely.

The path was long and the endless rows of trees were dizzying. Juniper knew where she was going. She *was* the forest—she knew every tree, plant, and animal as if they were part of her. Their spirits lived within her heart, and she used this connection to guide the way.

Her vision blurred from exhaustion—jumping through the trees telepathically had drained her, but she thought of Roscoe, alone and dying, and mustered enough energy to carry on.

When she and Rooney reached the clearing where Roscoe hung, Juniper knelt beside a large Kapok tree and placed her palm onto its trunk.

::*Are you okay?*:: Rooney asked frantically, nuzzling against Juniper's slumped-over body.

But Juniper's mind was back inside the trees.

She rocketed up the Kapok, through its branches until she reached the cocoon she crafted to keep Roscoe safe. Her spirit entered the vines and she could feel all of Roscoe at once. An ominous surge of cold energy blanketed Juniper's mind—Roscoe was barely hanging onto life.

The vines that hoisted Roscoe into the air unraveled from the branches, lowering his body toward the ground where Juniper could physically tend to him. The moment his body touched the soil, Juniper's mind exited the tree, reentered her body, and she raced to his side.

She fell to her knees, keeping her bare toes pressed upon the nearest tree trunk, and began ripping through the tangle of vines still ensnaring his body. His blood quickly covered her hands.

"I am so sorry I left you," she sobbed.

Roscoe's eyes darted around aimlessly as he tried to maintain consciousness.

She was losing him.

"Hold on," she begged as she searched for the bullet wound. "I will fix you."

Juniper struggled to see through the tears welling in her eyes. She squeezed her eyes shut, forcing the tears to fall and clearing her vision temporarily.

There was too much blood.

Roscoe coughed, splattering more on her face. She lifted a hand to wipe her eyes clean and brushed the back of her palm against the soil.

He will always be with you, Sofyla's voice filled Juniper's head, and she let her hand linger on the soil a moment longer.

He is lying in the dirt. Help me, Juniper begged her sister.

It doesn't work that way, Sofyla began to explain, but Juniper ripped her fingers from the soil in anger and broke the connection. She needed to focus on saving Roscoe—she was the only one who could.

Juniper placed her hand over the deep wound, which kept oozing blood. With pressure, she leaned into him, hoping to slow the bleeding while she channeled the energy of the trees into the wound. From her toes, through her legs, up her torso, and out through her hands, the trees obliged and sent the purest energy into Roscoe. Juniper was focused and unyielding in her connection, refusing to release the trees from this task until she felt life stir beneath her hands.

Roscoe remained immobile as the blood drained out of his body.

"Heal him!" she screamed up at the trees, to which she received no reply.

She intensified her focus, sucking every ounce of life she could from the surrounding forest. Her body was the vessel and the surplus of energy was overwhelming, but she held on, refusing to let the surge consume her. Roscoe needed the entire jungle to come to his aid; he needed help from every tree to survive.

Unrelenting, Juniper siphoned the life force from every tree she could latch onto and shoved it into Roscoe—an outpouring of desperation and hope. The rush was all consuming, and when she felt like it might be too much for Roscoe's body to withstand, she paused.

The wound was not healing.

Let me go.

Juniper's eyes widened in fear. It was Roscoe's voice, but his mouth hadn't moved.

I love you, he said. *Let me go.*

"Where are you?" she asked through the tears, touching the side of his face and examining it carefully for life. She kissed his lips then began to sob. "Come back to me."

I will always be with you.

"I need you *here*," she objected, refusing to speak telepathically with his spirit. "Alive and by my side."

My spirit belongs to the trees; it belongs to you.

"You need to fight!" she demanded. "Fight for me!"

Always.

"Fight for us!"

I love you, Juni.

She removed her toes from the tree trunk, breaking their connection.

The silence was crushing.

Juniper was angry, but not enough to be stubborn. She placed her toes back onto the tree.

I'm sorry, she confessed telepathically, but the other side felt hollow—Roscoe was no longer there.

Panicked, she began shaking Roscoe's corpse.

"Come back!" she begged.

Rooney nudged her thigh. ::*He will always be with you.*::

"That's not enough!"

Juniper collapsed onto Roscoe's body and wept.

Blinded by sorrow, she stayed there for hours and did not notice Clark, Teek, and the Wolfe brothers arrive on off-roaders. They waited patiently and did not disturb Juniper as she grieved.

When the sky began to darken, the sound of cicadas singing to the stars infiltrated Juniper's muffled mind. She turned her head, cheek covered in blood and tears, to see Rooney watching her intently.

"Thank you for staying with me," she said to the fox.

::*You are not alone.*:: Rooney tilted his head, and Juniper looked up to see her human friends.

She tried to give them a half-hearted smile, but the moment her lips curved, her attempt to appear strong crumbled into a quivering grimace.

"I lost him," she declared. "I had him here with me, and then I let him go."

"It's not your fault," Clark insisted, kneeling beside her. "Those outlaws killed him, not you. There was nothing you could do."

"He came back to me," she tried to explain through the tears. "And I let my anger get the best of me."

"You did nothing wrong," Clark reminded her, pulling her in close. Juniper buried her face into his shoulder and the onslaught of despair consumed her once more.

This time, her tears landed on a warm body.

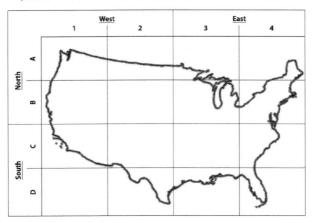

QUADRANTS OF LAMORTE'S AMERICA

Tier

15 years later

Chapter 1

Antarctica

Coral had promised to return.

The thought of her continued absence scorched Marisabel's icy heart—another promise broken. The Fresh Water Champion was alone on the continent of Antarctica, utterly isolated and living with the loss of everything she once loved.

Her own fault, perhaps—she once wished for this solitude, but its arrival brought with it something wicked: a transformation she never dreamt possible.

When she looked at her reflection in the icy pools covering the tundra, all she saw was a monster—a cold, wretched shell of her former self. Her flesh had formed a thin layer of frost over its surface, her royal-blue eyes were now snow-gray, and her dark hair was whitening. Within her body, she felt her insides transforming. Thick, unbreakable ice coated her bones, and her organs were encased in frozen armor. She could no longer enter the Davis Station for warmth—the heat made her sick. So sick, she suspected her innards were melting every time she tried to find comfort indoors.

Unable to stop the evolution taking place, Marisabel had no choice but to embrace the change. She let go of her desire to meet up with Zaire, lost interest in leaving to join Juniper in the

1

Amazon, no longer hoped that Coral would return with a boat. Marisabel's former potential was lost; she could no longer follow the path Gaia designed for her. She missed her opportunity to evolve with Coral underwater, and her attempts to catch up after everyone departed were futile—she was forsaken, and she had no one to blame but herself.

Marisabel couldn't recall how long ago Coral and their combined followers swam to the Caribbean. The sun had come and gone so many times since that fateful day. Each morning she awoke in her pile of snow to the blinding light of the sun reflecting off the expansive snowscape, and at night the all-consuming darkness blanketed her vision, erasing more of who she was each time it swallowed her.

Occasionally, when the skies were clear and her heart was open, she'd hold on to sight of the stars. Their tiny presence in the never-ending universe beyond gave her perspective: she was alive, she was still chosen, and though she was small, she could still serve a great purpose. But she could never hold onto the feeling of importance long.

The sun always returned, striking the white snowbanks and blinding her with its glory—reminding her that she was alone and unworthy of her title. She was the Champion of no one, of nothing. The Champion of a barren, arctic wasteland. And each time she let the landscape win, she lost another piece of herself.

Marisabel, a voice called to her. The accent was American—it was Juniper. *Please answer me. I miss you.*

Marisabel screamed in reply.

We all miss you, Juniper continued telepathically, unable to hear the hoarse cry echoing across the tundra of Antarctica.

Marisabel shrieked until she ran out of breath, then took a deep breath and released another bereaved cry. Anything to drown out the voice inside her head. Breath rattling and throat raw, Marisabel paused.

Juniper was gone.

Though Marisabel needed warmth, it was too late—she had not trained to survive underwater; she had not evolved like the others. Her home was within the ice. What once caused her great misery was now her only comfort. The cold numbed her aching heart, and within the unrelenting winter she was safe.

"She ignored me," Juniper informed her sisters as she arrived in the White Room. A chain of emeralds draped through her long, brown curls. *"It almost felt like she wasn't even there."*

"She ignores me too," Coral stated, her tone full of remorse. Her large, dark blue eyes darted toward the ground. Hints of pastels buried deep within her irises flickered as she averted her gaze.

"It's not your fault," Eshe insisted, waving her hand and creating a trail of black smoke in its wake. *"She chose this path. She chose frigid isolation."*

"We were all placed in scenarios that required we adapt. Everyone adjusted and made the best of their situations, except Marisabel," Sahira added. Her slate pink sari was lined with silver pearls, and her gray-mahogany eyes shone under metallic dusting.

Coral lifted her eyes, the shimmering opal undertones now brighter. *"I love her, but I had to leave."*

"No one blames you," Sahira promised.

"I can go back."

"No," Eshe stated plainly. *"You have an underwater kingdom to protect, as well as progenies to groom. The Coralen empire needs you."*

"How is Aria doing?" Juniper asked Sahira.

"She is due any day now," the Champion of the Mountains answered. *"Her belly is so large, we suspect she might be having triplets."*

"Just like me," Coral muttered with a smile.

"Yes." Sahira smiled, though she looked sad. *"It will be our first generation of progenies on the mountain."*

"How is Monte?" Juniper asked, her tone cautious.

"He has given up," Sahira stated plainly about her Second, her energy growing more bitter as she continued. *"The higher Aria*

4

and the air spirits lead us, the more cynical he becomes. His entire family is dead. Apparently, I am not enough to live for."

Coral's brow furrowed. *"Maybe you aren't supposed to climb higher. You aren't air, you are mountain—perhaps this is where yours and Aria's paths diverge."*

Sahira shook her head. *"The mountain tells me to follow. The spirits insist that I evolve with Aria. I obey, but I am not evolving. And the higher we climb, the more mountain disciples we lose. Sometimes, I fear my fate is designed for failure."*

"Impossible," Eshe objected. *"Nature would never steer you wrong."*

"I am keeping faith," Sahira vowed, though her conviction was not convincing.

"You must," Coral insisted. *"You cannot let this temporary difficulty defeat you as it has Marisabel."*

"I am doing my best."

Coral smiled. Her lips had turned blue from the cold ocean. *"I must return to Coralen—my people are holding a celebration for the triplets fifteenth birthday."*

"Say hello to the Coralene for us," Juniper expressed. *"And a very happy birthday to your children."*

Coral nodded with gratitude and disappeared in a swirl of sea mist.

"Goodbye, Sisters," Eshe said as a single flame swallowed her image, leaving only a thin film of smoke where she previously stood.

"You will be okay," Juniper promised as she took Sahira's hand. It was cold as stone. *"The hardships help us grow."* They shared an appreciative smile before Juniper vanished in a green glow.

Sahira was alone.

She took a deep breath before exiting the White Room and returned to the harsh reality atop Mount Everest.

The moment she arrived, she was greeted by an appalling sight: roaring planes circled their camp, creating dark plumes of exhaust that made the air taste like gasoline. The people were screaming, running about, unsure how to make the intrusion stop.

"Where is Aria?" Sahira demanded of Monte, who sat on a snow-covered rock, apathetically watching the chaotic scene unfold.

"In her tent, giving birth," he replied without looking at Sahira.

She cursed beneath her breath, aware that this horrible development was hers to deal with alone.

Sahira walked to the edge of the mountain, unafraid of the vile aggressors who had found their safe haven. With patient care she cleared a small patch, brushing the snow aside to create a clean circle. She stepped into the ring and closed her eyes. Bare feet pressed against the cool rock of the mountain, she channeled her element, lifted her arms, and summoned one hundred thousand shards of granite into the sky.

Head tilted downward, arms still raised, she opened her eyes—her irises had turned silver. She thrust her hands forward and sent the fleet of rocks at the planes. Like a swarm of bullets, they assailed the small task force, destroying the planes upon impact. Simultaneously, each metal aircraft exploded with fiery grace. The light show proclaimed Sahira's victory and calmed the frantic disciples of air and mountain, who looked to her for safety.

They joined her at the mountain's edge to watch their uninvited visitors plummet to their deaths.

"We are safe," Sahira confirmed to her worried disciples. "I will always protect you."

Chapter 2

Quadrant C2, North America

An empire of asphalt and steel: the truest honor he could gift to his late father.

Xavier had successfully transferred the loyalty of the populace from Sergei to himself, and his deep-rooted fear of nature shaped his rebuild of North America—not a single trace of vegetation or wildlife was welcome. Concrete covered every inch of the country, smothering any life attempting to grow beneath. The only exception was a small and highly patrolled vegetable farm in the flattened forests of Washington. There, food was grown for the masses and chemically altered in factories to taste like delicacies from the past.

Metal decorated the skyline from east to west, touching the clouds and blocking the views. A sprawling cityscape spanned the country—a feat no one dreamt possible. Comparisons to New York City were made, except Xavier made his empire grander. The grid ran north to south, east to west, until the entire continent was engulfed. The skyscrapers built on each of the countless blocks were so tall, they seemed to curve over when looking at the sky. Views straight ahead, down the infinite avenues were endless, but those to either side were limited by walls of metal and glass.

Buildings in the outer grids were hollow—built for show rather than livability, as were others scattered amongst the properly built towers. The population was still small—there weren't enough people to fill all the buildings—but the faux structures were erected anyway to ensure that no nature crept through.

Nature had spared the nuclear power plants, for which Xavier felt wicked delight. He reactivated the codes and brought the volatile energy source back to life, giving power to himself and the people.

Cedar City remained as Xavier's home base—its current glory rivaled every city from olden days. Sometimes, he found himself amazed by his own progress. He had created a glorious and complex empire with unnatural speed. A feat many told him was impossible, yet here they were, living in metallic splendor.

"Dear," his wife called from the kitchen of their penthouse apartment, which was the tallest building in North America. Through the glass walls they could see for miles; it was one of the few spots with a view. "Dinner is ready," Odette announced.

Xavier stood from where he rested on a plush, velvet couch. Not only had he revolutionized the mining and welding industry, but he also revitalized trades that provided classic comforts to his fellow survivors: furniture, clothing, food, beverage, electricity—and though he received high-end products, his populace was only given scraps. Plain clothes, plain furniture, plain food—but enough to ensure their gratitude. The items produced in these factories were so sparsely distributed that the factories only opened for one month every year.

The people couldn't pay, so Xavier minimized production—a vicious cycle, as closing the factories merely reduced employment opportunities for the poor. For most, poverty had become an inescapable fate.

The smell of factory-grown bacon filled the apartment. There were no pigs to farm, but the chemists came pretty close to replicating the exact flavor.

Upon entering the kitchen, he was greeted by the sight of his beautiful wife.

"Ms. Böhme, my German Queen," he purred, sauntering up to her and burying his face in her neck.

"I am Mrs. Lamorte now."

"Of course you are," he agreed, inhaling her scent and lustfully pinning her against the wall.

"My love," she giggled as he kissed her neck. "Aren't you hungry?"

"Only for you."

Though she enjoyed the affection, she playfully pushed him away. "Please eat."

Xavier took her hand and kissed it. "Only because you insist."

He sat at the table and Odette delivered his plate of food.

"Once the electricity project is complete and every avenue is alight with power, I plan to focus on finding the animals," Xavier revealed as he sat down and shoved a slice of bacon into his mouth. It was chewy and hard to swallow.

"Where do you think they might be?" Odette asked.

"I know where most of them are," he seethed, thinking of his fateful journey into the Amazon. "But I am hoping to find some north of here when I rebuild Canada."

"I have no doubt that you will succeed," Odette professed with a smile. She kissed Xavier on the cheek and then filled her own plate with food.

They ate in silence.

Odette accepted the role of subservient wife in exchange for a life of luxury. She stayed home and took care of their home while Xavier built his empire. She was content—a childhood of desperation and despair shaped her priorities: she would always choose survival over love. When her parents died, she and her sisters were left as orphans in the jungle with Juniper. Odette remained in the harsh living conditions beside her sisters until she couldn't stand another day of living with dirt caked beneath her fingernails. On her twentieth birthday, she left her sisters behind and found Xavier in Utah. He took her in without hesitation and soon after, they were wed. Their union was rushed and slightly forced, but Odette did not care. With him, she was given comforts she'd only known as a small girl.

The radio beeped incessantly.

Xavier exhaled, hardly containing his aggravation, before answering the call.

"Hello, Lucine," he said into the receiver.

"Manhattan is still in the dark."

"I'm doing my best. My men are moving east as quickly as possible."

"You're doing this on purpose," Lucine accused. "You don't want me to succeed."

"You are delusional," Xavier replied, bored.

"You sent me here, pretending this section of the country would be mine, yet you leave me in the dark. Literally. How am I supposed to garner respect from the people here if I cannot obtain the same electricity the rest of the country has?"

"It's on its way. I promise."

"You are my brother," she continued. "If you can't show me respect, your devoted populace certainly won't."

"You are exhausting."

"I am the only person who has the guts to stand up to you."

Xavier smirked. "True. Which is why you are so tiring."

"If I don't receive power soon, I will tarnish your empire from the roots up. I will twist the foolish love the Manhattanites hold for you until it rots. You know I am capable—I can turn their adoration into hatred."

"Slow down, crazy," Xavier replied. "You're supposed to be on my side."

"You're supposed to be on *mine*," Lucine corrected him. "I am all alone out here, by your order, and I have angry hordes of people banging at my door, demanding answers I can't give."

"You will have power by the end of the month," Xavier finally conceded. "The electricians needed to move in an orderly fashion to guarantee all of the grid was connected properly."

"End of the month," Lucine repeated. "I am holding you to that."

She disconnected the call without saying goodbye.

"She is infuriating," he complained to Odette.

"Is she right?" Odette asked, unafraid to request the truth from her tyrannical husband.

He glared at her for a moment before his expression shifted with a sly smile.

"I only do what's best for my dear sister."

"Leaving her in the dark is what's best?"

"Lucine needs to learn adversity. My father spoiled her."

"None of us were spoiled," Odette corrected him. "We all grew up in the aftermath of the apocalypse. We had nothing."

"Perhaps you and your sisters weren't spoiled—you did suffer alongside that jungle freak for quite some time."

"You surely suffered too when it first happened."

"Yes, it was hard. But Lucine and I were privileged—our father was the new ruler of the free world. The difference between Lucine and I is that I have faced adversity. I saw my father's murder. I had to pick up the pieces where he left off without any proper preparation."

"I see," Odette replied, sensing Xavier's rising aggravation.

"And Lucine just rode on my coattails. She is one of the wealthiest women in America, not because of her hard work, but because of mine. If I want to make her wait in the dark, I have every right to do so."

Odette raised a brow. "Seems childish."

Xavier's playful bantering rapidly turned violent. He stood from his chair and lunged for his wife, grabbing her by the neck and shoving her against the wall.

"Why do you test me?" he barked. Spit splattered her face as he choked her.

She could not reply.

As her face turned blue, Xavier's rage began to settle.

14

"You're lucky I love you," he sneered as he released her.

Odette fell into a heap on the floor, panting and silently crying as she massaged the fresh wound on her neck.

Xavier stormed out of the room and climbed the stairs to his observatory.

Domed glass kept the room safe from the toxic air at this altitude. Still, Xavier enjoyed the rush of danger. He put on his facemask and left the observatory, exiting onto a small deck exposed to the volatile elements.

The sky was still gray, though he no longer knew if it was because the ash clouds hadn't cleared or if his relentless construction created a new smog overhead. Either way, he had grown to love the overcast skies. The darkness suited him—it made him appear as a beacon of hope in a persistently cruel world. The people adored him and under his lead, the human race would thrive once more.

A punch, a slight twist to his gut, and Xavier lurched forward unexpectedly. He gripped the metal railing in time, stopping himself from plummeting over the edge to his death.

Terrified, he looked around, but he was alone.

Eyes wide and heart racing, he panted, trying to regain his composure.

Juniper, a voice clawed at the inside of his mind, and a bout of nausea overtook his body—cold sweat, shortness of breath, lightheadedness.

Xavier stumbled backwards.

Despite all his efforts, the spirits of nature still haunted him.

Chapter 3

The gift of eternal life was cruel indeed. Juniper Tiernan maintained her youth while everyone she loved grayed and disappeared.

First, Roscoe, then Rooney—the death of her little red fox came like the death of a child. Jeb and his wife, Alice, perished shortly after from pneumonia. None of her friends' parents were still around. Though her following grew each year, it did not diminish the sorrow she felt as she outlived those she cared about most.

The trees grew louder every year—Juniper suspected she was hearing the souls of her departed friends. Though they lost all memory of their mortal lives, their inexplicable bond to Juniper brought them back to her through nature. She appreciated their choice—to send their spirits to the trees. Choosing this afterlife for themselves helped Juniper carry on. It reminded her that she was never as alone as she sometimes felt.

She still hadn't told anyone about her gift from Gaia—not even her children, who were now young adults. Juniper planned to hold onto that secret for as long as she could. Everyone around her was aging, but she looked the same as she had on the day nature attacked, and her friends were beginning to comment on her lack of wrinkles.

Her secret would not survive much longer.

Most of all, she missed Roscoe. He was still with her—his cognizant spirit lived amongst the trees—but her desire to hold his hand, to kiss him again, never lessened.

They have found us, Sahira called out to Juniper.

Who? Juniper asked.

A group of rebels.

There are more of them on that side of the world? Juniper asked, dismayed. *But how? You and Aria are on top of the largest mountain in the world.*

They were in planes. They were circling our mountain. I knocked them out of the sky, so we are okay, but they know we are up here.

Should we initiate a meeting in the White Room?

No, I am telling each of the sisters briefly and individually. Aria gave birth to twins, so my consciousness must stay here to protect her, our people, and the mountain.

I understand.

As soon as I am able, I plan to investigate this further. We must know what threats live at the base of our mountain.

Let me know how I can help.

Thank you, Sahira expressed before leaving Juniper's mind.

"Mom?" Jasper called out as he searched the forest for her newest hiding place.

Juniper sighed, aware her moment of solitude had come to an end. "Yes, love?"

She lifted herself from the mossy patch hidden beneath a set of low hanging branches and greeted her son on the trail.

"Are you okay?" he asked.

Juniper smiled as she glanced up at her tall, 23-year-old son. He looked just like Roscoe.

"I am fine. I just needed some time alone," she answered.

Jasper nodded, though his expression remained concerned. "Elodie has run off again."

Juniper's shoulders slouched. "I see."

"She always comes back. I just wanted to let you know."

"Thank you."

"And Landon's leg has healed," he added, waiting for his mother's reaction.

"Already?" Juniper replied. "How wonderful."

Jasper studied her face, trying to siphon through the lies.

"He broke his femur two days ago," he reminded her. "A broken bone shouldn't heal that fast."

"I wonder if it is another evolutionary gift," Juniper replied, desperately wishing to hold onto her secret a little longer.

"Then why have so many people around us died from less severe injuries?"

"That is a good question," Juniper stammered.

Jasper stared at her defiantly. "Why won't you tell me the truth?"

Juniper looked up at her beloved son, tears welling in her eyes. "Because the truth isn't fair," she replied, doing her best to remain strong. "And I wanted you to remain little and pure for as long as possible."

"I am not a child anymore."

"I know," she replied. Jasper wiped away the single tear that rolled down her cheek.

"Tell me, please." His imploring eyes were kind, and Juniper caved. She took his hand and led him to a mossy spot to sit.

"Gaia granted me and the other Champions the gift of eternal life," she revealed. "I am still learning the full extent of this gift, but it appears that I passed it on to you and your siblings." She paused. "For which I am eternally grateful."

"So we will live forever?" he asked.

"No. We aren't immortal—fatal wounds and diseases can still kill us." She thought of Roscoe. Jasper sensed her returned grief and wrapped an arm around her.

"I miss him too."

Juniper nodded then continued, afraid she might begin to weep if she did not focus. "Gaia just gave us extra time."

"Do you think the gift will one day be given to all our people?"

"I'm not sure, but if it is hereditary, I suspect that eventually, many will receive it."

Jasper examined his mother's worried expression then smiled. "This is great news. You should be happy."

"I have many fears," she confessed. "The greatest being that I will somehow manage to outlive you and your siblings."

"Well, if Landon continues to think he can fly from tree to tree, and Elodie keeps running off to live with the lions, then yeah, I understand your concern."

"You aren't funny."

Jasper smirked and shrugged. "I just speak the truth."

"Don't tell your brother or sister yet."

"I won't. They don't need any motivation to be more reckless."

His infectious smile forced one onto Juniper's face. "I love you."

"I love you too, Mom. Now can you please join us for lunch? Clark made mango and salmon salad."

Juniper's stomach grumbled as she followed Jasper toward the clearing.

As they grew closer, evidence of her growing community became visible in the treetops. Small huts were constructed amongst the branches, and many of the tree trunks had notches carved into the bark. Juniper smiled—one day she suspected they'd all be able to climb to great heights without footholds.

Sunlight illuminated the clearing, where her people stood hand in hand around a large, moss-covered oak tree.

"I found her," Jasper announced, to which Clark rejoiced.

"Fantastic. Let's get started."

"What is going on?" Juniper asked.

"You'll see," Jasper replied. He kissed the side of her head and pulled her into the circle. They stood in front of the giant oak tree, facing those holding hands and rotating slowly around it. Her following had tripled in size since the start, and she often wondered how her perceived failure morphed into a thriving success. The families wore prideful smiles as they circled. The energy was blissfully content, and Juniper was reminded how lucky she was.

Zaire Nzile, Marisabel's Second, never made the trip from Africa to Antarctica. When Coral and her following left the frozen continent, Zaire was instructed to travel to the Amazon instead—his people had not evolved within the water like the others, and Marisabel insisted they stay where they were, so the soil and tree disciples welcomed them into the jungle; their connection to the rivers proved invaluable. Through them, Coral and Zaire were able to mend the broken connection between the water elements—the ocean and fresh water elements were now one, controlled primarily by Coral. With Marisabel refusing to participate, the Fresh Water spirits did not intervene and allowed the humans to make this call for the betterment of the people.

Complicated, but resolved, Juniper was grateful to have a cohesive community surrounding her. Zaire was gone now—he left the Amazon a few months prior and headed west toward the Andes Mountains in Ecuador. He hoped to find waterways within the deep volcanic caves of Cotopaxi through which he could eventually travel to Marisabel. Juniper told Eshe, who promised to help, but Juniper hadn't heard any updates regarding his progress since he left.

"Juniper Tiernan," Clark announced from the low branch he sat upon. Though the group was diverse, English was decided to be the common language amongst every Champion and their following, so the group was rapidly learning. "To you, we owe our lives."

"To you, I owe mine. I would not have survived long without support from all of you, my chosen family."

"Exactly," Clark went on. "We are family. And with you as our leader, we would like to unite the trees, the soil, and the fresh water under one common name."

"A name?"

"Yes. Our home, Tier. Our people, the Tierannites."

Shocked, Juniper looked to the faces of those who congregated around where she and Jasper stood. Their smiles remained steadfast.

"I am honored," she replied.

"You deserve more, but we hope this is a good start."

"Thank you."

Juniper leaned back and touched her fingertips to the oak tree.

Are you here with me? she asked Roscoe.

Always, he replied.

They are looking at me like I am more than what I am.

You are Chosen.

I feel too human.

That's why they love you.

Juniper took a deep breath, then stood taller.

"And this," she said, patting the thick branch of the oak tree. "Will be the heart of our community. A gathering place, a sanctuary, a symbol of unity."

The Tierannites cheered.

Their rejoicing grew so loud, the sound of the cracking tree branch was not heard. Only the thud of Clark hitting the ground.

"No!" Juniper shrieked, racing to Clark's side. He was hurt—a swollen ankle—but nothing fatal. "I can heal you."

"That branch was thick," Clark noted with a grimace. "Guess I need to lose some weight."

Juniper tended to Clark's wound, humming a healing song to lessen the swelling, but Jasper stared up at the sturdy old tree in wonder.

While everyone else was crowded around Clark to watch Juniper work her earthbound magic, Jasper kept his intrigue directed at the tree. Cautiously, he placed a hand on the trunk and closed his eyes to concentrate. He was greeted by the sound of an intense struggle.

Hello? Jasper asked despite the sounds of someone gagging.

Son!

Dad?

He found me, Roscoe revealed.

Who? Jasper asked, but Roscoe's spirit was gone and a dense darkness lingered in its place.

Chapter 4

"Is it ever enough?" Elodie asked Riad, pausing her sprint back to the giant oak. He was in a secluded section of the jungle, knuckle-deep in mud. With tireless practice, he and Sofyla learned how to communicate without Juniper's involvement.

"It's all I have."

"You've lost touch with the living."

"Sofyla's voice keeps me sane. It keeps me grounded."

"I can ease your suffering."

She took a step closer to the widowed Second, humming an enchanting melody. Once he was transfixed by her spell, she coaxed his fingers out of the soil and broke his connection to the deceased Champion of Soil. She then placed a hand on his forehead and sang louder.

Years of sorrow slammed against Elodie's palm as she absorbed his suffering.

The hypnotizing song radiated into Riad's skull, wiping his mind clean. Tears streamed down his face as he tried to cling to the memories being stolen, but he was powerless to the spell—Elodie was too strong.

When the aggressive energy within his mind lessened and she no longer felt it fighting her enchantment, she lifted her hand off Riad's forehead and took a step back.

Released from her spell, his mind began to clear. He shook his head and wiped the tears off of his face.

"Why am I crying?" he asked.

"You are releasing your demons."

"What demons?"

Elodie smiled. "They are gone. You need not worry about them anymore."

Riad's breathing quickened as he desperately searched for what he lost. In a panic, and out of habit, he began clawing at the soil.

"Stop!" Elodie demanded, but Riad was lost in a fit of hysteria. He scraped at the dirt, digging till he hit mud. Blood leaked from his fingernails, but he hardly noticed. Buried somewhere under the spell was all he lost, and he would not stop until it was recovered.

Riad? A voice entered his subconscious.

Riad paused abruptly, swatting at the sheets of fog in his mind.

"Sofyla?" he replied out loud.

"Damnit," Elodie cursed beneath her breath.

Riad looked up at the teenage girl imploringly. "Why would to try to take her away from me?"

"Because the dead should stay dead."

She darted away, disappearing in a blur as she ran. Her speed was fueled by disappointment. All her practice and training with the animals wasn't enough—her gift of mind control still did not possess the permanent hold she desired.

Another failed experiment.

One day, she'd master her craft, and though she only wished to use it for good, the road to greatness sometimes required sacrifices.

The route home was so engraved into her mind that she could run without fear of touching any of the trees—she hadn't spoken to her father in years, and she intended to keep it that way.

The clearing was in sight, as was the giant oak. A large group hovered around a body, and when she got closer, she saw her mother tending to a writhing old man.

"Clark," Elodie declared, pushing through the horde of bodies blocking her from her beloved, chosen grandfather. "Is he okay?" she asked Juniper.

"He will be fine. The branch he was sitting on broke."

Clark gave Elodie a smirk. "Guess I need to lay off the sugar cane."

Elodie returned his smile and watched as Juniper's touch rapidly reduced the swelling in his ankle.

Jasper broke through the group of people.

"It wasn't an accident," he declared.

"What do you mean?" Juniper asked.

"I felt a dark spirit in the tree."

Juniper lifted her hands from Clark's ankle. "Your father was in that tree."

"I heard Dad too." Jasper hesitated. "He was fighting the darkness then disappeared."

"Is he okay?" she asked.

Clark began to groan in pain again, so Elodie stepped in to finish the healing process while Juniper dealt with this grave news.

"It felt like Dad escaped," Jasper explained. "But I'm not sure. Dad was gone and the darkness lingered."

"Is it still in there?" Juniper inquired, ready to fight whatever evilness threatened her love.

"No, it disappeared a few moments after Dad."

Juniper took a deep, contemplative breath. "How is Landon healing? Is he able to walk yet?" she finally asked.

"I'd describe it as more of a hobble."

"Good." Juniper looked at Elodie then back up at Jasper. "The three of you will join me in the hunt for your father."

Elodie shook her head, refusing to break her concentration on Clark's ankle. "No, I won't."

"As soon as you finish healing Clark."

"No," Elodie repeated. "Not at all."

Juniper exhaled slowly, attempting to maintain her composure, then addressed the people crowded around them.

"If you could all please give us a moment alone," she requested of her people, who obliged and dispersed throughout the surrounding area.

"Why are you so selfish?" Jasper asked his sister as soon as the crowd was gone.

Elodie glared up at her brother. "Why are you such a pushover?"

"When was the last time you spoke to Dad?"

Elodie shrugged and turned back to Clark, unwilling to engage.

Jasper continued, "Unlike you, I miss him. Mom and Landon miss him too. If you can't do it for him, then do it for us."

"The dead should stay dead," Elodie mumbled, aware she was initiating a war.

"What about when I die?" Jasper asked. "And Mom and Landon?"

Elodie kept her eyes down.

"What about Clark?"

"Clark won't live on through the trees like we will."

"I will certainly choose the trees," Clark objected.

"You know what I mean," Elodie explained. "Your spirit will be in the trees, but you won't have a solitary voice like we will."

"Why do you reject this gift?" Juniper asked, utterly perplexed by her daughter's defiance.

"I don't like being controlled by ghosts."

"What do you mean?"

"Look at you," Elodie explained. "Look at Riad. You are both slaves to your dead counter parts. You haven't been fully present since Dad died. In fact, I'd gamble to say that you died that day too."

"That isn't fair—"

"And Riad has lost all connection to the living world. His fingernails are stained with dirt." She looked up at her mother wearing an expression of deep hurt. "You spend so much time lost inside the trees with Dad, you hardly know me."

"That isn't true."

"What's my favorite color?"

"Green."

"Wrong. It's purple. How about my favorite song?"

Juniper hesitated.

Elodie answered her own question. "The Beach Boys—*I Can Hear Music*."

"I love that song." Tears welled in Juniper's eyes.

Elodie's long held frustration boiled over. "You are absent from the life you are living."

"I'm sorry."

"Look at what's transpiring. Dark sprits? There is more to the afterlife than we can ever fully understand. We cannot protect ourselves from ghosts." Elodie pursed her lips in aggravation. "We cannot control the dead."

"It doesn't change the fact that our father is all alone," Jasper cut in, "outrunning something evil. We should try to help him if we can."

"I don't want him to suffer—I just can't conceive how we could possibly help him. He is a ghost."

"We have to try," Juniper pleaded.

Elodie caved. "Fine. But I'm not searching alone. I'm passing him off immediately if I happen to find him first."

"You can search with Landon," Juniper agreed. "He shouldn't be out in the jungle alone in his condition." She looked to Jasper. "Where is he?"

Jasper shifted his gaze upward then pointed at the sky.

Her 19-year-old was balancing on a tree branch fifty feet overhead.

"Really?" Juniper asked, exasperated.

"Hey, Mom," Landon called down with a wave.

"Get down here!"

Landon dove off the tree branch, which elicited a screech from Juniper, and caught himself on a branch directly below. He swung like a monkey from tree to tree until he lowered himself close enough to the ground that he could safely dismount. He landed in a crouch next to Clark.

"Hey, Gramps," Landon said to Clark with a smile.

"You're going to give your mother a heart attack."

Landon shot a curious look up at his mother. "I don't think that's possible."

"I thought you said he was hobbling?" Juniper demanded of Jasper.

"He was this morning."

"Time heals all wounds," Landon said, though his voice was lined with sarcasm. "Seems I don't need much of it though. I am invincible."

"No, you are not," Juniper corrected her rebellious son. "None of us are."

"Well, I've got some kind of Superman juice running through my veins." He eyed his mother. "Broken legs don't heal in a week."

"Enough. We need to focus on your father."

"What do you mean?" Landon asked.

"A dark spirit has found its way into our trees," Juniper explained.

"Dad is running from the Devil," Elodie said. "A devil we have no means to defeat."

"But we have to try," Jasper added.

"Obviously," Landon concurred. "Where do we start?"

"We will touch every tree in the forest until we find him."

"Oy." Landon groaned. "Can I do it from above?"

"No. You will remain grounded until he is located. Take your sister with you."

He rolled his eyes then looked to Elodie. "Ready?"

"No," she replied, but stood and followed her older brother into the jungle.

Once they were out of sight, Juniper looked to Jasper.

"Am I in the wrong?"

"Maybe a little."

"I never intended to make any of you feel unimportant."

"I never doubted your love, but Elodie was a baby when it all happened. She never got to know Dad."

"You do spend a lot of time lost within the trees," Clark interjected. "Especially when it first happened. I think Elodie was in my care more often than not right after Roscoe died."

"I was grieving," Juniper explained.

"I know. I'm not faulting you for anything, just stating the facts. The girl wants her mother. Can you blame her?"

"I will do better."

"I suspect you have plenty of time to amend whatever is broken," Clark replied with a wink.

Juniper gave Clark a half-smile—it appeared her secret wasn't safe after all.

Chapter 5

Quadrant B4, North America

An angry mob was gathered outside, thirty stories below her window.

Lucine was trapped. She could not leave—the people no longer believed her when she promised they'd receive power and their fury had turned volatile. Too perilous to risk walking the streets, her home had turned into a prison.

While their anger was potent, hers had turned vicious.

Living in the dark had given her clarity: her brother did not wish for her to succeed. He would be the sole Lamorte to rule the new world, and Lucine was just another puppet in his games. A familiar role, one she excelled at dodging, but an unacceptable role all the same. If her father were still alive, she'd be treated like a queen. She would not be at the mercy of her sociopath brother, and the masses would have idolized her too.

But Sergei was gone and she was left to fend for herself.

Her mother was no help; Marlaina started using painkillers after Sergei's death and the addiction rendered her useless. She was putty in Xavier's grip.

Uncle Dante and Aunt Renita had removed themselves from the expansion. They were still loyal to Xavier, but not nearly as involved as before. Lucine wondered if they grieved Sergei or if taking orders from Xavier was just too intolerable. She could sympathize with either. Her younger cousins were teenagers now, and while their parents had taken a step back from the spotlight, Lucine hoped she could still mold their loyalty. Callista, Freya, and Gideon had just as much right to the figurative Lamorte throne.

She had to bide her time, though. Callista was a lot like her Uncle Dante and Aunt Renita—she did not enjoy the attention or responsibility that came with receiving mass adoration. She did love Lucine unwaveringly, though, which would serve as an asset if they ever needed to take her brother down. Freya was twenty-seven years old and a lot like Xavier. While it worried Lucine that Freya craved the limelight and reveled in roles of authority, her loyalty usually landed with her younger brother, Gideon—whatever he wanted, she wanted too, and Gideon often sided with Lucine. Xavier paid his cousins no mind while they were little, unlike Lucine, who spent most of her time caring for them. Their bond would be a tough one to break.

Gideon was a wild card—he had grown into a picturesque image of a man: tall, strapping, intense, yet gentle. He adored Lucine, but he also was not blinded by loyalty to either of his powerful cousins. He appreciated honesty and transparency, to which their games of manipulation fell flat. To her luck, she had convinced Gideon to relocate to New York City. With him in

37

near proximity, she suspected it would be easier to keep him on her side.

Lucine wasn't sure what her next move would be. She hated relying on her brother, who reveled in her continued despair and dissatisfaction, but she also could not do anything drastic — the people depended on Xavier too much.

She glanced out the window again. The angry mob remained, furious expressions illuminated by the fire-lit torches they carried.

Lucine fell back onto her couch.

The quiet darkness was her friend.

She closed her eyes and let the shadows consume her.

The sound of clanging metal startled her awake in the wee hours of morning. She sat up, alarmed, and lifted the lamp off her end table. She was ready to fight whoever dared break into her home.

A vision rippled in the darkness.

"Who's there?" she asked, her voice unafraid.

No response.

"Explain yourself or I'll have you executed."

Another ripple in the unwavering dark.

Her eyes widened, but her vision did not adjust — the blackness was all consuming.

Lucine walked forward, swinging the lamp like a baseball bat, hoping the intruder's vision was just as impaired as hers and that they wouldn't see her coming.

But her wild swinging hit nothing—there was no one to make contact with. Out of breath, she paused, completely perplexed. She began to wonder if she was dreaming when the sound of banging returned.

"Show yourself!" Lucine screeched, her terror overtaking her confident calm.

No response, except for the frantic clamoring of metal.

She raced to the kitchen to locate her flashlight. The racket grew louder as she ran her hand along the top of her disconnected refrigerator, searching blindly for light. When her fingers found the aluminum wand, she snatched it, turned it on, and blared the light in the direction of the noise.

The room was empty.

She scanned her light, desperately searching for the source of the noise, but there was no one waiting for her in the faint glow of her flashlight.

Her breathing quickened, as did her heart rate. The noise was incessant; she was losing her mind.

A vision rippled in the glow.

Lucine held her flashlight still, afraid to breathe as she waited.

Another ripple in the faint spotlight.

Then the formation of a shadow, one with no origin.

Silence—the clamoring ceased while the shadow lingered.

Lucine closed her eyes, breath held, afraid to believe in the impossible.

Find me, a voice clawed at the walls of her mind.

The shadow disappeared and the sound of banging resumed.

Lucine dropped her flashlight, which rolled across the room and created a strobe effect on the furniture and walls. It stopped on the giant map of the world painted on her living room wall—a work of art, but also a reminder of the world as it once was. The lines of each country appeared to tremble. The world was not all right.

She dropped to the floor in a crouch with her arms cradling her head and rocked back and forth, unable to shake the sight of the undefined shadow. The clamoring was relentless—an adamant demand that she pay attention.

But she couldn't—she could not weaken herself by believing in ghosts. She was not a fool, though the longer the haunting carried on, the more she began to wonder if ignoring the call was more foolish than believing.

The noise grew so loud, her ears began to bleed. With age, she had learned to control her asthma, and she hadn't suffered an attack in years, but the fear she faced now was too great and she began to hyperventilate.

Lucine lifted her head in surrender, ready to face her fate.

The lights turned on.

Nerves shot, Lucine's heart thudded forcefully against her sternum. The shadow was gone, the room no longer shook, and the noise had vanished. She was alone.

She glanced toward the large picture window to see that the rest of the city was illuminated too.

Power was finally delivered to the quadrant; electricity once again graced the city of Manhattan.

She turned back to the inside of her home, expecting it to be destroyed, but nothing was out of order. Everything looked as it did in the daylight.

She touched her ears—no blood. The noise was imaginary.

The muffled sound of cheering echoed upward from the streets. Lucine walked to the window of her penthouse to find the angry mob rejoicing. Everything would improve now that she no longer ruled a city full of resentment.

She took a deep breath.

It was time for damage control—she would be respected, she would be loved.

Though her focus was on the repair of her reputation, her mind wandered back to the shadow. Its arrival and disappearance was an infuriating distraction, it was a mystery she felt compelled to solve. Whether friendly or nefarious, something about the incident felt familiar.

The flashlight was still aimed at the map.

She walked closer and ran a hand across the smooth wall. Everything appeared to be in place. She continued to scan the wall when she noticed the abnormality.

A long, black streak smeared the water lining the upper east coast of the United States. The ink was thickest near the coast of Maine.

The voice of the shadow returned.

Find me.

Chapter 6

Broadleaf, Tier

There were too many trees in the deciduous forest and not enough hands.

"We aren't doing enough," Juniper expressed.

"We are doing all we can," Jasper assured his mother.

"What if he is on the opposite side of Tier?"

"Then Landon and Elodie will find him."

Juniper placed her hand against a giant Beech. Each time she touched a new tree, she waited, praying Roscoe would appear.

He never did.

Juniper lowered her hand. Shoulders slouched, conviction wavering, she looked to her son, whose energy remained high.

"What if we lost him?" she asked.

Jasper broke his connection with a basswood to look at his mother.

"It felt like he got away." Jasper paused. "It was strange. Before he disappeared he said something odd."

Juniper furrowed her brow. "What did he say?"

"He said, *he found me*," Jasper replied.

"Who?"

Jasper shrugged. "I asked the same thing."

Juniper became visibly agitated as her mind raced. "Everyone loved Roscoe," she mumbled to herself.

"We still have enemies out there, beyond Tier," Jasper reminded her.

"The rebels?"

"Yeah, but it doesn't explain how they'd get to Dad within the trees."

Juniper didn't hear his logic—she had a new target.

She charged back to the Heart, Jasper tailing close behind. When she reached the oak, she shouted up at the tree homes.

"Böhme sisters! Please meet me at the Heart."

Her voice echoed and the Tierannites shuffled within the trees, murmuring with curiosity.

Jasper looked to his mother, prepared to back her up, but doubtful that this tactic was the right one.

Liesel, Beatrix, and Emeline Böhme left their individual families in the trees and joined Juniper at the Heart.

"Is everything okay?" Beatrix asked, examining Juniper's frantic demeanor with concern.

"Did we do something wrong?" Emeline asked, following her sister's line of questioning.

"No and no," Juniper replied, suddenly aware that her energy was hostile. "Sorry. You've done nothing wrong, but you might be able to give me some insight."

"Regarding what?" Liesel asked.

"Your sister. Odette."

"We haven't heard from her since she left," Beatrix informed Juniper.

"Nothing at all?" Juniper asked, her voice pleading.

"I wish," Beatrix said. "But no."

"How would we reach her, anyway?" Emeline asked. "We are cut off from the rest of the world."

"We don't have telepathic abilities like you do," Liesel added.

"I know," Juniper conceded with a sigh. "I guess I was just hopeful she somehow found a way to reach you."

"Why?" Beatrix asked.

"Someone has found Roscoe. They are hunting his spirit within the trees."

"Odette would never," Liesel objected.

"Of course not," Juniper assured the Böhme sisters. "But what about the Lamortes? Maybe their quest to hunt Champions hasn't ceased."

"Roscoe is dead," Liesel stated bluntly. "Why would they hunt ghosts?"

"To torment *me*," Juniper stated, as if this reasoning were obvious.

"Are they capable of reaching the dead?" Beatrix asked, her skepticism apparent.

"I don't know," Juniper said with a huff. "I was hoping Odette might know."

"You'll have to leave the jungle if you want to reach her," Emeline responded, her tone woeful.

Juniper considered this. She looked toward the sky—three falcons flew overhead. Maybe she didn't need to leave the safety of the trees to reach Odette.

"It doesn't make sense," Jasper interrupted her thoughts. "It can't be Xavier, or any of the other rebels. Nature would never allow it."

"Then who?" Juniper insisted.

"Only Dad can give us the answer."

Juniper surrendered. "I'm sorry to have bothered you," she expressed to the Böhme sisters.

"It's okay," Beatrix assured. "Let us know if we can help in any way."

"I will, thank you."

They left and Juniper looked to Jasper.

"The birds," she revealed in a whisper.

"What about them?"

"We can send them to Odette with a message."

Jasper was not convinced. "What if the polluted air kills them? Or worse, a Lamorte intercepts the message before it gets to Odette?"

"We've ignored the rebels for too long." Juniper shook her head, suddenly aware of her oversight. "They could be thriving. We have no way of knowing."

"We know their air is still filled with ash and pollution. The birds told us so."

"Doesn't mean they haven't found a way to endure despite it."

Jasper understood. "So you want to spy on them through the birds?"

"Yes. And further investigate your father's disappearance."

Jasper glanced upward. "Alright, let's summon the falcons." He lifted his fingers to his lips and released an ear-splitting whistle. The birds heard the call and redirected their glide toward the Heart.

::We have a task for you,:: Jasper began.

::I need you to travel into the northern darkness,:: Juniper explained.

::Where the air is ruined?:: the lead falcon asked.

::Yes, I'm sorry,:: Juniper replied. ::We need to check on the rebels — to see the status of their survival and to deliver a letter to Odette Böhme.::

47

The falcons circled overhead in quiet contemplation before the leader of the cast spoke again. ::*Anything for you, dear Juniper, but I do worry that you are sending us on a suicide mission.*::

::*What is your name?*:: she asked the falcon.

::*Finian.*::

::*Finian, I promise—if the air is too dangerous to breathe, we can turn around. I will be with you the whole time,*:: she promised.

::*Task accepted. When will we go?*::

::*This evening, at the start of nightfall. The shadows will mask your arrival into their territory.*::

The falcons screeched in unison before flying up and away.

Jasper looked at his mother with concern. "You have to protect them."

"Of course."

"Even if that means abandoning this mission before it's complete."

"I understand."

"I don't think you do," Jasper protested, knowing his mother too well. "The falcons' safety comes before Dad."

Juniper placed her hands onto the sides of Jasper's worried face and gently repeated herself, "I understand."

Everlands, Tier

"Haven't felt him yet," Landon declared as he hopped from a Pine to a Spruce.

"Might be because you're moving too fast," Elodie shouted up at her brother. She kept her arms crossed and refused to touch any trees in the coniferous forest.

"I need the speed to complete the jumps."

"Maybe you should be doing this task from the ground where you can move slower."

"If Dad is here, I'll know."

"If he is here, he probably can't keep up with you."

"He's a spirit," Landon objected. "He can move faster than all of us."

Elodie groaned, aware that her brother was too stubborn to alter his approach. The fate of this task fell on her.

She paused, took a deep breath, and uncrossed her arms. With a quick scan, she chose a Hemlock. Arm extended, fingers stretched, she made contact. The moment she touched the tree, a surge of sorrowful love coursed through her.

"You have got to be kidding," she cursed, as she fell to her knees, palm still pressed against the tree.

Elodie?

Her eyes brimmed with tears.

Hey, Dad.

Chapter 7

Body in the jungle, mind connected to the lead falcon, Juniper soared toward the dark skies covering North America. The farther they flew, the tighter the tether to her body pulled, but she held on tight. She had to protect Roscoe's spirit from the evil force threatening his survival.

She saw through the eyes of Finian, and though her body was not present, she could still feel the lurching sensation every time the bird dove and dodged through the sky.

When they reached the start of the ashy darkness, Finian faltered. His path forward turned crooked and he couldn't fly in a straight line.

::*What's wrong?*:: Juniper asked inside his mind.

::*The air is difficult to navigate,*:: Finian replied. :: *It's thick and hard to move through. It's also hard to see.*::

::*Volcanic ash?*::

::*Along the outskirts, yes. Maybe if I dive lower it will lessen.*::

Finian took an abrupt nosedive toward the ground, forcing Juniper's mind to somersault. Beneath the volcanic residue that still lingered in this part of the world, he found a safer layer of air. But after the ash cleared and the visibility improved, they both realized they had left one perilous scenario for another.

The landscape was draped in metal and asphalt. The air reeked of burning tar and the neon glow was disorienting.

Juniper's heart sank.

::*How is this possible?*:: she expressed, distraught.

::*This is worse than it was before the purge.*::

The falcon coughed up black soot.

::*Pollution,*:: he informed as he cleared his throat, ::*with a hint of volcanic ash.*::

::*Will you be okay?*::

::*Yes, but let's not linger long.*::

They flew east to west. The metallic view remained consistent, never changing or lessening. The expansive city was steadfast in its horrifying presence. When passing what used to be the prairielands of America, Juniper's concern intensified.

::*Where did all the mountains go?*:: she asked in dismay.

The land was flattened where the Colorado Rockies once stood and in their place was an asphalt grid covered with wall-to-wall steel structures.

::*How did I miss this?*:: Juniper asked herself. ::*How could I let this happen?*::

::*The skies were blocked and you were building new habitats for all the animals,*:: Finian replied. ::*You were obeying the trees' commands.*::

::*But I was also in charge of protecting the rest of the planet. Look at what they've done!*::

Finian soared over the sprawling metallic sore on the earth.

::It's like a virus infected the soil and then spread,:: Finian noted solemnly. ::It appears Gaia did not succeed in wiping out the disease.::

::I am so disappointed—with them and myself.::

::You did nothing wrong,:: Finian assured her.

::Then why do I feel so guilty?:: Juniper asked. ::Trees cannot grow here now. How am I supposed to fix this?::

Finian answered her with silence—there was no easy remedy for the cancer they flew over.

::And how did they cover so much land in such a short amount of time?:: Juniper continued.

::Humans are the cleverest bugs. Smart, capable, and motivated—but also selfish, greedy, and shortsighted. This form of resilience does not surprise me; it's what they know. It's what makes them comfortable. The greatest strength of the human race is survival, no matter the cost.::

::I'm sorry.::

::You aren't like them. Not anymore. You're an evolved human, a Tierannite.::

::I hope we are different. I hope we have learned from the past.::

::Everything you've done since the purge proves that you have.:: Finian coughed then continued, ::And your remorse for their atrocious actions further confirms it.::

::I need to find a way to undo this damage,:: Juniper stated, confidence returning.

::*Perhaps you ought to focus on finding a way to halt their progress first,*:: Finian suggested.

::*You're right. Stop the spread then remedy this destructive vandalism.*::

::*If anyone can do it, it's you.*::

::*We need to find the Lamortes' headquarters.*::

::*Easy,*:: Finian replied before picking up speed and soaring toward the tallest, brightest building in the grid.

Atop the roof, standing next to an illuminated glass dome was Xavier. Tall and grown, with sharper facial features, but age had not stripped him of the devious shimmer in his eyes.

::*Don't let him see you,*:: Juniper warned.

Finian flew higher, back into the shadowy clouds of rot and ash, then dove after rounding the building. He glided next to the top row of windows, circling the illuminated penthouse of the skyscraper.

::*Stop!*:: Juniper declared as she saw movement from within. Finian halted mid-flight and hovered by a window that revealed a woman inside.

:: *It's Odette,*:: Juniper revealed with a disappointed gasp. ::*I can't believe she went back to him.*::

::*Looks like she lives a pampered life by his side.*::

Though this discovery was wildly convenient, it left Juniper feeling betrayed—it was bad enough that Odette left to rejoin the rebels, but to partner up with the outlaw who killed Roscoe was true treachery.

::*Should we leave?*:: Finian asked.

::*No, we will finish our mission. Knock on the window.*::

Finian tapped his beak against the crank window, to which Odette jumped in shock. She walked briskly toward the glass and stared out in amazement at the sight of the falcon—she hadn't seen a bird since she left the Amazon.

Finian tapped his beak against the pane again, and Odette cranked it open. Through the small sliver of open space, Finian reached his talon through and dropped the note.

Odette untied the thin hemp rope, unrolled the paper, and began to read.

> *Odette,*
>
> *I am grateful to have found you. I hope you have found happiness away from the jungle, though you are greatly missed. Liesel married Noah Wolfe, and they have two little boys, Jack and Joey. Liesel did not think I would find you, and though she is tough in demeanor like your mother, she confessed that she misses you terribly.*

Odette's eyes shimmered with emotion as she continued to read.

Beatrix learned to ride our eco-dirt bikes—can you believe it!—so that she could collect her own spices and herbs from across the jungle. She is a fabulous cook. She has three little girls with Cade Culver: Mariette, Felicie, and Gretel. Felicie looks a lot like you. And your sister, Emeline, is a brilliant botanist. She and my son Jasper have found and cultivated countless medicinal flowers—together they've cured many illnesses and extended the lives of our people.

They love and miss you, always—they wanted me to tell you that.

A tear fell from Odette's eye, staining the page with an inky watermark.

Now, on to the matter of my search—I hope that you still feel some loyalty to me, as I need your help.

Odette paused where she read and looked up at the bird, very aware that Juniper was there too. She returned to the note.

We have not heard from the rebels in years, but I am beginning to worry that my attention has been misplaced. Should I be worried? Do they still desire to hunt the

Champions? I do not know where I will have found you when I deliver this note, but something is amiss within the trees, and the only dark force I know to exist is that which comes from the rebels. Do you have any information that you can share with me?

Either way, I do wish you a lifetime filled with happiness, and I hope that I can trust you to keep this note between us. If it falls into the wrong hands, who knows what the consequences will be.

Take care, Odette.

Lots of love,

Juniper

Odette looked up at the falcon.

"I'm sorry you found me here. It wasn't my intention to link up with Xavier, but he had been my friend during those years my family spent in Cedar City, and it felt natural to return here. Our relationship blossomed naturally. It was not out of spite toward you—you saved my family and I. For that, I will always feel love and gratitude toward you." She looked at the falcon, who showed no emotion toward her confession. Juniper could not respond, so Odette continued, "To answer your question: No. Xavier hasn't mentioned the Champions much since his father died. He hates nature, he has made sure it cannot exist in his empire, but he's never shown any signs of resuming the hunt." Odette paused, glancing down at the letter again, her eyes glassy with nostalgia. "And yes, you can trust me. This update on my sisters is a gift. One that I will cherish and keep private."

::Is that enough?:: Finian asked.

::I can't question her further, not now anyway, so I suppose it has to be,:: Juniper replied.

Finian tapped his beak twice against the window in thanks and then flew backwards, far enough away that Odette could no longer see him.

Odette folded the letter and stuffed it into her bra. A moment later, Xavier appeared from the staircase that led to the observatory. Odette quickly wiped her eyes and successfully hid the fact that she had just received the most beautiful gift from a bird.

Chapter 8

Quadrant C2, North America

Xavier wrapped his arms around Odette and repeatedly kissed her neck. She melted in his embrace, accepting the warmth of his unpredictable love.

A knock sounded at the door.

Odette's brow furrowed. "Are you expecting company?"

"Yes." He kissed Odette's cheek, then left to open the door.

Killian Halloran stood on the other side, dark hair graying but as handsome as ever.

"Killian," Odette greeted him with a smile from the kitchen. "It's been years. How are you?"

Xavier stepped aside so Killian could enter.

"I've been great. I met a nice girl in Oklahoma City a few years after the tragedy." Killian chose his words carefully, afraid to set Xavier off with unpleasant reminders of the past. "So I moved there with her. Dominic and Brianne followed me there." He looked to Xavier. "It's been amazing to watch your empire grow."

"You could've been part of my team," Xavier informed Killian, his tone harsh.

"I know. I'm sorry. It's great to see you now, though."

Xavier refused to let any weakness slip. "And it's not called Oklahoma City anymore. It's called Quadrant C2."

"You might face some difficulty forcing people to forsake the city names that existed for centuries."

"State borders have been erased—everything lands under my rule. But for the sake of clarity, it's easiest to refer to each region by their electrical quadrant."

"Feels a bit impersonal," Killian stated cautiously.

"It's simplified. It's easier. We are united."

"It's wonderful that you found love," Odette cut in to break the growing tension. "Did you enjoy your trip back to Cedar City?"

"I don't know if *enjoy* is the right word to describe it—the walk took five days and I had to sleep in a hostel each night." He pointed over his shoulder to his stuffed backpack. "But when the president of the new world calls, you answer," he finished, attempting to mask his sarcasm.

"You didn't send him a car?" Odette asked, her attention snapping to Xavier.

"Hardship builds strength," he replied, his conviction unwavering.

Killian sighed. "Haven't we all suffered enough? If you rebuilt the automotive industry the people could be free."

"They *are* free," Xavier objected.

Killian eyed him knowingly. "They are trapped in their 'quadrants' of the country. They have no means of transportation."

"You got here just fine," Xavier argued.

"C'mon," Killian countered. "You can give us electricity, but not cars?"

"Cars are not a necessity."

"You're in your trucks daily."

"I have to attend to all quadrants across the land. The rest of you just need to survive and procreate."

"That's shallow."

"It's the truth. Repopulation is the only aspect of my empire's continued growth that I cannot control. The rest I can handle."

"Why did you ask me to come here?" Killian asked, no longer able to mask his rising anger.

"Come with me." Xavier departed for the observatory, leaving Odette behind. Killian followed him up the stairs, out of the domed glass and onto the roof. The air was dense and stale.

"Right here," Xavier began, gripping onto the handrail. "Something punched me in the gut and knocked me back to my senses."

"Ok …" Killian replied hesitantly.

"It whispered a name into my ear."

"Whose name?"

"Juniper."

Killian paused, suddenly aware where this conversation was heading. "I'm not interested."

"You were a leader back in the day. What happened?"

"Sergei died and I woke up. We were fools. We were evil. Leave the people in the jungle alone."

"How can I when every ounce of my being desires to return—to enact long overdue vengeance for my father."

"You should silence those desires."

"Why?"

"Have you learned nothing? We cannot beat them. Honor your father by staying alive."

"He wants me to finish his task. I know he does, I can feel it in my bones."

"I am certain he'd be prouder if you finished the rebuild of America."

"It's almost complete. What then?"

"Bring back the automotive industry! Or better yet, the educational system."

Xavier's glare was devious. "You know I cannot do that."

Killian pursed his lips together in frustration. "Then move north into Canada. Or south into Mexico. Don't embark on a suicide mission. The people need you."

"The only way I can truly keep them safe is by eliminating the Champions."

"They've left us alone. They've never once tried to stop your rebuild."

"A single woman wearing a ram's-horn crown shot Japan's planes out of the sky. Not with guns or bombs. With rocks."

"I did not know this."

"They are dangerous."

"Did the Japanese enter *their* territory?"

"Yes, but that is not the point."

"I don't think it is wise to start a war—the people out there have just settled in. It took years for most to exit survival mode and relax. They are finally enjoying the comfort and safety you gave them."

"You cannot have peace without war—not when the enemy lives right outside your door."

Killian realized he'd never change Xavier's mind. "Have you told your uncle yet?"

"No."

"How about the Palladons?"

Xavier shook his head.

"Your mother or sister?" Killian asked.

"Only you."

Killian hesitated. "Why me?"

"Because you're far enough removed from the politics that have unfolded between those who rank directly below me, and because you understand the enemy as well as I do."

"Do you plan to tell Dante and the Palladons?"

"No. They will only try to stop me. Maybe the younger Palladons, though," he contemplated. "Dennis and Oliver have shown great loyalty to me over the years."

"How about Gino, Vincent, and Benny?"

"Vinny is a menace. He has been working hard to bring back the weather—directly disobeying my orders. I've had him arrested twenty times."

"But you always let him go."

"I am not a heartless man—the Palladons were like family during my childhood. I hoped he would change."

"Has he?"

"I think he has only grown sneakier. I suspect he's organized an underground coalition of climatologists, but I promise you, if he emerges with some grand plan to bring back the sun, I will arrest him and he will die in jail."

Killian sighed. "So that set of Palladon brothers is out. Why haven't you told your sister?"

"She still blames me for our father's death."

Killian nodded, aggravated that he had just stepped into Xavier's inner circle. Now that he was there, Xavier would never let him go.

"I am trusting you," Xavier said. "Do not betray me."

"So it's just you and me against an army of nature warlocks?"

"I have an entire continent of soldiers ready to fight for me," Xavier scoffed. "I will plant the seed of war slowly. I will explain to them *why* we must eliminate our fellow survivors, and when the time is right, my army will rise."

"Dante will rocket into the spotlight to stop you, to save the masses from a sure slaughter."

"I will have already sealed their commitment by then." Xavier glared at Killian. "You're on my side, whether you like it or not."

"I've gathered."

"And if you attempt to betray me, I will know," he warned. "I always know."

"There is no need for threats," Killian promised. "I have no interest in making my life any harder than it's already been."

"Wise."

"But I won't lie to you either."

"Nor should you."

"And I do not agree with this plan."

"When the Champions fall and we no longer have to share this world with murderers, I think you'll come around."

Chapter 9

Everlands, Tier

Roscoe's spirit was gone as fast as it had arrived. Stripped from Elodie's mind, she lost her father all over again.

"The darkness," she exclaimed. "It's here."

Landon swung down from the treetops and joined his sister at the base of the Hemlock. Palm to trunk, he felt it too. A cold surge, a prickly aftereffect, pinging back and forth throughout the tree trunk. The frantic nature of this energy felt juvenile.

"Dad escaped?" he asked.

"Yes. He left right before the darkness arrived."

"At least we know he's still out there and okay." Landon focused on the frigid tingling sensation in his palm. "It feels underdeveloped," he noted. "Desperate and infantile."

"All I felt was a tidal wave of ice wash over me."

"It's gone now," Landon informed his sister before removing his hand from the tree.

"I don't want to go any farther," Elodie confessed.

"We can take a break. Let's go tell Mom the news."

They raced toward the heart, turning to blurs as they ran south, but when they reached it, Juniper was nowhere to be found.

Clark sat by the tree with Aldon, chatting and eating berries.

"Hey!" Clark shouted at them. "Come talk to your grandfathers."

"Have you seen Mom?" Landon asked.

"She left with Jasper."

"Where to?"

"Someplace quiet and private, I assume. She was planning to take a trip with a falcon."

Elodie's brow furrowed and Landon opened his mouth to ask why, but Aldon cut him off.

"Did you find my son?" he asked, his voice raspy from age.

"Yeah," Landon replied. "Dad's spirit is still out there."

"Good." Aldon nodded, resuming his consumption of berries.

"We felt the darkness, too," Elodie added. "It's potent."

"That's why your mother left—to investigate what's causing it. She thinks it might be the rebels."

"The Debauched?" Elodie asked, unconvinced. "She thinks they are traveling through our trees?"

Clark shrugged. "Gotta start the search somewhere."

"How's your ankle?" she asked.

"All healed up," Clark answered with a smile. "Thank you."

"Let's go find Mom," Landon said, tugging Elodie forward.

They ran at blurred speeds through the jungle, Landon slightly faster than Elodie, and headed northeast toward the mossy spot in the rainforest Juniper usually chose whenever she left her body to visit the White Room or to travel through the trees.

Halfway there, Elodie's swift pace was painfully halted when something seized her by the ankle. She fell to the ground and released a terrified scream as she was dragged backwards. Elodie clawed at the ground, shaking her leg frantically as she tried to escape—but to no avail. She glanced over her shoulder and saw a blood-red hand with daggers for fingernails clutching her ankle. The grip was unbreakable.

"Landon!" she shouted, but her brother was gone. He was too fast; he already vanished through the trees.

Elodie fought, refusing to surrender despite the terrifying reality that she was not stronger than that which had captured her. She looked backwards once more and saw that she was being dragged toward a hole in the ground.

Nails scraping dirt, blood leaving a trail where she failed, Elodie calmed her panicked heart and refocused.

I hope you can hear me, she called to the trees. *I need you now more than ever.*

The trees remained silent.

Save me, please!

Her pleas went unanswered and she was tugged closer to the pit. She channeled her energy into the soil and a vine dropped from a nearby liana tree, but by the time it lowered far enough, she was already out of reach.

"No!" she screeched as her body plummeted into the pit.

She landed with a thud and the light above disappeared as the shadowed figure repositioned a boulder over the hole.

"Who's there?" Elodie demanded, fear overriding the pain.

She was answered with silence. The fiery energy of her captor lingered, seemingly circling her where she knelt on the ground.

Elodie lifted her arms, attempting to use them as a shield, and began to sing. She sang a song of compliance, a melody of submission.

Before she could mumble enough of the song for the enchantment to take hold, she was grabbed by the jaw and shoved against the wall.

Silenced.

"Interesting," the voice cooed, hot breath singeing a few strands of Elodie's hair. "Can't you see me?"

Elodie mumbled and shook her head.

"You need to learn to see in the dark," the voice instructed before lowering Elodie to the ground.

Elodie paused—she was still alive. Her fear lessened. "Tell me your name."

A flame sparked and set fire to a torch. Behind the glow was a beautiful face with blood-red skin, crimson eyes, and daggered teeth.

"Are you the darkness?" Elodie asked.

"I am Eshe, Champion of the Core."

Chapter 10

Ahi

"You are a Champion?" Elodie asked, her horror turned to awe.

"I am the Mother of Fire, quite the opposite of darkness," Eshe explained before stepping closer and placing her uncomfortably warm palm against Elodie's forehead. "And you are a progeny."

"Excuse me?"

"A direct descendant." Eshe smirked. "You can call me Auntie."

"You didn't need to scare me like that."

"I couldn't risk exposing my tunnel to too much jungle air."

"What do you want from me?"

"The darkness you mentioned," Eshe began. "Tell me more."

"It's been haunting us. It lives within the trees."

Eshe nodded. "We have an unwelcome darkness as well."

"My mother was investigating the cause. I was running to find her when you stopped me."

A voice shouted from above.

"Elodie!" Landon's voice rang clear. "Where are you?"

Eshe ignored the small search party. "Tell your mother that we need to meet in the White Room. We need to work together to solve this problem."

"Okay."

"And you cannot tell a soul about this entrance into Ahi, the underworld of fire," Eshe said, her glare threatening. "Only your mother."

"Landon is up there right now … he will figure it out when you let me go."

"Which is why I cannot do that." Eshe's eyes flickered in the flame and then the flame was gone.

Darkness resumed.

"Come on!" Elodie shouted. "You're really going to leave me here?"

Eshe's intense energy had vanished.

Elodie slammed her fists against the ground, and then looked up to where she believed the rock door was. She squinted her eyes, attempting to see despite the blinding dark, but nothing changed. Her sight had not yet evolved.

"Landon!" she shouted, but he could not hear her. His search grew more faint the farther he traveled from the pit.

"He's gone," Elodie called into the endless black tunnel. "Let me go!"

Her plea echoed with no reply.

For hours, she sat alone in the dark, plotting how to save herself but unable to execute any of her plans. She jumped as high as she could, fingertips scraping the bottom of the boulder. She surveyed the dirt walls, hoping to find some footholds, but the walls were smooth. So she tried climbing instead, but her rounded fingertips were too dull to lock into the wall and hoist herself upward. She made an attempt to channel her connection to the jungle, but the trees remained quiet and she was too far beneath the flora to call it to her aid.

Elodie fell back to the ground, exhausted and ready to surrender when a flash crossed her vision. She blinked rapidly a few times, before turning her head and realizing she could see again. The tunnel stretched farther in both directions than she originally imagined. She then looked up and saw all the bloody scratch marks she had left on the dirt wall.

She smiled, excited—she could see in the dark.

<<*You are ready now,*>> the trees proclaimed as their roots slithered along the tunnel ceiling. With little effort, they moved the boulder and Elodie was able to jump high enough to grab solid ground and pull herself out of the pit.

"Landon!" she shouted, looking in all directions for her brother. Behind her, the trees' roots snaked through the dirt and closed the tunnel door.

Elodie began running toward the northeast point where her mother usually meditated.

She ran fast, her adrenaline fueled by excitement—she had received another evolutionary gift. When she reached the mossy clearing, both of her brothers were there, protecting their mother.

Juniper sat on her knees with her head tilted toward the sky. Her mouth was open, her expression blank, and her eyes were the brightest shade of green.

"Where'd you go?" Landon demanded.

Elodie decided to temporarily protect Eshe's secret tunnel. "Sorry, I fell behind. My vision went wonky, but I'm fine now."

"Wonky?" Jasper asked.

"Yeah, I think something changed. I think I might be able to see in the dark now."

"Night vision?" Landon asked, his tone jealous. "Are you sure?"

"Pretty confident. It's nighttime now, and it looks like daytime with extra hints of green."

"Why you?" Landon scowled in disbelief. "How'd you make it happen?"

"I'm not sure," she replied, afraid to reveal too much. "How's Mom?"

"She's been gone a while," Jasper answered. "The sun will be rising soon and she promised to make it back before then."

The Tiernan siblings sat around their mother's vacant body, waiting patiently for her to return.

The sky shifted from black to light purple as morning light graced the new day. A falcon soared overhead, tearing through the orange clouds.

Juniper opened her eyes.

"We found Dad," Landon declared, excited to share the good news. "He is okay."

Juniper nodded then doubled over.

"Mom," Jasper said, racing to her side. "Are you okay?"

"Yes, I'm fine," she replied, still disoriented.

"Did you find the source of the darkness?" Elodie asked.

Juniper shook her head. "According to Odette, it isn't coming from Xavier."

"Then who?" Jasper asked, frustrated.

"We might have bigger problems," Juniper stated. "They've grown."

"What do you mean?"

"They've expanded. They are thriving. They have covered the world in asphalt and steel."

"How?" Jasper asked. "I thought they were oppressed beneath ash clouds."

"Apparently not—a terrible oversight on my part."

"Nature can't possibly expect you to control those ingrates from afar," Elodie commented. "They are rotten. They are Debauched."

"Rodents," Jasper added.

"Don't insult the rats," Landon joked.

"I need to consult my sisters," Juniper stated, her senses slowly returning.

"Yes," Elodie agreed. "That is a great idea."

"Tomorrow," Juniper went on. "I need to rest before traveling again."

Jasper and Landon lifted their mother, placing each of her arms over their shoulders, and helped her walk back to the heart.

When they arrived, a group of Tierannites stood around the Heart wearing grave expressions of concern.

The sturdy oak tree was shaking violently.

"What is happening?" Jasper asked, leaving Juniper with Landon and marching forward. But before anyone could answer, the ground began to tremble and a shrill shriek echoed through the sky. The noise was deafening and sent most of the Tierannites to their knees. Arms cradling their heads and covering their ears, they shielded themselves from the unnatural noise.

When it finally stopped, the world became still and Jasper opened his eyes. The ground was covered in leaves.

He peered upward.

The tree was barren—not a single leaf remained on its branches.

Jasper raced forward and slammed his hand against the tree trunk.

Death.

Not the death of the tree, but the presence of something dead existing within.

"Impossible," he said in awe.

"What do you feel?" Juniper called out.

Jasper looked over his shoulder at his mother, his expression alight with bewilderment.

"I think we're experiencing an actual haunting."

Chapter 11

Quadrant B4, North America

"I don't know *what* it was, Gideon," Lucine expressed, "just that it left me this message."

She slapped the wall near the black smudge.

"It doesn't look like much of a message to me," her younger cousin confessed, his skepticism apparent. He walked closer to the mural of America. Being much taller than Lucine, he was able to lean in close to examine the mark. "Looks like soot."

"Then what about all the things that happened before the mark appeared?"

"You want me to believe in ghosts?" Gideon asked.

"I don't know what else it could be." Lucine plopped herself onto the couch in defeat. "Unless Xavier found a new way to torment me."

"He's too busy to bother with petty nonsense like that."

Lucine looked up at Gideon in disbelief. "He waited months to activate the northeast grid, particularly *my* quadrant—the one he 'gifted' to me to govern. He wants me to fail," she expressed earnestly. "And now I'm starting to think he might be playing games to mess with my mind."

"This is a dangerous thought process," Gideon stated. "You're safer believing it was a ghost."

"Ghosts aren't real," Lucine scowled. She felt like a prisoner within her family's empire.

Gideon sighed and dropped onto the couch next to her. "I'm sorry I can't be more helpful."

Lucine nodded. "Thanks for listening."

"Maybe you just need some rest," he suggested. "You've taken on a lot recently. And the people have not been kind."

"No kidding," Lucine mumbled.

"But now they have electricity and their moods should shift. Let me help you win their favor."

Lucine gave Gideon an intrigued sideways glance—he was a poster boy in the new world, the first socialite in their budding society. The women adored him, the men admired him, the younger generation looked up to him. While Xavier was stern and unreachable, Gideon stepped forward into the limelight wearing an infectious smile—someone beautiful and positive that the masses could look to for hope.

"How?" she asked, despising the feeling of inferiority.

"Hang out with me more," he replied simply. "Show the people that you can be relatable."

"I'm not relatable?" she asked.

"No. You are distant and unreachable. Just like your brother. They worship him because he provides comforts and luxuries they could never have acquired on their own, but their adoration is based on fear. They see his power and his refusal to grant them all the freedoms they had in their old lives. They aren't stupid."

"I am not my brother," Lucine objected.

"No, but you sit on a pedestal slightly below his. You might not be controlling this new empire, but you've made no effort to show the people that you are on their side. They want the educational system restored. They want the autonomy that having an automobile provides. Stand up for them, petition your brother for their rights."

Lucine exhaled heavily. "It might be easier to hide in this penthouse."

"This penthouse will turn into a prison and you will go insane. You're already seeing things that aren't there," Gideon noted. "You need to get out and socialize."

Lucine groaned. "Fine."

"Fantastic. You will join me tonight at a power party downtown."

"Power party?"

"To celebrate the return of electricity."

"I wasn't invited."

"*I'm* inviting you. It'll be way more fun than the stuffy gatherings we usually go to."

"I've never been to a *real* party," Lucine commented.

"You are going to love it. Get dressed."

"Is it formal?"

Gideon laughed. "No. Not even a little bit. Wear jeans and a T-shirt."

Lucine followed her cousin's instructions and topped her casual outfit with an antique leather jacket.

"Perfect," Gideon approved. "Let's go."

Lucine stifled her anxiety and left the safety of her skyscraper with Gideon by her side. Her appearance attracted countless glares, but she did her best to ignore the scrutiny. No one gave her any trouble—she was accompanied by the golden boy.

Gideon didn't seem to notice the angry stares; he actively remained oblivious to most negative things in life. Lucine quickly realized that this was how he survived: she and Xavier dealt with their grave reality, while Gideon and his sisters gallivanted about without any cares. They could be the poster children of hope for the new world because they didn't have any real responsibilities when it came to keeping the surviving populace alive and happy. Lucine felt annoyed and slightly jealous, but understood that Gideon had no control of his fate. This was how he was raised; this is what Xavier crafted for them—relation to new age royalty, but no power.

Her jealousy shifted to admiration. Perhaps she could learn from her younger cousin. With his help, she could acquire some of his popularity and combine it with her power.

Lucine stood taller, unafraid of the masses who quietly despised her.

Gideon led her around the maze of streets, all illuminated by the recent gift of electricity. Lucine lost count of how many turns they made before they reached a set of steps leading to a basement beneath an apartment complex.

She shook her head in amazement. "How did you manage to make friends in this neighborhood?"

"I socialize," he replied with a shrug. "The less wealthy a person is, the more fun they are to hang out with."

Lucine raised an eyebrow. "I doubt that."

"You'll see," he answered with a smirk.

He led her down the stairs and knocked three times on the door at the bottom.

"Password," a voice shouted.

"Juniper," Gideon replied. He looked over at Lucine, whose eyes widened in shock.

"State your name," the voice on the other side of the door directed.

"Gideon Lamorte." The door cracked open and a set of eager eyes locked onto Gideon. Gideon continued, stepping aside as he spoke. "I've brought a guest."

Lucine came into view and the eyes narrowed on her.

"She isn't safe."

"C'mon, Drew," Gideon pled. "She's my cousin."

"She's *his* sister."

"Lucine isn't anything like Xavier. Give her a chance and you'll see."

The door shut and Lucine and Gideon were left to wait.

"Sorry," Lucine expressed.

"For what?"

"For ruining your night."

"They'll let us in," he replied, unconcerned.

Lucine leaned in and whispered, "Why was the password Juniper?"

Gideon hesitated. "They know."

The door swung open before Lucine could ask any more questions, and Drew yanked them both inside.

The room was dark and Drew's voice was threatening.

"If you betray us, you will not survive." His breath was hot against Lucine's ear.

"I just came for the party," she replied, heart racing.

"We outnumber you. Your last name won't save you."

"I get it," Lucine insisted, pushing Drew away.

"Leave her alone," Gideon stepped in, shoving Drew with a hard push. "She just needs a night of fun."

Drew's expression was ravaged by doubt. His fear and hatred for Xavier read clearly in his eyes and transferred seamlessly to Lucine.

"I don't want to cause you any trouble," she promised, then looked to Gideon. "I'll go home."

"No," Drew answered for Gideon. "You're here. This is your chance. Prove yourself."

The unexpected pressure to perform heightened Lucine's barely controlled anxiety. She wanted to run, to hide away in her penthouse, but there was no escaping now. The only way to survive the night was to put on a show.

"Okay," she conceded.

Drew nodded. His energy remained volatile as he ushered them into the living area where the party had congregated. The room was packed, leaving little space to move. Drew left the Lamorte cousins, and Gideon was bombarded by his female fans.

He wore a charming smile as they swarmed him into a corner, asking questions and vying for his attention.

Lucine no longer had a wingman.

She scanned the party to find that the skeptical glares had not ceased. As she steadied her nerves, an outstretched hand holding a drink appeared. She looked up to see a handsome man smiling at her.

"Loads of liquor, minimal water," he stated, still wearing a kind smile. "But I guess Xavier can't control nature, no matter how hard he tries."

Lucine accepted the drink and took a small sip, eyeing her pursuer with caution.

"My name is Max."

"I'm Lucine."

His smile widened. "I know who you are."

"Right," Lucine said, shaking her head in embarrassment. "And yeah, my brother can't control nature, though I'm sure he wishes he could."

"But he can control what we are given in the new world, correct?"

"Yes."

"Can you?"

Lucine's stomach lurched. "It's complicated."

"I figured as much." His smile faded. "Still, you possess the correct last name."

"What are you getting at?" Her defenses returned. "Do you think that because you have a pretty face I'll be smitten and let you use my name for your own purposes?"

"No, no. Not what I was implying at all," he insisted, his expression sincere.

"Then what?"

"That *you* could be the change."

Lucine's chest rose and fell as she struggled to contain her anger.

Max continued, "You have the power, you just need to learn how to use it."

"What makes you think I'm not happy with the way things are?"

Max shrugged. "Just a hunch."

She had no retort.

"It was nice to meet you," Max stated and began to turn away.

"Where are you going?" she asked, offended.

He laughed. "Should I stay?"

Lucine stammered, "Oh, I mean, you can do whatever you want."

Max nodded, his confidence radiating. "I'll stay."

The tension building inside Lucine's chest relaxed and her guard lowered slightly. Max stayed with her the entire night.

They talked about everything from their drastically different lifestyles to their dreams for the future, realizing by dawn that they weren't so different after all.

"You are the loveliest paradox," Max confessed, his eyes gleaming with genuine intrigue. "I thought I had you pegged, but I was wrong."

"How did you think I would be?"

"Stuck up, condescending, unable to listen. But you aren't any of those things."

Lucine laughed. "Happy to hear that."

"I'm sorry. I'm just pleasantly surprised. I feel hopeful for the future."

A smile crept across Lucine's face. She leaned in and kissed Max, who returned her affection. When she pulled away, Max was wearing the happiest grin.

"I was not expecting that," he stated.

"Neither was I."

Max leaned in and kissed her again—so passionately it was hard for either of them to find its end. Lucine pulled away first, leaning her forehead against his and smiling widely. They held each other's gaze for a moment before Max spoke.

"You have a beautiful heart, Lucine Lamorte."

Her chest swelled—receiving compliments felt foreign. "Thank you."

Faded orange light from the hidden sun began to creep into the cellar apartment.

"I have to get going," Max informed her as he caught a glimpse of the time. "I hope I'll get to see you again."

"Yes, I'd like that." She grabbed a pen. "Here's my radio frequency," she said as she scribbled her number onto the back of his hand.

He smiled. "I'll find you."

He kissed her once more and then left.

Lucine fell back into the couch, happier than ever, and noticed all the sleeping bodies sprawled out on nearby couches and along the floor. She didn't recognize any of them.

The exhaustion from not sleeping finally kicked in.

There weren't many windows in the sub-terrain apartment, so the room remained dark despite the faint glow of daylight. Lucine shut her eyes, ready to surrender to a quick nap, when a shadow rippled through the ribbon of faint orange sunlight.

Lucine sat up straight, terrified that she was seeing things again. She rubbed her eyes, but that only made everything blurrier. Her exhaustion was too severe.

An invisible force shoved her backwards, knocking her hard into the back of the couch.

Find me.

It was the same voice as before.

A set of hands grabbed and squeezed her shoulders from behind.

"Let's go."

Lucine screamed in fright, startling everyone around her. The sleeping bodies rustled, half waking, but returned to their sleep upon realizing that everything was fine.

"Sorry," Gideon whispered. "I didn't mean to startle you."

Lucine looked up to ensure it was truly her cousin, but couldn't calm her heart.

"I saw it again," she confessed.

"Saw what?"

"The shadow."

"You're probably just tired."

Lucine didn't have the energy to argue. She stood and Gideon led her toward the door.

As she followed him out of the apartment, the voice returned, latching onto the back of her neck and nestling into her mind.

Find me.

Chapter 12

Tier

Juniper followed Elodie to the secret entrance into Ahi.

"There," Elodie stated, pointing to a huge boulder.

"I thought you said it was a tunnel," Juniper replied, confused.

"The rock conceals a doorway—an opening into the tunnel."

Juniper moved closer and attempted to push the boulder aside, but it did not budge. She looked to her daughter, who shrugged.

"I got yanked in by Eshe. And the trees opened it to let me out."

"The trees," Juniper commented before digging her toes into the mossy ground and channeling the tree spirits. At her command, thousands of vines dropped from the branches, tangled around the boulder, and lifted it into the sky.

She smiled at Elodie, who did not look relieved.

"Do you want me to follow you down there?" Elodie asked.

"Yes."

Elodie hesitated, aware that Eshe only locked her down there to help her gift of night vision emerge, but she was still slightly shaken by the fear it initially caused.

Juniper jumped into the hole and landed in a graceful crouch. Elodie followed.

"What do you see?" Juniper asked her daughter.

Elodie rubbed her eyes as her vision flickered. "I haven't mastered this yet."

"You're trying too hard," a familiar voice with a thick Kenyan accent said.

"Eshe?" Juniper called out into the darkness.

"Please drop the boulder. You are letting too much outside air into Ahi."

Juniper obeyed, and all light vanished the moment the trees obeyed her command.

"Eshe?" she asked again, her tone more cautious now.

A flame ignited before them, illuminating the space. Juniper had to readjust her eyesight to the dim light, but once she did, the source of the light caused her and Elodie to pause in awe.

Eshe stood before them, holding an orb of fire in her palm. Her golden brown eyes held flickers of red as she smiled.

"Welcome to Ahi," Eshe greeted. "It is so nice to meet you in the real world, dear Sister."

Juniper's bright green eyes glowed with love. "Finally," she agreed.

"I gave your daughter a slight fright the other day," Eshe stated. Her playful tone was infectious, and Elodie found herself less frightened by the dark this time.

"I am grateful," Elodie replied. "You pushed me to be greater."

Eshe grinned then looked back to Juniper. "She is a very strong progeny."

Juniper nodded in agreement, glancing at Elodie as she spoke. "She impresses me every day."

"I am expecting my own soon," Eshe revealed.

Juniper's expression lit up with joy. "That is wonderful!"

"I am frightened to lose my strength."

"You won't," Juniper promised. "I grew stronger with each of my children. They helped me evolve."

"Keahi has been so supportive."

Juniper replied with a sad smile. "Yes, the process is exciting, but scary. I would have hated to go through it without Roscoe by my side."

Eshe understood. "Does he still live within the trees?"

"Yes. I speak to him as often as possible, but the spirit haunting my forest still threatens us."

"We are all better off with our Seconds close by."

Juniper thought of Zaire, Marisabel's Second. "Does this tunnel lead to the Andes?"

"Yes. I made contact with Zaire. Fascinating fellow. He is trying to create underground rivers to reach Marisabel."

"He told me of his plans before he left. Do you think he will succeed?" Juniper asked.

"So far, he is only creating steam."

"Maybe Coral can help," Juniper suggested.

"Have you seen her progenies? They are otherworldly."

A voice shouted from above.

"Mom!" It was Jasper. "Landon broke his femur again!"

Juniper sighed. "That's my eldest son, Jasper. Landon is my second-born, and he thinks he is a monkey." She paused. "Sometimes I believe he is too, until he breaks his bones and reminds me that he isn't." Jasper's shouting became more distant. Juniper turned to Elodie. "Can you let him know I'll be back soon?"

"Sure," Elodie agreed.

Eshe scaled the walls, using her dagger-sharp nails to stay elevated, and with her free hand she clutched the bottom of the boulder and dragged it far enough for Elodie to launch through the tiny opening. Once Elodie was gone, Eshe resealed the tunnel.

"The air is delicate here, and with all the pollution still emanating from the rebels, I've grown very strict about protecting this space."

"Speaking of the rebels, I have very grave news. I traveled there in the mind of a falcon and learned that they've plastered a city on top of the land. Every inch is covered with asphalt and steel."

"No wonder I can taste the distant, yet familiar stench of fumes when I travel here."

"I can't believe I let this happen. I was so consumed by Roscoe's death, I buried myself in my work, creating habitats for all the different animals, and totally neglected checking in on the Lamortes."

"It's not your fault," Eshe replied. "We all got lazy, thinking they'd die off naturally. How did they expand so quickly? It's only been 15 years since they attacked you in the Amazon."

"Determination, I suppose. Seems the trees properly spooked the little Lamorte."

"Aria said there is a similar spread happening in France. They've been calling them the Debauched."

"Elodie used that term to describe them recently too. It's quite fitting."

"Very. I wonder if the French are in contact with the American Debauched."

"Perhaps. We need to figure out how to stop their growth."

"Which is the bigger threat: the Debauched or the dark spirits?" Eshe asked.

Juniper paused in thought. "I need to protect Roscoe."

Eshe understood. "We have had strange hauntings in Ahi too. They don't feel as directed as what you've been experiencing, so I wonder if we are receiving the aftereffects from your visitor. Perhaps its energy filters through the roots of the trees and into the underground."

"Anything is possible," Juniper replied. "All I know is that it is aiming to hurt me however it can."

Eshe furrowed her brow. "I wonder if we can tackle both threats at once."

"How so?"

"With spies. My people and I can dig tunnels beneath their cities. We can keep an eye on them from the underground. It won't fix the problem, but it will keep us better informed."

"That is a fabulous idea."

"Great. We will get to work on that. I have plenty of idle hands down here in need of a purpose."

"Thank you."

"But first, let's evolve your sight," Eshe said with a smirk before smothering the flame that illuminated the tunnel, returning them to darkness.

The Heart, Tier

"If it's just ghosts, maybe they'll go away if we ignore them," Clark suggested. "Sort of like bullies. It's no fun to pick on someone who doesn't care."

"Is it even possible?" Misty asked. "Ghosts?"

"*A lot* of people were killed during nature's purge," Noah Wolfe reminded everyone at the meeting. "And the trees talk to Juniper. Don't forget that she can also make things grow with her mind." Noah smirked and shrugged. "I'd say anything is possible."

"She also isn't aging," Zoe noted, a hint of jealousy in her voice.

"You wear your wrinkles well," Irene teased her sister, touching Zoe's crow's feet. Zoe slapped her hand away.

"What's most important is that we remain steadfast for Juniper," Clark reminded the group. He looked around at the original group of survivors—from the Hall of Mosses to the Amazon, these people endured the worst of times by Juniper's side. "We all would have died a long time ago if it weren't for her. We cannot understand what she is feeling or experiencing when she says Roscoe's spirit is in trouble. All we can do is remain firm in our loyalty."

"Of course," Liesel agreed.

"Even if it feels like another round of crazy," Zoe added.

"What does it matter?" Beatrix challenged. "We are safe."

"It's just tiring," Zoe replied, her tone less bitter.

"No one is asking you to be a shoulder for Juniper to cry on," Clark tried to explain. "Just don't make it worse by openly doubting her."

"Juniper can't be *that* crazy. Her kids believe her," Irene stated. "They claim to feel it too."

"That whole family has powers we cannot fathom," Clark stated. "Personally, I'm honored to be here for the ride."

"And her evolution is being passed onto the next generation," Noah added. "Jack and Joey show more traits similar to the Tiernan's every day."

"Our girls too," Beatrix agreed. Cade nodded in confirmation.

"Irene's kids received nothing special," Zoe spat.

"They weren't born in Tier," Irene countered her sister. "I suspect my grandchildren will be born with gifts."

Zoe rolled her eyes. "I'm not trying to be difficult. I just don't like babying her. She's a grown woman. I don't believe in ghosts, and I'm not going to sugarcoat it when she asks me."

"You are being difficult," Irene pointed out.

"Juniper and I fixed years of damage and mistrust. But ever since Roscoe died, we all went back to walking on eggshells around her. Just like we did in the beginning when she was leading us to the Amazon. Why is everyone so afraid to upset her a little?"

"Because she saved our lives," Clark explained, his patience on edge. "We've watched people doubt and betray her time and time again. She is strong, yet fragile. We are the last remaining people from her original group of survivors—everyone else has died. She values our opinions of her."

"One day, she will be alone," Zoe stated solemnly. "I suspect she will long outlive the lot of us."

"I think she fears that too," Clark agreed.

"I can't be fake with her," Zoe concluded. "We've repaired too much painful history for me to be soft with her. She deserves honesty."

"Just don't be cruel," Irene pleaded.

"I'm not looking for a fight." Zoe looked around at the rest of the group. "I suggest you all rethink your approach too. Lying to her won't help her."

Zoe departed.

"She might be right," Teek commented.

"Jasper might be right too," Clark countered. "This might be an actual haunting. There's no way for us to know, and I've trusted Juniper this far ... I'm not going to stop now."

The group mumbled in agreement.

"Hey," Elodie announced as she approached. "What's going on here?"

"Just convening the troops to make sure the arrival of ghosts hasn't spooked anyone too much."

"I see," Elodie said with a nod. "It's weird for sure, but I felt it too. If my Dad's spirit can live on within the trees, I don't see why other spirits couldn't find a way to do the same."

"Let's just hope it can't *leave* the trees," Noah commented playfully, though his fear was warranted.

"Maybe it isn't even an evil spirit," Elodie went on. "Just a lost soul trapped and trying to break free."

"Let's hope that's the case," Clark said with a smile.

As the words left his mouth, the ground began to shake and an eerie cry echoed through every living mind. Everyone lifted their hands to their ears, but could not block the noise—it was happening inside their heads.

"What is that?" Dedrik shouted over the telepathic noise.

"It's horrible!" Zoe shouted in reply, adjusting her hands but failing to muffle the sound.

The forest was quiet, but their minds were loud.

Clark shook his head and lowered his hands, revealing a bloody mess on his palms. His eyes widened in fear as he felt the stream of blood running down his neck.

He stood in a panic, putting pressure on his ears and pacing, unsure how to stop the flow.

"Enough!" he screamed, but the imaginary noise did not cease.

The entire group became frenzied. Some ran hoping to escape the phantom's reach, others screamed and scratched at the sides of their heads, futilely fighting a force they'd never defeat.

Mom, hurry. The phantom is back, Elodie called to her mother.

A minute later, Juniper ran into the chaotic scene, terribly confused. Everyone was shouting and running in circles, clawing at their ears and drawing blood. She ran to Clark.

"Stop it," she demanded, grabbing his wrists and yanking them away from his face.

His expression was ravaged and deranged. "Let me go!" he responded, struggling beneath her firm grip.

"You are hurting yourself," she replied, horrified. "You've nearly scratched your face off!"

"It's in my head," he explained. "The noise, it's making my ears bleed."

Juniper looked closer at his ears, but all the blood appeared to be coming from his self-inflicted wounds. She looked over her shoulder at all the others who were in similar states of hysteria.

"Your ears are fine—" she tried to tell him, but he cut her off.

"Are you saying I'm crazy?"

"No—"

"You're the only one who can't hear it!"

"So it seems," Juniper agreed, her alarm heightened.

"It's awful," Clark expressed as he broke into tears. He sobbed, "Make it stop."

"Do everything you can to ignore the sound. Keep your hands by your sides, sing a song to yourself ... whatever it takes. Don't let the darkness win."

He nodded, but his expression was already defeated.

Juniper fell to her knees near the closest tree and placed her palm against its bark.

If the darkness planned to haunt her friends, she would return the favor with a hunt of her own.

Chapter 13

The Heart, Tier

Juniper left her body and entered the tree. The moment she became one with it, she felt the lingering darkness. It was all around her and its devious energy was potent.

She remained quiet and still as she assessed her options. Vision a blur from her racing adrenaline, she took a deep breath to refocus.

Beneath her, her friends were still imprisoned by the madness. Blood decorated their ravaged expressions as they slammed their fists against their ears.

Juniper needed to work fast.

She extended a shadowy arm toward the phantom, hoping to snatch it before it could flee, but the darkness stirred with a jolt the moment Juniper's energy moved.

The chase was on.

Juniper tore through the trees, traveling at speeds she never dreamt possible. The world below became a streaked smudge as she moved, but she was not there to survey the land—she was hunting a phantom.

The darkness jumped swiftly from tree to tree. The ear-piercing buzz it created left a stinging itch in its wake, which Juniper swatted through as she tailed the demonic energy. As it increased its speed, the horribly uncomfortable sensation intensified, encasing Juniper's spirit as she struggled to keep up. Her chase began to feel dire—if she lost the darkness, she could not save her friends.

She carried on, unsure how the prickling sensation taking over her would affect her living body. She pushed through, determined to win this race.

The closer she got, the more details she could pick up from the phantom: a salty sea water breeze, the smell of tar and fumes, a deep voice muttering French poetry in an American accent.

The clues made no sense.

Juniper lost track of where they were, or how far her spirit had traveled, but she felt the tether to her body grow tighter. The tug became impossible to ignore. She tuned in to her surroundings, maintaining her grasp on the phantom's energy, and noticed that she was in the Dunes of Sandfire, the southern territory of Tier where she created the four desert habitats. The rattlesnakes hissed at the darkness as it raced through their home. But the farther into the desert they went, the harder it was for Juniper to follow. There were less trees here and she had to take more time to map out each jump from shrub to cactus.

She was losing the phantom.

"Come back!" Juniper shouted, but the darkness did not obey. *"Tell me what you want from us!"*

The cacti were spaced too far apart; she couldn't keep up.

A viper slithered nearby, so Juniper jumped from the cactus into the snake. While the viper glided atop the rocky sand as fast as it could, it wasn't fast enough.

::*I need a faster vessel,*:: she called out to the animals.

Heeding the call, a caravan of camels came charging from behind. Juniper jumped from the viper into the lead camel and continued her chase.

The camel moved fast, hitting its maximum speed, but its endurance was weak and quickly began to slow.

::*I am failing you,*:: the camel expressed, short on breath.

::*You are doing wonderfully,*:: Juniper insisted, though she began to worry she was losing the phantom again.

::*Down here!*:: a tinier voice shrieked.

Juniper looked down to see a skulk of fennec foxes running alongside the camels.

::*Thank you,*:: she expressed to the camel before hopping into the fox. The tether to her body pulled tighter with each transition.

::*Let's go!*:: the fennec fox declared. The skulk of foxes cheered as they sped forward.

Their speed was intense, much faster than the other desert animals, and Juniper was grateful. The smell of salt water and gasoline returned—she was gaining on the darkness.

But as her hope increased, so did the distance between her and her target.

The eastern shoreline came into view and as the fennec foxes screeched to a halt, the phantom catapulted beyond Juniper's reach.

It was gone.

Juniper groaned in dismay.

::*We're sorry,*:: the foxes expressed in unison.

::*Don't be. I am grateful for your help.*::

Juniper's tether finally pulled too tight and she was ricocheted back into her body.

Her body reanimated with a gasp.

"Where did you go?" Clark asked. He appeared to be back to normal, though the bloody scratches along the sides of his face remained.

"On a hunt for a phantom."

"Did you catch it?"

Juniper shook her head. "But I will."

Chapter 14

Quadrant C2, North America

She betrays you.

Xavier awoke with a jolt.

He glanced at Odette, who slumbered peacefully, then down at his chest. It felt like his heart might burst through.

He closed his eyes. "It was just a dream."

She betrays you.

Xavier's eyes shot open and he sat frozen in place. After a moment of contemplative silence, he spoke.

"Who?" he asked in a whisper.

She betrays you, the voice repeated itself.

Xavier nodded slowly, then looked back over at Odette. There was only one way to learn the truth.

He exited the bed, careful not to wake his wife, and began rummaging through her drawers. He wasn't sure what he was looking for, or if he was being sent on a witch hunt, but he could not share a bed with a traitor.

His search yielded nothing — her drawers only held the clothes and jewelry he bought her.

Xavier crawled back into bed, terrified that his mind was playing tricks on him. Odette was the only female he was close to, the only one with the potential to betray him. He shook his head and fell back asleep.

Odette woke Xavier a few hours later with a tender kiss. He opened his eyes to find her smiling down at him.

"What do you want for breakfast?" she asked.

The options were few.

"Do we have eggs?"

"The few that exist in the country," Odette confirmed.

"That'll do." He pulled her in close to kiss her again before she departed for the kitchen.

Xavier remained in bed, alone with his thoughts. Sunlight struggled to break through the gray sky, casting the world in a grayish orange glow. Light filtered into his bedroom through the slits where the curtains did not touch, and Xavier stood to face the day. He walked to Odette's dresser and checked the first drawer. Everything was scattered about—it hadn't been a dream, he really did hear a voice and search Odette's possessions for some sign of treachery.

Xavier carefully refolded all of her clothes, hiding the evidence of his mistrust, then joined his wife in the kitchen.

The aroma of eggs cooking filled the room, and for a moment, Xavier was reminded of his childhood before the purge. Sunday mornings with his mother cooking omelets filled with red peppers, sausage, and cheddar cheese. Marlaina would juggle between preparing breakfast and helping Sergei find the correct page for sports in the Cedar City Times newspaper. Sergei would read the sports highlights first, before switching over to the weekly crossword puzzle. Lucine always brought an army of stuffed animals to the breakfast table, and Marlaina always made her put half of them back into her bedroom.

Xavier sighed. Those were simpler times—a time of innocence and purity; a time long before nature destroyed him.

"You make this place a home," he expressed to Odette, who smiled in reply. "I love you for that."

"I love you for everything," she replied sincerely. "This life I live with you—I am so grateful."

"I know you are. You would never do anything to jeopardize it," he replied, his baited comment loaded.

"Of course not! I am yours, faithfully."

"Forever."

"Forever," Odette agreed. She left the stove to kiss Xavier. He accepted her promise with relief.

The radio beeped.

Odette returned to the painfully plain eggs she was cooking, and Xavier stared at the tactical radio from across the room.

It beeped again.

"Are you going to answer?" Odette asked.

"I'm debating who it might be."

"If you brought back telephones you could have caller ID."

"No. Certain luxuries hinder progress."

The radio beeped again, more frantically this time. The noise was maddening.

Xavier stood, read the numbers dialing in, and lifted the receiver.

"Hello, Lucine," he stated, suddenly curious if his sister might be who the mysterious voice was referring to.

"What took you so long?"

"I wasn't sure if I wanted to talk to you today."

"That's rude."

"Why have you called?" Xavier asked.

"Are you alone?" Lucine asked, her tone softening.

"I am with Odette. Whatever you have to say can be said with her around."

Lucine hesitated before unloading. "I am being haunted."

"Excuse me?"

"Something is visiting me in the night—a shadow figure."

Xavier chuckled. "The prolonged darkness affected you more than I intended."

"You're a jerk," Lucine scoffed at his confession.

"C'mon, it was a joke."

"You made the masses hate me."

"But I gained you one ghostly friend," he remarked with a chuckle.

"This isn't a joke."

Xavier thought of his own unnatural visitor, but refused to let Lucine think they were bonded in any way.

"Is it a friendly ghost?" he asked, his tone dripping with sarcasm.

Lucine ignored his vicious quip. "It hasn't given any indication that it wants to hurt me."

"Then why worry?"

"I shouldn't have called you."

"What does it say to you?" he asked more seriously, as he did wish to know what the voices were telling her.

"Find me." Lucine paused. "That's all it ever says."

"I see," Xavier said. "Then you better go find it."

"I hate you," Lucine stated with a growl before ending the call.

The conversation turned to static.

Xavier, wearing a cocky smile, looked up to Odette. "Pissy little brat hung up on me!"

Odette rolled her eyes. "You could go easier on her."

"What fun is that?"

Odette shook her head, wise enough not to interfere in the Lamorte sibling drama.

Xavier lowered the radio receiver, content with his victory—everyone around him knew their place. Still, he had a traitor to find.

Or maybe he was losing his mind.

Lucine was hearing the voices too, so he rested a little easier with that knowledge, but he remained content with his decision. The line was drawn—they would deal with their ghosts separately.

Chapter 15

Quadrant B4, North America

No one believed her—no one even wanted to listen to her. Lucine felt more alone than ever.

She sat in her quiet penthouse, watching the clock. The hour hand passed so slowly it didn't appear to be moving at all. She had hours left before nightfall and she dreaded the looming dark. The thought of its arrival and the secrets it carried in its shadows plagued the hours of sunlight keeping it at bay. She could not escape.

The buzzer to her apartment rang. Lucine's attention snapped toward the door—she wasn't expecting visitors.

She went to the intercom and held down the call button.

"Who is there?" she asked.

"Gideon." His voice sounded crackled through the speaker. "I'm here with Max and Drew. Are you busy?"

Her heart fluttered at the mention of Max, but Drew was not a person she wished to see again.

"I wasn't expecting company," she replied.

"I figured. That's why we decided to stop by."

Lucine wasn't sure whether to feel offended or delighted. "I'm good," she finally replied.

"C'mon. Let us up. I know you don't want to be alone."

Lucine felt trapped. She growled softly before pressing the 'unlock' key and buzzing them into the building.

She had a few minutes before they'd reach her floor, so she began tidying up, realizing quickly that there wasn't much to clean besides the few books scattered across her coffee table and a jacket that she left on the floor from the night before.

A loud knock sounded at her door. She took a deep breath, then opened it.

Gideon charged through first, giving her a hug before entering. Drew came next, wearing the same scowl he had when she first met him. He gave her a curt nod before following Gideon into the living room. Max entered last. He held Lucine in a tight hug, one she wished to never leave. He discreetly kissed the side of her neck before pulling away.

Lucine felt like she was floating. She shut the door and turned back to her guests. Drew's nasty grimace brought her back down to earth.

"Thanks for the visit," she stated, though it sounded more like a question.

"They were hanging at my place," Gideon explained. "And you live so close, I thought it would be nice to swing by."

"Did you have fun at our party?" Drew asked, his expression still rotten.

"Yes," she replied cautiously, unsure why his question felt like a threat.

"You're one of us now," Drew stated.

"What does that mean?" she asked.

"We let you in," he explained. "You accepted our outstretched hand. You made a promise."

"I didn't make any promises except not to talk about the party to people who weren't there."

"I warned you what entering the party meant." Drew's anger was rising.

"I had a drink, got to know Max, and that was it. I don't understand what the big secret is," she countered, her own impatience growing. "Who cares if you throw parties?"

"Swear that you can be trusted," Drew demanded, stepping closer to her.

"Trusted with what?" Lucine shouted in reply. Unafraid, she countered his approach and stepped toward him.

"Okay, okay," Gideon cut in, moving his body between theirs.

"Your friend is a madman," she barked at her cousin. "Why did you bring him here?"

"Tensions are high, I'm sorry." Gideon turned to Drew. "You are out of line."

"I didn't come here to waste time."

"Zero tact," Gideon spat. "Don't talk again."

"So there *is* an ulterior motive behind this visit?" Lucine asked, feeling hurt. She looked over at Max, who wore a sympathetic expression.

"I love you," Gideon answered. "You know that. I want you to be part of our group. I don't want you to feel so alone."

"I'm fine," she replied, embarrassed.

"I brought cards," Gideon revealed, taking the deck out of his coat pocket.

"And I have a bottle of gin," Max added. "Impromptu game night?"

Lucine's tense energy softened. "Sure. That sounds fun."

They spread out on the floor of her living room and began playing slapjack. The game was intense and the more gin they drank, the livelier the commotion became. Lucine lost herself in the merriment and completely forgot about the time.

Three rounds and a bottle of gin later, the foursome abandoned the card game and sprawled across her carpeted floor, happily chatting.

"Do you think we will ever make it into outer space again?" Gideon asked.

"At the rate Xavier's moving, we will be in space next month," Max retorted, to which everyone laughed. "I suspect he might try to conquer the moon next."

"Not before he finishes covering what's left of Earth in a steel blanket," Drew retorted.

"He won't go farther south than Mexico," Lucine revealed with a hiccup.

The three men became quiet with curiosity.

"Why's that?" Drew finally asked.

"He's afraid of trees."

"That explains a lot," Max said in contemplation.

"What a stupid thing to be scared of," Drew noted with a laugh.

"Why is it stupid?" Lucine asked, her guard lifted. "Trees killed millions of people not too long ago. The trees killed my father," she spat.

"It's okay, Lucy," Gideon said, placing a hand on her shoulder. "No one meant to upset you."

Lucine took a deep breath and accepted his apology on behalf of his friends. She was drunk—she wanted to have fun. More importantly, she did not want to be alone. "How about a game of spoons?"

"Oh, I love that one," Gideon agreed.

Lucine went to the kitchen, grabbed three spoons, and plopped back onto the floor.

"It's better with more people," she informed them as she dealt each player four cards, "but it'll still be fun."

The game commenced and the competition grew just as intense as it had with slapjack. They were all laughing and play fighting between rounds. After Lucine won three times in a row, they finally called it quits.

"I am exhausted," Drew confessed.

Lucine looked at the clock and a sense of dread washed over her—it was nearing midnight.

"You can all crash here," she offered.

"Excellent," Drew replied to her suggestion.

"There is a spare bedroom next to the bathroom," she told him.

He stood and stumbled into the room, slamming the door behind him.

"He's easier to deal with when he's liquored up," she noted, to which Max and Gideon laughed.

"He has trust issues," Gideon explained. "But once he's on your side, he's there for life. Drew is one of the most loyal guys I know."

"He seems to have a lot of secrets," Lucine commented.

"Don't we all?"

She looked at the clock, which revealed the late hour, then at the light switch, which would stay on all night, then back at her cousin.

"I suppose we do."

"Can I ask you something?" Gideon's tone shifted, and Lucine felt the loaded question coming.

"What?"

"What do you want out of life?"

This forced Lucine to pause—no one ever asked her this before. She had always been assigned tasks and roles that served her family's legacy and grew up believing there was no room for personal desires.

Gideon added to his line of questioning, "Do you like the way things are?"

"I usually avoid thinking about these types of things," she confessed.

"Why?"

"Because it doesn't matter how I feel or what I want. Xavier always gets his way."

"I know, it's been like that for a long time," Gideon sympathized, slurring his words slightly. "I watched it firsthand as we grew up. But it doesn't need to stay that way."

"He's too powerful," she whispered, her gaze lowering.

"You should not fear him," Max cut in. "He should fear *you*."

Lucine lifted her eyes, her expression skeptical but intrigued. "He tormented me when we were little."

"He was awful to you," Gideon agreed. "But you are grown now, and so am I."

The statement was loaded.

"Two against one?" Lucine asked.

Gideon smiled, not ready to reveal all his cards yet. "Just know you aren't alone." He rolled over and kissed his cousin's forehead. "I'll take the room across from yours," he said before getting up and heading to bed.

Lucine and Max were alone.

She looked over at him and smiled.

"Finally," he expressed, inching closer and wrapping his arms around her. Eyes closed, they kissed tenderly, and for a moment, Lucine forgot the terrors that waited for her in the dark.

"There's something about you," Max confessed. "I feel like you're meant to be in my life. Like a missing piece of my whole has finally been found."

Lucine grinned. "I like you too."

Max laughed and kissed her again. After a moment, he looked at her more seriously.

"I need to know," he began. "What *do* you want out of life?"

This time, the answer came easily. "Love," she stated confidently. "For myself, of course, but also for everyone who has stood by my family's side all these years. For the people who supported us and helped us rebuild this country. I want everyone to feel loved. I want everyone to feel safe and protected. And I want to give them opportunities to live a life that isn't just about surviving day to day. I want them to have dreams and goals. I want them to have a fair chance at achieving all their desires."

Max leaned in and gave her a small kiss. "I want that too."

Drunk and happy, they fell asleep on the floor in each other's arms, and Lucine was safe from the terrors for the night.

Chapter 16

Camp III, Mount Everest - 21,300'

The camp appeared barren, but even from a distance, it felt familiar to Aria. She cradled her twin daughters in her arms as she led the charge upward. Erion manned the back of the group with Aria's younger brothers, Ölvir and Tístran, while Sahira and Monte stayed in the middle.

Most of Sahira's mountain disciples had perished during the ascent, only Monte, four young male Sherpas from Nepal, and Sahira's youngest sister remained.

How are Ástríd and Birgitta? Erion asked.

Aria looked down at her beautiful daughters nuzzled contently in her arms. *They are perfect,* she replied. *I can see the camp. We are almost there.*

Great.

How's my mamma and pabbi holding up?

Your mom is great, your dad has expressed that his hips hurt.

Aria hated watching her parents age. *They will be able to rest soon.*

The snow was shin-deep and most of her following was too cold to complain. They trusted her and followed without protest.

Camp III was moments away when Sahira released a bereaved shriek from the middle of the group.

Aria turned to find her Champion sister on her knees, cradling her youngest sister, Gita.

"What happened?" Aria asked.

"She coughed a couple times then collapsed," Sahira sobbed, stroking Gita's long, black hair. "I've lost everyone. I cannot lose her too."

"You won't," Aria promised, desperate to help Sahira. *Erion,* she called out telepathically. *Gita needs to be carried to camp. Send one of my brothers ahead.*

Ölvir is on his way.

Monte stood beside his Champion while they waited, his expression cold. "I told you. This plan is designed for our failure."

Sahira glared up at him, appalled. "Do not talk to me," she demanded. "You only make me sad."

"I'm sorry if the truth brings you sorrow," Monte countered.

Aria stepped in. "Nature would not lead any of us astray."

"Then how do you explain the death of almost all our followers? Every innocent person who chose to follow me or Sahira has perished. We are following orders from the air when we ought to be listening to the mountains."

"The mountains told Sahira to follow me to the summit of Mount Everest," Aria countered, then looked to her Champion sister. "Did they not?"

"They did, a long time ago. I haven't heard from them since we left the base camp."

Aria sighed. "If you wish to stop at Camp III, you can."

"We have no one left," Monte shouted. "Just me, Sahira, Gita, and my four Sherpas. How do you expect us to build a community?"

"I am sorry," Aria promised in a whisper, cautious not to wake her sleeping daughters. "I will speak to the spirits of the air."

"You cannot undo what has already been done."

Ölvir's brisk jog came to an abrupt halt between Aria and Monte. Oblivious to their tense argument, he bent down next to Sahira and carefully lifted Gita into his arms. Once she was secure, he looked to his sister. "Let's go."

Aria turned back around, Ástríd and Birgitta in her arms, and marched toward camp. She was furious—utterly perplexed why she was being blamed for something that was completely out of her control. She loved Sahira, but Monte's growing negativity was beginning to feel like hatred.

Upon reaching Camp III, she found a safe place to put her daughters down to rest. Her parents found comfort in the same tent and agreed to watch the twins while Aria got to work. They'd be stationed here for a few weeks; the air insisted each stop last a while so everyone had time to acclimate before climbing higher. They spent years at the first two base camps, so being told that they would only be at Camp III for a few weeks seemed odd. Aria did not question the instruction, but planned to adjust her methods of creating a home for her people. Insulated ice igloos took too much time to build, so she'd make the existing, abandoned tents comfortable for this short stay.

The vicious winds were no longer a formidable contender to their survival; Aria possessed full control over their direction. She could not lessen their intensity, but she could conduct their swirling patterns.

Kneeling in the center of camp, Aria inhaled deeply, cast her bright blue eyes toward the sky, and let her spirt jump out of her body and into the wind. The powerful rustle of the crossing currents tore at Aria's spirit, but she had learned how to manage the constricting sensation. She was the master of air; she feared no squall.

The currents continued to tangle around her, forcing her to jump from stream to stream to avoid getting consumed. When she found the lead current—that which orchestrated all the surrounding airstreams—she harnessed its power and seized its reins.

Reflection from the sunlight and the snow below turned the thinner streams into beautiful ribbons of color that danced and darted beneath the airstream she rode. With a tender touch, she began snatching the smaller threads of air and knotting them together. Cross-stitched and woven into tight, colorful braids, she made domed columns that covered the camp. The air still flowed through each strand, but the streams were now contained and unable to roam freely. They were also laced so tightly together that foreign winds from beyond could not penetrate the dome and pester those who lived below. From Aria's vantagepoint, her creation was a glimmering shield of color.

She tied the final current into the ceiling of her dome and returned to her vacant body. Her lungs contracted dramatically as she adjusted to the slower flow of oxygen. Eyes already fixated on the sky, she no longer saw her colorful masterpiece, just a beautiful blue sky.

"We are safe," she told Erion, who came to her side while her body was vacant.

Erion kissed the side of her head.

"How is Gita?" she asked her beloved Second.

"Ölvir took her to that tent over there. It's a good setup inside: plenty of beds, sufficient insulation. He and Tístran went to look for medical supplies." Erion looked over his shoulder. "Not sure if they found any. I came to be with you."

"Do they know what's wrong with her?" Aria asked.

"It's happening just like the others," Erion revealed, his eyes remorseful. "She fell during the walk because of her severely swollen ankles. She can't move her toes anymore. When she woke up, she was having trouble hearing us, so we gave her a taste test." Erion paused. "She couldn't taste the apple."

"Oh no," Aria expressed. "Has she started bleeding?"

"Not yet. We are hoping that staying still for a few weeks might help her heal."

"We can stay longer if it helps. As long as she needs."

"You'd disobey the air spirits?"

"For Sahira? Yes. She needs her sister."

Erion smiled. "I love you."

"I love you too." Aria paused in thought. "I wish Monte was more supportive."

"He has lost everyone he loved."

"He still has Sahira," Aria objected.

"Yes, but he's grieving. He will come around."

A scream echoed from Aria's tent, which sent her into a sprint toward her family.

"What's wrong?" Aria asked as she barreled through the curtained flap, but her question was answered by the sight of floating babies. "What in the heavens," she gasped, terrified to see her sleeping daughters dangling in the sky.

"I cannot explain it," her mother Reyna expressed. "I was tending to your father and when I turned around, they were up there."

"How on Earth," Erion stated in awe, walking closer to his baby girls and delicately touching them where they rested in the air. He looked back at Aria, who still wore a look of shock by the tent's entrance. "Should I bring them down?"

"They are evolving," Aria stated in a low voice, ignoring Erion's question.

"Future generations will be able to fly?" he asked.

Aria shook her head and walked to Erion's side. She looked up at her daughters, curious and concerned. "I'm not sure."

She reached up toward Birgitta, but the moment she plucked the child out of the air, the infant started wailing. Aria cradled her close to her body, rocking her and kissing her head, but Birgitta would not settle.

"Oh no," Erion commented, pointing at Ástríd, who was beginning to toss and turn where she hovered. "You better put Birgitta back before we have two crying babies."

Aria looked up to see that Erion was right, so she held Birgitta above her head and the child levitated upward toward her sister. The moment their tiny hands touched, the girls fell back asleep and slumbered peacefully in the air.

"How am I supposed to navigate this?" Aria asked, her tone defeated. "Will they fall and hurt themselves when they wake up?"

"We will need to watch them closely to find out."

Their nap ended within the hour, and as they began to rustle awake, their bodies slowly lowered back into their bassinette. No need to catch them or break their fall; they descended with grace.

Aria looked to Erion, amazed. "This is incredible."

"Our quest toward the summit of Everest is starting to have a whole new meaning," he replied.

<<*It's your turn, dear Champion,*>> the Air Spirits declared as they swirled around Aria's head, lifting her long, white hair in a subtle breeze.

The cool air overtook her senses as her body levitated. Erion and her parents watched in awe.

A numbing chill overtook her senses as she rose into the air. Beneath the tingling cold, sharp pain seared through her nerves.

What are you doing to me? she asked, teeth gritted.

<<*Hollowing your bones.*>>

A single tear fell down Aria's cheek as she endured the agonizing transformation. She focused instead on the freezing current that enveloped her. It danced along her skin, prickling her flesh and leaving a trail of goose bumps as it came and went. It did not numb the pain completely, but it served as a sufficient distraction.

Aria did not realize it was over until her bare toes touched the ground again. She opened her eyes and the circling breeze vanished.

"What just happened?" Erion asked.

Aria arched her feet and lifted herself to her tiptoes, then rose a few inches into the air. She hung suspended for a few seconds before lowering herself. When her feet touched the ground, her illuminated gaze shifted upward to Erion.

"I've been given the gift of levitation."

Chapter 17

Tier

Landon swung into a scene of chaos at the ape and monkey sanctuary. Gorillas were fighting orangutans, who were swatting at the mandrills, marmosets, and baboons from where they hung from their tails.

::*What is going on here?*:: Landon demanded, but his question went ignored.

The cacophony of apes and monkeys screeching at each other was deafening—Landon could not make out what they were fighting over. He grabbed an Emperor tamarin by its tiny body and yanked it out of the fray.

::*Tell me why you're all fighting,*:: Landon ordered. The small monkey screeched and flashed its fangs, but Landon was not rattled. ::*I thought we were friends.*::

::*The son!*:: the tamarin shrieked. Its long, white moustache matched its ancient sounding voice.

::*The son!*:: the other monkeys and apes repeated in unison.

Landon paused, his concern apparent. Announcement of his arrival halted their fighting and their angry energy was now aimed at him.

::*Hey, friends*—::

::*The son!*::

::She is to blame!:: a giant gorilla growled.

::She is to blame!:: the rest of the apes repeated.

::Who?:: Landon asked, his voice stern.

::Juniper.::

::For what?::

::She is to blame!:: the monkeys chanted in a chorus, repeating this line as they tore off in the direction of the Heart. Terrified, Landon did all he could to beat them there.

I miss you more than ever, Juniper confessed with her hand pressed against the giant oak—the heart of Tier.

I am always with you, Roscoe replied.

It shouldn't be this way.

But it is. We are lucky that we can stay connected through the trees.

Juniper nodded. Roscoe reminded her of this blessing many times, and while she recognized their good fortune, it did not change the fact that she wanted to feel his arms around her.

Any signs that the darkness has returned? she asked, changing the subject.

None. It has been enjoyably peaceful within the trees. It's nice not having to be constantly on the run.

What do you think it would do to you if it caught you?

I'm afraid to imagine ... It can touch my spirit. I think it could rip me out of the trees.

We need to discover who is conjuring this magic.

We will. It always finds me when I stay still for too long.

Then I will enjoy every second you are here with me.

"Mom!" Landon's voice shouted from overhead, shaking Juniper out of her bliss.

"Be careful," she replied as she watched her son jump from branch to branch.

"The monkeys are freaking out."

"What do you mean?"

"They will be here any second," Landon revealed, looking over his shoulder frantically. "I hardly got a lead on them."

"What are they freaking out about?"

"They blame you for something."

"Me?"

"They sounded possessed."

It's back, Roscoe informed Juniper. *It's racing toward us.*

The darkness?

Yes. I have to go.

Roscoe's spirit disappeared and Juniper looked back to Landon. "They are possessed by the darkness."

"What do we do?"

Juniper placed two fingers in her mouth and released an ear-splitting whistle. Finian the falcon came swooping down a moment later.

"I plan to chase it back to its source."

"Can I help?" Landon asked.

"Protect my body."

A roaring discord of savage shrieks arrived with the rumbling stampede of gorillas. From ground to treetops, a wall of angry primates swung and charged toward them.

Juniper fell to her knees, palm still pressed against the Heart, as she vacated her body. Inside the tree, she felt the icy chill of death.

I am here, she proclaimed. *Come and get me!*

Juniper, a deep voice hissed. The moment the darkness sensed her presence, a small flame sparked within the frigid cold and all the primates were released from its spell.

Its focus was locked on Juniper.

Juniper's heart skipped—she was ready for the chase.

She could feel the darkness soaring toward her, ripping through the trees at light speed. An arm reached out of its black energy, grazing her spirit's neck, and the moment it threatened to take hold, she ricocheted out of the tree and into Finian.

The darkness howled in protest as she evaded its grip. Through Finian she was able to follow it, sensing its energy as it fled north.

The chase ensued over the Everlands and across the sea. Salty air lashed Finian's face and Juniper could taste the ocean mist through him—his senses became her own while they were connected.

Unable to deviate its course, the darkness led Finian straight to its hideout—a small, wrecked fishing village off the coast of Maine.

::We shouldn't linger,:: Finian advised.

::But I want to learn who's tormenting my home.::

::I think it would be wiser not to reveal that you've found your enemy's hideaway. If I fly overhead, I will be spotted and you will lose the upper hand.::

::There must be another animal I can jump into here,:: Juniper stated, frantically looking for any living creature.

::I can feel the tether to your body tightening. I think we should come back another time.::

Juniper hesitated—the only other living energy she felt radiated from the cockroaches skittering around below. ::You're right. Let's go.::

Finian circled south and headed back toward Tier.

Juniper marked the location in her memory. It would be impossible to forget the little, rickety fishing town built on stilted docks.

Chapter 18

Quadrant B4, North America

The rippling shadow figure stopped visiting Lucine. She suspected Max's constant company played a role in their absence. They were together every day, forming a bond Lucine never dreamt she'd find in her lifetime as a ruling Lamorte of the new world.

She kept her budding romance a secret from her brother—if Xavier knew she was dating below her societal class, he'd demand she never see Max again, so she kept their growing affection private. Only Gideon and Drew knew of their developing relationship.

Lucine couldn't imagine her life without Max—he gave her hope, helped her define her own desires and dreams, and supported her in every way. For the first time, she had someone who loved her for who she was; she didn't need to pretend to be something she wasn't to win his affection—a welcome change.

Her association with Gideon, Max, and their group helped alter the public's perception of her, which was another welcomed change. Everything was falling into place and Lucine had never felt happier.

"Can I show you something?" Max asked as they snuggled on the couch of his sub-level apartment, to which Lucine nodded.

Max took her by the hand and led her into a side room.

The warmth and brightness forced Lucine's eyes shut, but once she adjusted, she reopened them to the most beautiful sight.

A small plant in a pot—a shade of green she hadn't seen since she was a small girl.

"How?"

"We salvaged multitudes of seeds from the trees and plants before your brother leveled everything and built this sprawling city."

Lucine suddenly realized her involvement with Gideon and Max and all their friends was much bigger than she ever dreamt—it wasn't just about giving the people fundamental rights like education, it was about changing everything Xavier and her father built.

"So Xavier is right to be suspicious," she commented in fear.

"Will you tell him?"

"Never."

Max smiled. "We are the revolution."

"Does Gideon know about all of this?"

Max nodded. "Without him, we wouldn't exist."

"And that surprise visit the other day," Lucine went on. "*This is what Drew was so stressed out about?*"

"Yeah, he doesn't trust anyone, understandably. You are the riskiest recruit."

"How many plants have you grown?"

Max took her hand, leading her through another door and down a flight of steps. He pulled a string hanging from the ceiling and the room was illuminated by hot fluorescent light.

Rows upon rows of various vegetation lined the damp basement.

"It's nighttime for the plants," Max explained.

"I didn't mean to disturb their sleep," Lucine joked.

Max smiled. "Weren't you curious how we had a party stocked with gin, vodka, and beer?"

"I just assumed you hadn't run out of your stash from the old days."

"We ran out years ago," Max corrected her with a laugh. "Once the electricity returned, we were able to begin brewing. We built the equipment a while back, but without the heat lamps, we couldn't grow anything. So we saved the seeds and waited."

"I see," Lucine replied, still in awe of the underground greenhouse.

"The power party was also a launch party for our liquors." He grinned. "First time any of us have gotten drunk in years."

"You can't go public though," Lucine warned.

"We know," Max replied solemnly. "For now, this is enough. The brewery and distillery are in my buddy's basement next door. We are working on bourbon and whiskey next, then hopefully wine."

"Building an empire that can never flourish," Lucine commented in a sad whisper.

"It's one of the few things we can control, one of the few luxuries we can provide to the people. I'm kind of surprised your brother doesn't want alcohol in the new world—it's a fabulous way to further oppress us."

"He doesn't see it that way. He sees it as a treat—a gift. He doesn't want anyone to be *too* happy."

"Alcohol is a depressant," Max stated.

"One that makes the masses happy," Lucine corrected. "Even if the happiness is only temporary. Alcohol is a tool used for bonding and creating friendships—something Xavier will never allow."

"Ah, I see."

"Enslaving people to the bottle *would* serve his end goal, but I doubt he will ever see it that way."

"Good for us, then," Max concluded with a grin.

"Just don't let him find out," Lucine warned.

"You're the only one with access to him, and I trust you."

Lucine smiled as he pulled her in close. They swayed to the silence, creating music with their bodies as they pressed against one another and kissed. Foreheads locked together, they enjoyed a comfortable connection before Max guided Lucine back to his bedroom. Flesh to flesh, they became one, and for the first time in a long time, Lucine felt loved.

They lay entwined for a long time in quiet happiness, Max tracing the outline of Lucine's shoulder blade. When his bladder became too full, he kissed her forehead and turned to leave. He sat at the edge of the bed, putting on his shorts, when Lucine noticed his tattoo.

An enormous tree colored in black and green ink covered his left shoulder.

"The trees killed my father," Lucine stated plainly.

"Did they?" he asked, looking over his shoulder. "Or did your father try to kill Juniper first?"

Lucine knew this day would come.

"The password to enter your party," she recalled in a whisper.

He nodded.

"How much do you know?"

"Everything."

"How?" she asked, skeptically.

"Your brother denounced the Devereaux family from his elite circle of trustees, and they wasted no time telling the rest of us the truth."

"I can't even pretend like I'm surprised."

"Phineas wanted us to rally against Xavier's reign, but all he did was ignite a different kind of spark. One of hope. One that craved change."

"Where is Phineas now?"

Max shrugged. "No one knows."

"I represent everything you don't like," Lucine realized, her heart heavy. "Why would you want to be with me?"

"Because you aren't like your brother. You have a good heart."

"Sometimes I'm not so sure."

"Why?"

"Something dark lives inside me too."

Max wasn't buying it. "Well, *I* am sure. I wouldn't have let you in if I wasn't."

His confidence filled her with joy. This was who she wanted to be—someone to believe in.

"I hope I can live up to your expectations."

"You already do."

He leaned over and kissed her forehead, then left for the bathroom.

Lucine stirred uncomfortably; she didn't like to be alone in dark places. She waited for the shadowy ripple to appear, but it didn't.

Max returned.

"I need to tell you something," Lucine confessed. Her expression was grave.

"What?" Max asked, concerned.

"I am not alright."

"None of us are," Max replied with a laugh, but when his lightheartedness was not returned, his expression became stoic.

"I hear voices," Lucine confessed. "And I see things that aren't there."

Max eyed her cautiously, wanting to make a joke, but ultimately deciding against it. "What do the voices say?"

"Find me."

"Ah, a challenge. Have you received any clues on where to start your search?"

"Only one."

"Go on," Max coaxed.

"I have a painting of a world map on my wall and after a particularly aggressive visit from whatever is haunting me, the lights turned on and revealed a charcoal smudge off the coast of Maine."

"That's not too far away," Max stated optimistically. "Let's take a trip."

"I'm afraid of what I might find."

He leaned in and gave her a tender kiss. "I will be by your side the entire time."

Lucine exhaled deeply. "What if it can hurt us?"

"Then it would have already."

Lucine nodded. "Yeah, I guess you're right."

Max leaned in and brushed his nose along her ear. "I won't let anything, or anyone, hurt you. Ever." He kissed her cheek.

"I love you for that," she confessed.

His eyes gleamed with elation. "I love you too."

Chapter 19

Tier

"Roscoe's been absent for weeks," Juniper said with worry as she paced.

"He'll come back, Mom," Jasper promised. "After what happened with the primates, he is just trying to keep the darkness far away from us."

"We cannot live like this."

"It's been working for a few weeks now," Jasper countered hesitantly. "There haven't been any hauntings since Dad lured the phantom elsewhere."

"It isn't fair."

Jasper sighed. "What else can we do?"

"I need to go back to that fishing village. I need to eliminate the root of this evil."

"I still don't think it's wise. What if you being so close makes it easier for this person to kill you?"

"I've stalled for too long because of all your warnings."

"You need to rest. You need the energy to make your tether stretch farther."

"It has been three weeks since I've left my body. I am well rested now."

Jasper groaned. "You don't know what you will find there."

Juniper stood taller, her conviction unwavering. "I appreciate that you, your siblings, Roscoe, and Clark are looking out for me, but we cannot live in hiding. I get that you're all trying to protect me, but I need to start protecting all of *you*. And that starts with a trip north."

"Let me come with you, then. I will keep an eye out over head."

Juniper hesitated. "If I let you come, you will *not* follow me into that village. You will stay overhead as a lookout."

"Understood."

"Elodie," Juniper shouted. "Landon!" To which her younger children eventually appeared from opposite sections of the forest—Landon from the Everlands and Elodie from the Vale of Night.

"Yeah, Mom?" Landon asked as he approached.

"Watch our bodies."

"Where are you going?" Elodie asked.

"On a hunt for phantoms."

Elodie furrowed her brow and looked to Landon, who appeared outraged.

"I want to go with you," he objected.

"If there is a next time, you can come then," Juniper promised. "But let's hope this is a one-time trip."

Landon grunted in annoyance, but did not argue further. Elodie grabbed a long stick and began drawing letters in the dusty dirt around where Juniper and Jasper knelt.

"What are you doing?" Juniper asked.

"An experiment," Elodie mumbled, unwilling to break her concentration. Each letter was enormous, forming a perfect circle around her mother and brother. When she finished, the word she wrote read *PROTECT*. She stepped back, examined her work, and then lobbed a rock at her brother's head.

Jasper shouted in horror as the heavy rock flew toward him, but the moment it tried to cross Elodie's dirt-carved letters, it hit an invisible wall and fell to the ground.

Jasper, Juniper, and Landon each wore an identical expression of shock.

"Looks like it works," Elodie said with a satisfied smile then turned to leave. "I'm going back to the Vale of Night."

"Excuse me?" Juniper scoffed.

"You don't need me."

"How did you do that?" Jasper demanded.

"I'll teach you when you get back."

"I'll stay," Landon promised, sans enthusiasm. "In case Elodie's witchcraft doesn't hold."

"It's not witchcraft," Elodie spat. "It's manifestation and intent. I've been practicing in the dark valley. For this shield, I asked the forest to protect them, and the forest obliged."

Landon rolled his eyes. "Whatever. Go back to your vale of creepy critters and darkness."

"No," Elodie protested, turning back around in stubbornness. "Now I'll stay."

"We don't have time for this," Juniper stated, then looked to Jasper. "Are you ready?"

He nodded.

Juniper whistled loudly and Finian swooped through the trees, landing on her outstretched forearm.

::It's time,:: she revealed.

::I am ready.::

::Jasper is going to come too.::

::He can tether to Faris.::

Juniper looked over to Jasper, who was already whistling for his falcon.

As soon as Faris appeared, Juniper lifted her arm and Finian joined Faris in flight.

Together, Juniper and Jasper left their bodies and entered the minds of the birds circling overhead.

With the pounding of their enormous wings against the warm jungle air, the falcons were off and the tethers began to stretch. Juniper ignored the pull and focused on their destination—the rickety maze of docks lined with wrecked shacks off the coast of Maine.

Halfway there, a flock of seagulls appeared.

::Follow me,:: Juniper commanded through Finian.

::Juniper?::

::Juniper?::

::Juniper?::

The seagulls squawked her name repeatedly as they shifted the direction of their flock to follow the falcons.

When they arrived, the village looked exactly as it had before.

::Are you ready to make the jump?:: Finian asked.

Juniper replied with an abrupt departure, hopping into a seabird without warning.

::I'll remain close by, with Faris and Jasper, but out of sight,:: Finian promised as he soared south.

::Be careful,:: Jasper requested.

::I will,:: she promised before diving toward the docks.

Juniper surveyed the abandoned fishing village. Every house was wrecked from the purge and left in a state of disrepair—flooded, gutted, and rotted. Yet the docks were bustling with people. Tons of bodies moved about below, aimlessly wandering up and down the piers, hardly interacting with one another. The peculiar sight heightened Juniper's concern.

In the distance stood a pristine white lighthouse made of white dolomite and sedimentary rock. From afar, it appeared as though humans had sculpted a lantern room into the top of the lighthouse, but when she soared closer, she realized no human had ever touched this rock at all. The intense glow was otherworldly—it was not fire or electricity. There wasn't even a mirror reflecting sunlight.

Unnatural.

That was the only way to describe the illuminated rock formation.

The eerie energy emanating from the lighthouse gave her chills, and when a chorus of bereaved cries echoed from the cove below, Juniper had seen enough. She shook the terror from her spirit and directed the seagull back toward the village. She had a phantom to find.

An old mansion far from the bustling piers came into view— it looked like a haunted house off an old movie set. Juniper flew lower to investigate more closely. She soared through a broken windowpane and scoured the musty house for her phantom.

The sound of a deep, muttering voice emanated from a back room.

Juniper soared into the great room, immediately darting upward and landing on a rafter above, undetected.

Adrenaline racing, she peered over the edge of the rafter to find a man sitting below. His face was buried in an old book, so she could only see the back of his head. Dark hair, large body, an American accent uttering French sayings.

Libérez en moi.

Libérez en moi.

Libérez en moi.

The room remained still as the man waited for a change that never came.

He released a groan of savage frustration.

"Release into me!" he shouted, reciting the spell in English.

Still, he yielded no result.

"Give me magic," he cried, the desperation in his voice came from years of failure. "They need to see me!"

He slammed his fists into the book and then shoved it away.

The seagull Juniper resided within ruffled, knocking loose a white feather that tumbled slowly downward, landing gently on the man's arm.

He lifted the feather, examined it for a moment, then turned his gaze upward. His former anger shifted into a glazed stupor.

Gray eyes, crazed by prolonged failure, and sickly white flesh stared up where Juniper hid.

"Birds," he stated. Life stirred behind his vacant stare and the sight of the seagull ignited a memory buried deep within his soul. He smirked wickedly and repeated, "Birds."

The man stood and walked directly beneath the beam Juniper was perched upon.

Juniper held her breath, finally recognizing the man.

"Is that you, Juniper?" he asked.

Sergei Lamorte's dead eyes narrowed—the malice contained within his soul jumpstarted his flatlined heart.

Chapter 20

White Room

Juniper escaped the horrifying discovery, flew back to Tier, and immediately recoiled into the depths of her mind and called for her Champion sisters.

In the White Room, she waited.

Sofyla's spirit was already there, dressed in sand and soil. Her amber eyes radiated kindness as she held Juniper's shaking hand.

Eshe arrived, wearing a blood-orange aura gown. Her skin was decorated with leopard body paint and her crimson eyes held deep confusion.

"What is wrong?" she asked.

"I'll explain when everyone gets here," Juniper replied, her energy wholly shaken.

Aria arrived next dressed in shimmering diamond dust and owl feathers, followed closely by Sahira, who wore a crown adorned with ram horns.

"Are you okay?" Aria asked.

"None of us are," Juniper replied.

Coral appeared next. Her jet-black braids concealed countless seashells, and her blue aura gown appeared electrified like the tentacles of a jellyfish.

"Marisabel isn't coming," Coral informed in her thick Indonesian accent.

"Why not?" Eshe asked, infuriated.

"She doesn't want to be seen."

Flames brightened Eshe's fiery stare as she disappeared in a twister of fire.

The remaining Champions watched her angry departure in silence. Before they could wonder aloud about where she went, Eshe reappeared, dragging Marisabel into the White Room by her forearm.

"Your touch is too hot," Marisabel screeched in protest.

"Maybe it'll revive your frozen heart," Eshe spat.

"Let me go!"

Eshe released her with a slight push, sending Marisabel stumbling forward.

"We already lost one sister, I refuse to lose another," Eshe growled in reply. *"Answer us when we call."*

As the heated interaction calmed, the room zeroed in on Marisabel's appearance. Her flesh was coated in ice, and her sapphire colored eyes had turned so light they were almost white. She wore the furry skull of a polar bear like a helmet, and her aura gown had morphed into arctic armor; pointed icicles and razor-sharp frost adorned her outfit.

Marisabel looked up at her sisters, ashamed. *"Ice is a form of fresh water,"* she said defensively.

"I don't think this is what Gaia intended for you," Aria replied, her tone as gentle as a light breeze.

"We have bigger problems right now, Juniper cut in. *Sergei Lamorte found a way to return."*

"But you killed him," Coral said. *"The trees saved you from his hunt."*

"I thought so too, but as the hauntings in Tier grew more intense, I was forced to investigate, and I found him on a small isle off the coast of Maine."

"So he's alive?" Sahira asked, perplexed.

"I don't think so," Juniper answered, her expression conflicted. *"I think he is a ghost."*

"You can see ghosts?" Coral asked, brow furrowed.

"I think the whole fishing village is filled with ghosts. I don't fully understand it either, but the town remains in a state of disrepair from the purge, yet countless people are living there, seemingly unfazed by all the rotting damage. It's so strange."

"How is this possible?" Sahira asked.

"We need to consult Gaia," Aria insisted.

"Sergei said something about needing magic," Juniper revealed.

"If he's dead, is he really a threat?" Coral asked, unconvinced that this was a battle worth fighting. "He's been trapped on that isle for how long? Failed to impact us for how many years?"

"He is getting stronger," Juniper asserted. "Whatever magic he has channeled has reached my jungle and is affecting my people and my animals. It is ruining our peace."

"How do we fight a ghost?" Aria asked, looking to Sofyla. "You live on the other side of life. Any ideas?"

Sofyla's serene gaze never faltered. "I am a spirit, yes. But I am bound to the soil, tethered to my element. This room is the only break I get from the dirt and sand. I know little about the experiences of normal spirits."

"We need to learn his weaknesses," Eshe stated, aggravated.

"So far, we've managed to distract him and lead his hunt astray, but we will not be able to hold him off forever," Juniper informed the others. "If I don't find a way to send his soul to Hell, he will eventually catch me."

"We need Gaia's help," Aria repeated.

"She only comes to us on Her terms," Coral reminded her sisters.

"If we all call out to Her continually, She will sense our distress and heed our call."

"There's no guarantee of that."

"It's worth a try," Aria said with a huff.

"It is *worth a try*," Eshe agreed. *"We need to protect each other. This devil has sunk his claws into the core as well—I feel him in the walls of my tunnels. He will get to each of us if he isn't stopped."*

All the Champions looked sullen, except for Marisabel. She wore a look of determination—an expression that hadn't graced her face in years. She said nothing, but her mind danced around her dark and mysterious flirtation with death.

"For now," Juniper continued, *"all we can do is remain alert and informed. If anyone has an encounter with Sergei, let the others know. We will find a way to defeat him."* Juniper paused. *"We must."*

Eshe nodded. *"We ended his hunt for the Champions once, we will undoubtedly find a way to thwart him again."*

The sisters departed one by one, vanishing in puffs and whirlwinds crafted by their elements.

Marisabel lagged behind, lost in her thoughts.

For the first time since shifting into ice, she felt like she had something to offer. Her never-ending waltz with death might finally serve a worthy purpose.

Chapter 21

Nether Isle

"Why?" Bianca Wrey screamed into the sky. "Why did you send me back here?"

The lighthouse remained silent.

Bianca looked around at the empty docks—all that remained in Nether Isle were ghosts.

She had grown to like the abyss; she found a peculiar sense of peace in the eternal darkness, but her temporary contentment was stolen and replaced with a new kind of hell.

Bianca glared at the lighthouse, furious with Kólasi. He gave her no explanation. He simply pushed her through the portal and into the place she hated most. Except now it was worse: there were no living bodies to possess, no purpose for her in this wretched place. Everyone was dead.

"Tell me why!" she screeched. "If I must live with ghosts, let me live with them in Your darkness!"

<<*Finish what you started,*>> Kólasi's voice echoed from the lighthouse.

Bianca's face contorted with rage. "How am I supposed to do that? I am surrounded by ghosts!"

Silence.

Kólasi was gone.

Bianca trekked down the rickety dock, making no noise as she stomped her feet angrily with each step.

The first set of gaunt faces she passed were familiar: Delilah Clement, Clementine LeClair, Rupert Chevalier—all part of the Wiccan tribe Bianca detested.

"Hello, Clementine," Bianca greeted maliciously. Clementine's attention turned, but her expression remained blank. Bianca continued, "How does it feel?"

Clementine halted, forcing Delilah and Rupert to pause too. "How does what feel?" she asked.

"Death," Bianca answered with a sneer.

"I am of the light," Clementine protested, her eyes glazed and glossy.

"You are dead."

Clementine lifted her hands and examined them, flipping them slowly in confusion.

"No," she objected half-heartedly. "No. I am still here."

"Your spirit, sure. But your body is gone," Bianca stated. "Washed out to sea with the rest of them."

The trio turned their heads toward the rough ocean that lapped against the rickety piers.

"Am I dead?" Rupert asked, his voice creaked with desperation.

"Very," Bianca confirmed. "Just like me. You too, Delilah."

"For how long?" Delilah asked, alarmed, though she sounded far away.

"Oh geez. I don't know. A decade, at least."

At this revelation, Delilah slipped into a fog, disappearing mentally from the group. The farther away her mind wandered, the more she retreated from reality.

"I don't want to be dead," Rupert declared. "I want to be alive."

"Unfortunately, death is an irreversible fate." Bianca smirked. "You could join me on a hunt for living bodies, though."

"Never!" Clementine proclaimed. "You failed once before, you will fail again."

Bianca laughed. "Your memory is returning, I see."

"I remember everything," Clementine scoffed.

"What is my name?"

"You are the ghost girl who tricked that boy and—" Clementine paused in thought, her determined expression softened as the answer evaded her. "Little Ruby, you wanted her body."

"What is *my* name?" Bianca repeated.

Clementine went blank.

"What is *your* name?" Bianca asked, deepening Clementine's maze of confusion.

"Stop," Clementine shouted. "Stop. I am me." She placed her hands over her ears and shook her head. Frantic, she paced in a circle, repeating to herself, "I am me."

Her panic sent Rupert into a tizzy as well. "How did we get here?" he asked. "I was home just a moment ago."

Bianca chuckled to herself. "This is too easy."

Feeling a little better, she left the frenzied trio to wallow in their turmoil. Within the hour, they'd forget they ever saw her, as was the curse of a weak-minded ghost.

She wondered if the Ouijans handled their existence as ghosts with more grace — darkness was the foundation for their magic after all, accepting death ought to come naturally to them. Bianca scoured the piers, looking for familiar faces, but only found more Wiccans and ghosts she knew from decades ago.

The faces of strangers were countless; every living person in Nether Isle seemed to have stayed after the purge. Fear of the lighthouse and the mysteries it concealed remained rampant and prevented most from choosing a fate in the afterlife. None wanted to go near the lighthouse, therefore they did not receive the option to be born again in nature or to enter the infinite abyss. Instead, they remained bound to this realm as ghosts — existing in Nether Isle as tangible spirits, but wholly invisible elsewhere.

Bianca never dreamt she'd want to return to the abyss—she hated it there—but seeing the state of the living world was far worse. The gloom consumed her spirit, making it hard for her to maintain her sharpened wits.

"Do not lose focus," she said to herself. "Do not lose yourself to the fog."

"Why are *you* here?" a crackled voice asked.

Bianca snapped out of her daze to find Poe Lesauvage sitting on a nearby bench, staring at her with venomous hatred.

"I thought we sent you into the light," Poe scowled.

"Yeah, well, I'm back," Bianca replied with a growl.

"Why?" Poe interrogated.

"Your guess is as good as mine."

"Hmph." Poe's tense focus relaxed and he slumped back against the bench.

"You're the first Ouijan I've encountered since returning."

"They're all here," he stated, unenthusiastically.

"You're quite lucid."

"I'm thriving," Poe replied. "Can't say the same for the rest of them, though."

"Your fellow Ouijans?"

"Eh, they're doing okay. They have good days and bad days. But the rest are zombies. I tried to teach them how to stay in the present, but it's like trying to teach a fish how to walk. I might as well spend my days chatting with a wall."

"The curse of a weak mind. I just ran into a few Wiccans. Their aversion to the dark is keeping them oppressed."

"They're a lost cause," Poe quipped.

"Have you been able to work your Ouijan magic in this realm?"

Bianca's question struck a nerve. Poe's posture straightened and his face contorted with rage.

"Why? Do you want to fight me?"

"No, I was just curious."

"If you try to ruin my afterlife I will personally destroy yours," Poe fumed.

"Calm down. It was an innocent question."

"Nothing you say or do is innocent," Poe barked. "Why are you here?"

"Like I said, I'm not totally sure. I think I'm here to restore order."

"Everything is perfectly fine as it is."

"For the Mother of Life, maybe."

Poe considered her response before replying. "How? Everything is dead—any Mother of Life is surely the most distraught of all."

"She orchestrated the purge. She killed the masses."

"Then who are you restoring order for?"

"Her brother. The Father of Death."

Poe was intrigued. "We are all dead, shouldn't He be happy?"

"I think I am here to deliver chaos."

"I like chaos," Poe smirked.

"You won't like how I plan to go about it, though."

"Tell me."

"Possessing the living," Bianca stated bluntly.

To her surprise, Poe remained calm.

"Impossible," he replied.

"I know, it's everything you stand against."

"No, not because of that," he corrected her. "Because there are no living souls left on Earth. Just ghosts. That purge wiped the planet clean."

Bianca groaned. "Are you sure?"

"Yes."

"You've left Nether Isle to explore?"

"No," Poe spat. "But I've used a little magic to scan for life. You think you're the first to want to feel alive again in a new vessel?"

"Death has changed your principles," Bianca sneered. "Not too long ago you banished me into the light for doing just that."

"Yeah, well, death has given me a new perspective." Poe huffed. "Regardless, you'll need to find another way to deliver chaos. There aren't any living bodies left to take."

Poe resigned from his interrogation and resumed his relaxed state of being.

Bianca was more frustrated than before. She marched toward the old house where the Wiccan coven used to congregate. She needed crystals to channel energy and charcoal to sketch runes. She needed to recall her knowledge of magic in order to reclaim control. Years spent in the abyss without access to her hard-earned powers left her rusty, and now she needed to focus on rebuilding what was taken from her.

So much was taken from her.

Bianca's thoughts knotted together. Life before death—Cadence, her parents, the garden. Her discovery of magic—traveling the globe, endless hours of research, trials and errors on the living. Her attempted takeover—her female commanders, her ghost army, Theodore.

Bianca halted.

Theodore.

Determination redirected, she marched down Peddler's Way and took a hard left onto Cricket's Pier. House after house was left in shambles, drenched wood corroding with rot, wind howling through the broken windows, roofs cracked and caving in. At the end of the row sat the home she sought. Bianca charged forward and burst through the precariously attached door.

Inside sat a man, one with dark hair and soft skin. He held blue chalk in one hand and a black crystal in the other. Hundreds of circles with X's crossed through them were drawn on the wooden floor.

"Theodore?" Bianca announced, wondering if she was seeing the ghost of the boy she once loved all grown up.

The man looked over his shoulder with an unfamiliar gaze.

"Is that you?" she asked.

"Theodore is gone," the man replied, turning his attention back to his sloppy runes. "Probably pacing atop the ocean. Useless." He threw the piece of chalk across the room.

"Who are you, then?" Bianca asked.

The man turned back around, his glassy eyes appeared crazed. "Sergei Lamorte."

Chapter 22

Quadrant C2, North America

Odette kissed Xavier awake.

"It's almost noon," she informed him.

Xavier rolled over, tangling himself within the sheets.

Odette gave up trying to force him out of bed and left.

The words still haunted him. *She betrays you.*

Xavier opened his eyes, frustrated that he still did not know who the warning referred to. With a grunt, he exited his bed and jumped into the shower.

His building was one of the few with access to running water; still, he moved quickly to avoid wasting his precious— and limited—supply. Despite his speed, he felt the water pressure dwindle to a trickle. The need to eliminate the Champions was more imperative than ever. Once he removed their guard over the last remaining natural resources on Earth, he could run pipes into North America and provide fresh water to the masses—a luxury he did not mind sharing.

He wrapped a towel around his waist and stared at himself in the mirror. Lines etched his face, creating subtle streaks near his eyes. The years were beginning to show.

He ran his fingers through his black hair and searched for the only pair of tweezers they owned—cosmetics were a luxury found only in the ruble of the past. They were not where he left them, so he retrieved Odette's toiletry bag from under the sink and began to dig.

Five weathered toothbrushes, a packet of floss she used sparingly, a broken blush palette, empty lipstick tubes, and countless hair ties filled the bag. Xavier sifted through the rubbish, searching for the tweezers. When his hand reached the bottom, he felt a piece of paper. He retrieved the folded note to find dirt marks all over the white page.

His anger began to rise.

Carefully, he unfolded the paper, prepared for what he might find. His eyes darted to the bottom of the page.

Lots of love,
Juniper

Blinded by rage, Xavier crumpled the paper in his clenched fist and stormed out of the room. He entered the kitchen in a fit of fury.

"What is this?" he shouted, slamming the note onto the counter.

Odette jumped in shock.

"What is what?" she asked, her voice meek.

"This letter," he demanded.

Odette shifted her focus from her crazed husband to the dirty piece of paper crinkled into a ball. Her heart stopped.

"I haven't seen her," she insisted. "That letter just arrived."

"It *just arrived*?" Xavier spat.

"With a bird," she confessed. "A bird delivered it to me."

"You are a traitor."

"Everything is okay," she pleaded, tears falling from her eyes. "I told the bird nothing."

Xavier's eyes widened as he snatched the note and read its full contents. When he finished, he lowered the letter slowly and glared up at Odette.

"I told the bird that you lost interest in the Champions years ago," she vowed, her breathing panicked. "That you have moved onto bigger and better things."

Xavier's eye twitched. When he finally spoke, his demeanor was blanketed by an eerie sense of calm.

"Do you miss your sisters?"

Odette had not expected this line of questioning. "I do."

"How much?"

She took a deep breath. "Not enough to leave you."

Xavier flattened the letter and traced his finger along the watermark her tears left on the page.

"It's you," he stated in a low voice. "It's been you all along."

"What does that mean?" Odette asked, bereaved by guilt.

"I was warned that there was a traitor in my midst, and I did not want to believe it was you. I was blind." He shook his head. "You have wronged me."

"No, I haven't. Who cares about the Champions anyway? You haven't spoken of Juniper in years."

"You don't know me," Xavier commented. "You don't know my desires."

"Are you saying that you *do* want to continue hunting the Champions?"

Xavier's eyes went dark. "I cannot discuss sensitive matters with you anymore."

"You can trust me!" she insisted, her desperation smothering.

Xavier shook his head, his calm rage more terrifying than when he lost control.

"I love you," she declared, stepping in closer to kiss him. But the moment she got too close, he palmed her face and slammed the back of her head into the wall.

She whimpered as he pinned her to the concrete slab, one side of her face pressed against the wall and the other trapped under Xavier's grip.

"You disgust me," he sneered in a whisper.

"I'm sorry."

"Your guilt embarrasses me."

Odette trembled at his mercy.

He let go and she fell to the floor.

"I have matters to attend to," he stated simply, his calm returned. "Be gone when I return."

"Gone?" Odette asked, confused.

"Yes," he stated, his tone condescending. "Gather your belongings and leave. I don't ever want to see you again."

Odette stared up at him in shock.

Xavier continued, "And if you think I'm joking, let the bruises on your face remind you that I'm not."

He stormed out of their apartment and Odette was left alone. She lifted her hand to the tender skin and winced—even the gentlest touch hurt. She raced to the bathroom to find that her cheekbone was already bruising.

She began to sob. Hastily, she grabbed a bag, packing only what she'd need. Thoughts of where she might go only furthered her despair—she had no friends, no allies to call upon. Only those in the jungle, and each time her mind returned there, her pride intensified her grief. Going back to Juniper was demoralizing; it meant she failed. It was also Juniper's fault that she found herself in this harrowing position.

Odette only knew this world under the protection of the Lamortes—without Xavier, she was alone and susceptible to the perils lurking in the streets.

She grabbed the note from Juniper and shoved it into the side pocket of her bag.

With tears in her eyes, she bundled up in her nicest jacket, threw her duffel bag over her shoulder, and left the comfort of the penthouse.

The outside air felt clammy as she exited the building—she hadn't left her well ventilated home in weeks as there was no need to. Food was delivered to them and she had no friends outside those walls. As she began her trek down the long, asphalt sidewalk, the dirty air filled her lungs. She coughed violently and wished she had packed a few more scarves.

The avenues were long and seemingly endless as she wandered aimlessly.

She had no place to go.

As the gray sky shifted to black, she realized that she also had nowhere to sleep. Terrified, but determined to carry on, she located a hostel on the corner of the nearest intersection. This hostel was one of many she had passed—they were everywhere, and they were all filled with people who lost their homes when Xavier initiated the rent tax.

Odette hurried inside, hoping she might have stumbled across one of the nicer hostels.

Her hopes were squashed the moment she scanned the establishment. The open layout was scattered with dirty beds, and the walls were decorated with foundation cracks. Rats and cockroaches—the only surviving rodents after the purge—scurried throughout the room, skittering over the people passed out on the floor. The overcrowded hostel had no open beds, so Odette found an empty space along the wall to rest for a while.

From riches to rags, Odette struggled to adapt to the harsh and abrupt change. Xavier portrayed his metal empire as a flourishing and healthy home for all, but what she was discovering was far from that.

The hostel reeked of sickness and despair. The beds were saved for those sick from the polluted skies, who coughed their contamination into the shared air. A group of motherless children ran about, creating a scene as they stole items from the bags of the elderly. There were no parents to discipline them. Chaos ran rampant. Tears filled Odette's eyes as she covered her nose and looked at the old man to her left—he was filthy, dressed in tattered clothes, and smelled of mildew and body odor. He slumbered peacefully beside her, unaware that she was there.

"Don't wake him," the woman to her right whispered.

"I didn't plan to."

"Good." The woman was missing most of her teeth. "He's a cranky old geezer."

Odette nodded and turned her attention back to her clasped hands resting on her lap.

The woman leaned in closer, breathing her rotten breath onto Odette's neck.

"I know you," she stated. "I've seen you before."

"Perhaps," Odette replied, not wishing to discuss her exile from the Lamorte inner circle.

"You are the president's lady trophy."

"I was his *wife*," Odette corrected her.

"Was?" The woman dug her elbow into Odette's thigh and rested her chin on her hand. "What happened?"

"It's complicated. I won't be here long."

"Lucky you," the woman spat, sitting back.

"How long have you lived here?"

"Since your husband initiated the rent tax," she spat. "I'm all for earning my way through life, but it's a bit unfair to ask for money from people without also offering them jobs."

"I see."

"When the sprawling cookie-cutter build of his empire finished, the masses were left jobless. There's no paying work anywhere, except for a few factory jobs that are impossible to qualify for," she explained. "I've tried. Always got denied. Only way to make a buck now is to join his army."

"Army?" Odette asked.

174

The woman dug into her canvas bag, ruffling through layers of garbage until she found the flyer she was looking for. She shoved it in Odette's face.

"To hunt this monster," she explained.

Odette snatched the flyer and stared at it in horrified awe. It was a picture of Juniper, except she looked different—whoever sketched her image turned her into an ugly, sinister looking devil. In large lettering it read: Juniper, the traitor.

The woman continued, "Apparently, she killed Sergei years ago, and now she and a few other women have threatened to dismantle the Lamorte empire. The president is offering housing, food, and money to anyone who joins his army." The woman paused in thought before continuing, "I considered joining ... then I also considered that I'd like to see his kingdom fall."

Odette looked around at the crowded hostel. "Looks like a lot of people would like to see him fail."

The woman shrugged. "He's a false prophet. Everything went to shit when his father died. Xavier isn't half the man that Sergei was."

Odette held her tongue, knowing that Sergei would have done no better for these people.

Odette felt betrayed; she felt dirty—while she lived a comfy life ignorant to all that happened a few stories below her, thousands of people suffered. Xavier merely put a glamourous bandage on a worsening wound, and she never questioned him. She didn't take a stand when she had the power to do so.

The fresh wound on her face stung, reminding her that maybe she couldn't have made a change anyway, that she might have been thrown onto the streets far sooner if she had tried.

It didn't matter now. She had no say, no power to make things better. She looked to the woman again.

"What's your name?"

"Marley."

"Nice to meet you, Marely. I'm Odette."

"I know."

"This woman in this sketch." Odette lifted the flyer. "I know her, and she isn't evil."

Marley nodded. "I figured as much. Besides the food and shelter, most people are joining the army to avenge Sergei, not to protect Xavier's reign."

"Juniper didn't kill Sergei."

Marley furrowed her brow. "How do you know?"

"I was there. I was a child in the jungle when it happened. I lived with Juniper for a long time before coming back here."

"You chose *this* place?" Marley asked in disbelief.

"I was young, and I didn't think I was cut out for jungle living. Regardless, Sergei entered the jungle to kill Juniper. He is to blame for his own fate."

"Why is Xavier gunning for her then?"

"He is delusional," Odette stated, beginning to see his true nature for herself. "He is his father's son."

"Sergei was a great man," Marley countered.

"I don't want to argue about Sergei's integrity with you—he is irrelevant now."

"And we are stuck with his satanic spawn of a son. The man knows nothing. Where are the schools? How can we build a functioning society without educating our youth? The next generation will produce no doctors, no scientists, no scholars. Our history and all the knowledge humans achieved will be lost within the forthcoming century."

Odette had no reply, nothing to say in defense of Xavier.

Marley continued, "He wants us to fail so that his elite group of chosen individuals can thrive." She shook her head. "But what he is failing to see is that he cannot control *who* will help our society progress, and if he denies education to the masses, he will lose great minds in the process."

"I agree with you."

"Did you ever challenge him?" Marley inquired.

Odette shook her head. "I'm ashamed to say that I did not. Until I left, I wasn't aware of what was going on outside my home. I only knew what Xavier told me—he never mentioned the absence of schools, and I never thought to ask."

"Go back and tell him. You're his wife. You have pull."

"It's not like that." Odette exhaled deeply, her breath rattling with suppressed anxiety. "I can't go back."

"Why not?"

"He kicked me out. It's a long story."

"That's a shame," Marley expressed, disappointed. "You missed your chance to make a change."

Odette felt ashamed. In the span of one setting sun, her entire world transformed. From a life of luxury to poverty, from in love to heartbroken—she was transforming too. Despite all she lost in such a short timeframe, her mind was focused on the surge of information she was acquiring. Her inactive role in oppressing an already suffering society weighed heavily on her heart, and she found herself motivated to fix what she involuntarily let transpire.

"Lucine likes me," Odette mumbled to herself.

"The sister?" Marley asked, then shrugged. "Still a better connection than the rest of us have."

"She's not like Xavier."

"That's why she has no power," Marley noted. "But she could. Can you reach her?"

"She's in Quadrant B4."

"Old New York? That's quite the hike."

"I don't have any other options."

"A lot of travelers pass through here," Marley explained. "The hostel organizers can give you some food and a map of safe spots to rest."

Odette nodded, thinking of Juniper again, whose fate depended on her courage. "I'll need all the help I can get."

Chapter 23

Hostel, Quadrant C2, North America

Morning arrived with the sound of voices echoing across the large open hall.

The hushed chattering woke Odette out of a deep yet uncomfortable slumber. She opened her eyes to ragged people bustling around the shabby establishment. Their stares were empty—no hope lived within—and their expressions were blank as they stood in a long line, waiting for the unappealing scraps being served for breakfast. The harsh reminder of her new reality fell on Odette's chest like one thousand bricks.

She closed her eyes and remembered her new mission: reach Lucine and help Juniper. She thought of Xavier and her heart ached—despite her love for him, she was never safe in his care, nor did he ever truly return her love. It was a cruel reality to accept, but she suspected he wouldn't miss her at all.

Odette looked over at Marley, who snored undisturbed, and decided not to wake her new friend before leaving. She flipped the unattractive army recruitment flyer over and scribbled the words *Thank you* onto the blank white page. She then folded the paper and left it on Marley's lap.

The trek across the country would take weeks, so she took what the hostel workers offered: a map of the country marked with every hostel location and a small bag of food. Odette peered into the soggy paper bag and sighed. Processed garbage that would last her two days.

She took for granted the fresh food she received while living with Xavier—very few had access to the vegetation and grains grown in the small patch of Washington that Xavier did not cover with asphalt. Her stomach might revolt, but she'd have to learn to adapt.

Odette zippered her jacket as high as it would go and exited the building. The thick, stale air made her eyes water. Her pores clogged up and she felt a layer of oil form on her forehead. The pollution was potent.

She shook her head, ashamed that this devolution happened right beneath her and she never did anything to stop it. Juniper would be so disappointed.

Through watery eyes, she peered outward at the never-ending stretch of sidewalk. It reached so far into the distance, the buildings appeared to touch and she could not see the end. She looked at her map, which showed this road led directly to the east coast of Quadrant C4, but no light came from that direction. The buildings were too tall and too tightly spaced. The roads were empty, but every so often, a Lamorte armored truck drove past. Being on the other side of the social divide,

181

Odette felt the flagrant insult of superiority each time one of these vehicles sped by.

Time was elusive without sight of the sun to guide the day, only faint shifts from gray to black. When Odette felt nighttime approaching, she examined her map and found a nearby hostel where she could rest.

Inside, she was greeted by a familiar sight: an open gymnasium covered in dirty cots and walls with cracked foundations. Numerous flyers of Juniper—an aggressive, unrelenting call to join Xavier's army—adorned the walls. Too many bodies shuffled about, and once again, she was stuck with a tiny space of wall to lean against.

She took her place and waited out the night, leaving quietly the moment the light gray sky illuminated the large space. She tiptoed around the countless bodies that lay strewn across the floor and out the front door. She was exhausted, but determined to reach Lucine.

The days passed in a tiring blur, and she began to lose track of how many nights she had spent in each identical hostel, but her end goal kept her moving forward.

The overbearing police presence kept the people indoors. The roads were empty, outside the occasional Lamorte vehicle. The sidewalks were clean, as were the shiny sides of every building she passed. Very few people crossed her path as she traveled east, leaving her wildly alone with her thoughts.

When she crossed into Quadrant C3, the sights began to change. People wandered the streets here: orphans begging for food, a widowed man asking for spare change to feed his baby, a sickly woman coughing as she hobbled by.

Odette also noticed that the sanitation crew was far less diligent here—there was litter everywhere. Trash was scattered along the streets, garbage was piled in heaps on the sidewalk, and graffiti decorated the asphalt and steel buildings in sporadic bursts. Such disrespect for Xavier's empire was not tolerated in Quadrant C2, but here, the rules appeared to be less strict.

In addition to the lack of order, the placement of the army recruitment flyers here was more public. Juniper's unbecoming portrait was everywhere. On posters, on flyers littering the streets, on billboards hung across the buildings. The propaganda was impossible to escape. What was subtle in Quadrant C2, where most of Xavier's relatives resided, was blatant and persistent in Quadrant C3. Odette felt the shift and wondered if she was in for greater trouble here.

Upon entering her first C3 hostel, a woman rushed up to her, eyes glowing with adoration.

"I love you," she blurted out as she grabbed Odette's hands and kissed them repeatedly. "You are everything I aspire to be."

"Thank you," she replied, alarmed.

"You are the face of the female plight. You are strong, as we will need to be in this fight."

Odette struggled, but eventually broke free of the woman's grip.

"Are you here to inspire the women who haven't yet joined the army?"

"No."

Odette's blunt reply startled the woman.

"Then why are you here?" she asked, looking over Odette's shoulder. "Is the president with you?"

"He is not."

The woman glanced at the wound healing on Odette's face, then at her battered appearance.

"Are you here on his behalf?" she asked, her excitement fading.

"I am not."

Her gushing idolization for Odette vanished as fast as it had arrived and her energy turned vile.

"Then you should go," she stated, her glare threatening.

Odette nodded and backed away. As she neared the door, a large man burst through, shouting orders at the masses who stopped what they were doing and formed attentive lines.

"This place is a mess," he shouted, storming forward. "Everyone! Drop and give me fifty!"

The large group obeyed and everyone fell to the floor, racing to complete fifty push-ups.

When Odette did not fall with the rest of them, his attention snapped to her.

It was Killian.

Thankful, Odette opened her mouth to speak, but Killian quickly shook his head and his eyes widened with concern. Odette swallowed her relieved greeting, and the overwhelming feeling of terror returned.

Killian took slow steps toward her, still shouting at the others to keep going. When he was right beside her, he whispered, "Go outside. Around the corner into the alley. I will meet you there."

Odette slipped out of the building as the first solider finished his set of push-ups and jumped back to attention.

Terrified, Odette obeyed Killian's instructions and waited in the alley. Though her initial feeling was relief, perhaps his unexpected arrival into her journey was not welcome—he *was* one of Xavier's closest allies.

Still, she waited, praying that he might help her.

An hour passed before he joined her in the alley. He wore a look of grave concern as he approached.

"What are you doing here?" he whispered frantically.

"Xavier kicked me out."

Killian noticed the healing bruise across her face. "Quite literally, it appears."

Odette nodded. "I'm trying to get to Lucine."

"Why?"

"I thought she might take me in."

Killian paused in thought. "It's not a terrible idea. Lucine is much kinder than her brother. But you'll never make it there alive."

"Why do you say that?"

"The Midwest and lower eastern quadrants are volatile," he told her. "The farther you go, the more devoted to Xavier they are. If they see you and realize you're no longer with him, they will think you are a traitor."

"Like Juniper?" Odette asked.

Killian exhaled heavily. "Something like that."

"Why are you helping him?"

"I don't have a choice. He threatened my family."

Odette shook her head. "I'm sorry."

"So am I. I saw what happened to Sergei. We are leading these innocent people into a slaughter."

"I saw one recruitment flyer in C2, but here, it's everywhere."

"Xavier is trying to hide his intentions from his family. Dante would never allow the reinstatement of the hunt for Champions. B4, where Lucine lives, looks a lot like C2 as well."

"But everywhere else looks like this?"

"Yes."

"What do I do?"

"I might be able to help you get to B4, but Xavier can never know."

"I won't tell a soul."

He trusted her.

"Come with me."

Killian led Odette down the corridor into a second alleyway where the backs of the buildings nearly touched. The dark maze seemed to go on forever as Killian used the labyrinth to sneak her around the city.

He stopped next to a door marked with green paint.

"We are here," he informed her as he pulled out a key ring. He sorted through them, eventually locating a gold-painted key amongst the steel ones. Killian unlocked the door.

"Is this where you live?" Odette asked. The narrow hallway gave her anxiety as he led her farther inside.

Killian nodded. "I've stopped using the front door. It's too dangerous."

"Seemed like the people at the hostel respected you."

"They either idolize me because I am in direct contact with Xavier, or they hate me. There is an underground revolution plotting against the Lamorte regime. They haven't found their voice yet, but they are growing."

"Does Xavier know?"

"Not yet."

"Will you tell him?"

Killian shrugged. "I think I might've chosen the revolution over this war if I hadn't been blackmailed into picking a side."

He stopped and looked at Odette. "My family is hungry," he confessed. "Even with decent rations shipped to us, it isn't enough. I don't mean to sound ungrateful—I know that so many others have it far worse—but the world Xavier is building isn't sustainable. Humans need nature. We need fresh air, clean water, and vegetation."

"He is terrified of nature," Odette said.

"I know. But he is wrong. We will all die if something doesn't change."

Killian turned back around and led Odette up a tightly wound staircase. They climbed until they reached another door marked with green paint.

"What does it mean?" Odette asked.

Killian examined the green paint for a moment before lifting his key ring. "The green paint is sort of like a white flag. For a while, the revolutionists were secretly assassinating the die-hard supporters of the Lamortes. Then the Lamorte extremists began publicly slaughtering small groups of the revolutionists. It only lasted a year, news of it stayed local, but those of us caught in the middle began painting green streaks on our doors as a sign of neutrality. We did not pick a side, we did not want to be involved." Killian paused, key pressed into the lock. "Except now, if the revolutionists saw *my* door with green paint—the lead commander for Xavier's army—everyone with this mark would be in danger. They'd see the truce as a lie and come after all of us."

"The maze of alleyways keeps the location of your home undiscoverable?"

Killian nodded. "And I can't show any signs of doubt in Xavier—I can't play both sides. Doing so would surely be reported back to him and then my family would be in direct danger."

"I understand. Thank you for taking this risk to help me."

"We go way back," Killian stated as he opened the door. "I've known you since you were a little girl. You might as well be family."

Odette smiled with gratitude and followed Killian into his home.

The apartment was small and dilapidated—for someone directly connected to the president, Killian's life was far from luxurious. Far better than the hostels, but only because there weren't hundreds of people crammed into the small space. He and his family had some privacy here.

"Karli," Killian announced their arrival. "We have a guest tonight."

Karli exited the room their children shared wearing a smile, but upon seeing Odette, her expression dropped.

"Is everything okay?" Karli asked, the worry in her voice apparent.

"I'm not with him anymore," Odette explained, sensing the root of her concern. "He kicked me out."

"Why?"

"He thought I was working with Juniper, which I wasn't, but now, perhaps I will."

Karli looked to Killian. "What if Xavier finds out?"

"He won't. She isn't staying long. I'm just going to help her map a safe route to B4."

Karli nodded then looked back to Odette. "Are you hungry? I have some leftover boxed potatoes."

Odette nodded. "Thank you."

While Karli heated up the cardboard-tasting potatoes, Killian got to work. He spread a map of the country out on the table and began showing Odette her safest options. Odette paid close attention.

"The further east you go, the worse it will be for you. C3 is a mess, but it's much worse in B3, so don't go north. You'll need to travel into C4, then up into B4. C4 is a lot like C3, so be careful." Killian uncapped his pen and began circling specific street corners. "These hostels should be safe. The guards here aren't too extreme … still, you'll want to be disguised. I'll have Karli lend you a pair of sunglasses and a scarf." He counted the rows of streets and began placing X-marks on the map. "Do *not* go to these hostels. You won't make it out alive." He then traced the southern border to quadrant B4. "Dennis and Oliver Palladon patrol this border. They are just as rotten as they were when they were kids. Don't try to cross into B4 here. Follow the border line up into B3, but don't spend a lot of time there—cross into B4 before nightfall. Once you're in B4, you should be fine. Most of the hostels there are a lot like the ones in C2. Relatively tame, not too many extremists. The revolution is there, but they aren't as angry as the ones who live here. You should be able to get to Lucine without much trouble."

"Thank you," she expressed as Killian folded the map and gave it to her.

Odette ate and understood why Killian's family was still hungry after eating a government-rationed meal. It wasn't enough—there were zero nutrients in the chemically processed food. She had been on the streets for days, possibly weeks—she lost count—and she too was beginning to feel the lack of energy from malnutrition. There was no food available like that which she received while living with Xavier. He was starving the masses, driving them deeper into poverty in an attempt to force compliance. The more Odette saw the truth, the more disgusted she became. She had to reach Lucine. She had to talk sense into the only Lamorte who might listen to reason.

When morning arrived, Odette awoke to the sound of children laughing. She opened her eyes and saw Killian lying on the floor, pretending to be a monster while his twin toddlers crawled all over him, giggling. The sight brought a smile to her face—joy still lived in this ugly world.

The moment she sat up, a surge of nausea coursed through her, forcing her to run to the bathroom and vomit.

"Are you okay?" Karli asked.

"Yes," Odette replied, cleaning her mouth and panting. "I think my stomach is revolting. I'm not yet used to all the chemicals in the processed foods."

"I see. You will adjust," Karli stated with a smile.

Odette ate a quick bowl of Sugar Bombs cereal, hoping the almond milk and sugary grains might coat her stomach before gathering her belongings.

"Thank you both. That is the first time I got a full night's sleep since I left C2."

"You could stay a little longer if you'd like," Karli offered.

"I appreciate that, but I must go. Juniper's fate depends on me convincing Lucine to take a stand against her brother."

"I hope you succeed," Killian expressed. "I wish we could follow you there, but Xavier would be able to find us anywhere."

"Not in the jungle," Odette suggested.

Killian's brow furrowed in thought. "Will you return there?"

"Possibly." Odette saw the intrigue hidden within Killian's eyes. "I will try to find a way to let you know if I do. Then you and your family can join me."

Killian nodded, afraid to agree to too much. "Yes. Let me know if you can. I'm a dead man where I currently stand—the revolutionists will kill me if they take over, and a life ruled by Xavier is always one small mistake away from death. I am trapped."

"I owe you for your kindness," Odette expressed. "If I can get you out of here, I will."

Karli lunged forward and buried Odette in a hug. "Thank you," she expressed with tears in her eyes.

Odette realized her mission was much bigger than the fate of just Juniper—hundreds of oppressed people would be set free if Xavier was removed from power.

She wasn't sure how her quest would unfold, be it the Champions or the revolution, but someone needed to end the Lamorte reign.

Chapter 24

Cricket's Pier, Nether Isle

Sergei examined the mysterious girl—dark brown curls hung over her shoulders, cascading down her white nightgown like shadows streaked across the fullest moon. Purple circles cradled her wide eyes and her face looked as hollow as death. Her pale flesh held undertones of blue, and in the daylight she appeared translucent. She looked like a child, yet her presence felt ancient.

"Are you dead like me?" Sergei asked.

"Not like *you*," Bianca spat in reply, her tone condescending.

"Then like who?"

"I am not like anyone," she informed the infantile ghoul. "I am evolved. I am powerful."

"Show me," Sergei taunted.

"I don't need to prove anything to you."

Sergei's eyes narrowed and he turned away. "Then leave."

"What are you trying to do?" Bianca asked, stepping closer to his mishmash of crystals and runes.

"I am trying to make my children see me."

"Did they stay bound to Earth? Or did they go through the light?"

"What?" Sergei spat. "One is in Utah. The other is in New York. Percival gave me this book and Theodore led me to this house. He was *supposed* to show me how to use the crystals," Sergei groaned.

"Theodore?"

"Yes. The back bedroom is loaded with pretty rocks, but as soon as we got here, he left. Jumped off the pier and walked across the ocean into the horizon."

Bianca glanced out the broken window, but saw no signs of her lost friend. She returned her focus to Sergei's earlier comment.

"If your children's spirits are earthbound, you shouldn't need magic to reach them."

"They can't see me when I visit."

"Why not?"

"I suspect it's because I'm dead," Sergei replied with a grunt.

"The dead can always see the dead."

"My children aren't dead."

Bianca paused. "Everyone died during the purge."

"Not everyone."

Bianca stepped closer, her intrigue amplified. "Tell me more."

"What more is there to say? All I've managed to do is scare them."

"How many people survived the purge?" Bianca asked, ignoring his confusion.

"Loads." He paused in thought, his eyelids lowering as he tried to recall what he could not remember.

Bianca refused to lose him to the groggy fog of purgatory.

"Focus," she demanded. "Your children," she stated, bringing back the memory Sergei clung to most dearly. "What are their names?"

Sergei blinked a few times, returning to his former clarity, and eagerly refocused on a matter he could recall.

"Xavier and Lucine," he replied.

"They are alive?"

"Yes."

"Why do you wish for them to see you?" she pried, hoping there was more to his quest than sentimental drivel.

"They need to finish my mission," he replied, his brow furrowed. The fog threatened to take over again, but he managed to remain alert. "They need to complete the hunt."

"The hunt for what?"

"Champions," Sergei replied. His eyes cleared and his expression contorted with rage—thoughts of his enemy lived on within him more potently than that of his children.

Bianca grinned, satisfied that they were getting somewhere. "Explain to me what a Champion is."

"They killed us all," Sergei shouted. "They are the reason so many died!"

"How so? I saw the purge from the infinite dark. Kólasi pulled back the curtains so we could watch."

"The Champions can talk to nature," Sergei replied, his tone manic.

"They told nature to attack?"

"No, but they were warned. And they didn't warn the rest of us. My family survived by sheer luck."

"Did the Champions save anyone?"

"Yeah, but not enough," Sergei spat. "They each have a following."

"How many Champions are there?"

The search for specifics in the depths of his mind opened the door for the fog to return. As he clawed his way through the recesses of his memory, he dug up a number before the haze took over.

"Seven," he replied, clarity fading.

"Xavier and Lucine," Bianca stated. The mention of their names snapped Sergei back to the present.

"I must reach them," Sergei insisted as his awareness returned.

"I will help you."

Sergei hesitated. "Why?"

"Because we are friends."

"We are?"

"We've known each other a long time. Don't you remember?"

Sergei paused, unable to recall how long he'd been in this house, sitting on this floor, talking to this child-ghost. He looked down at the black crystal in his hand then back up at the girl.

"You do look familiar," he stated.

"That's because we have been working together for a long time now. I've been trying to help you reach your children. I knew Xavier and Lucine. They were my best friends."

"You miss them too?" he asked.

"I do."

"We must reach them."

"We will." She extended an arm toward where he sat. "Take my hand."

The moment their spirits touched, they were whisked away into a vortex. All he could see was Bianca spinning around him in blurred speed.

"Show me your enemy," she instructed.

Sergei wobbled with dizziness. "How?"

"Think of them."

Sergei closed his eyes and pictured the forest. Within the tightly spaced trees, in the darkest shadows of the woods, appeared Juniper's face.

They were taken there.

When the spinning stopped, Sergei opened his eyes. They were inside the trees, looking out onto the verdant jungle.

"I have been here before," Sergei stated.

"I can tell," Bianca replied. *"You've left messy trails of black magic all over this place."*

"I've done some damage to those out there as well," he stated, hoping to impress her. *"I bewitched the apes. They almost killed Juniper for me."*

"We need to discuss your intent to kill her," Bianca stated.

Before Sergei could object, movement came from beyond the trees.

They became still and watched.

A woman was collecting berries, moving slowly and calmly, unaware that she was being observed.

"That is Liesel Böhme," Sergei replied, his memory electric with adrenaline. *"She lived with my people when she was a young girl. Her family betrayed me."*

"I see."

"Let's kill her."

"No."

"Why not?" Sergei asked, outraged.

"Because we cannot possess a dead body."

"I don't understand."

"You will."

Bianca dragged him forward, jumping from tree to tree with ease. She followed the sound of distant voices until she reached a small oak tree surrounded by taller trees covered in huts. She transported into the shorter oak and reveled in the 360-degree view of the little community.

The people bustled about, living harmoniously in simplicity.

"There are so many of them," Bianca noted in awe, salivating subconsciously at all the bodies there were to take.

"They've been reproducing," Sergei explained, displeased.

"More bodies than I could ever possibly need." She looked to Sergei. *"Which one is the leader?"*

Sergei turned his attention beyond the golden-green swirl of the tree's spirit and located Juniper mending a sparrow's wing with her daughter Elodie.

"There," he stated. *"The one with brown hair. The blonde is her daughter—she's a freak, just like her mom."*

"And there are six additional Champions with similar sized followings?" Bianca asked.

"At least five. We killed one of them a while back."

Their conversation was interrupted by an unwelcome presence.

"Show yourself!" a man shouted.

Sergei rolled his eyes at the sound of the righteous voice. Bianca looked to Sergei, confused.

"Roscoe," he explained. *"Juniper's husband. His spirit lives in these trees."*

"Maybe we can recruit him," Bianca stated.

Sergei laughed in reply. *"Not a chance. He would die a second time to protect Juniper if he could."*

"I can sway his allegiance."

"He's more fun to taunt."

Bianca saw Roscoe's stubbornness as a challenge, but dropped her interest for now. *"Let's go. I've seen enough."*

She began to spin, carrying Sergei with her as they traveled away from the jungle. When they returned to Nether Isle, they landed back in the abandoned hut where Theodore used to live.

Bianca paced, deep in thought. She *could* finish what she started so many years ago. She *could* try again.

"What are you doing?" Sergei asked, his faded attention returning.

"Thinking."

"About what?"

Bianca paused, then glared at Sergei contemplatively. "What do you think about opening the portal?"

"The portal to where?"

"The infinite dark."

"Why would we do that?"

"You said that you hate the Champions because they stood by idly while millions perished. That they had the information to save countless lives yet did not warn the masses. You want to avenge the fallen by killing the Champions."

"Exactly." Sergei's rage reignited his focus.

"What if, instead, we brought them all back?" Bianca asked wearing a sly smile.

"Bring back the dead?"

Bianca nodded. "Into the bodies of the living."

Sergei stared at her blankly, too bewildered to completely understand what she inferred.

Bianca took his silence as compliance. "Excellent." She smiled. "But first, I need to teach you dark magic."

She left the rickety hut on Cricket's Pier, beckoning Sergei to follow. He obeyed and together they made their way toward the Ouijan mansion.

This world would be hers.

She would taste the intoxicating breath of life once more.

Chapter 25

Antarctica

"Nothing is as it should be," Marisabel expressed with her fingers dug into the snow. A frigid breeze swept past, but she no longer felt the cold—she *was* the cold.

A thin layer of ice coated her flesh, cracking and falling off, only to reform again. It came back stronger each time, and soon, she suspected that only intense heat would be able to break her armor.

She kept her fingers in the snow, focusing on the feeling of death she'd grown so fascinated by—that which surrounded her and those fleeting moments she wished to know what death felt like.

Concentrated on her morbid fantasies, she was startled when an ethereal voice entered her mind.

<<*You are exactly as I need you to be.*>>

Marisabel's spirit lifted and she lost her grip on her grisly thoughts.

You came, Marisabel expressed, in awe that Gaia chose to visit her.

<<*The aftermath of the purge has not transpired as I hoped.*>>

We are very sorry about that.

<<You are not to blame. There are forces beyond your control intervening.>>

The Debauched?

<<A force far greater than them; one that rivals my own power. What matters now is that I give you the required tools to defeat your new adversary.>>

The snow around Marisabel lifted and danced around her in a snowy cyclone. Divine energy sparked from the revolving flurries, striking her icy skin with heat. It hurt, but she let the magic run its course, accepting Gaia's mysterious gift without question.

When the warmth of Gaia's touch began to melt all of Marisabel's iced armor, the snowflakes fell back to the ground and the cyclone vanished.

Marisabel felt the same, as if nothing had changed.

Why don't I feel different?

<<Because you've already welcomed death as a friend.>>

Marisabel's alarm heightened. *Am I dead?*

<<No, of course not. You need to be alive to help your sisters protect the living world. I simply gave you access to the bridge connecting life and death.>>

Like a medium?

<<Much more powerful than that. You will understand the full potential of this gift over time. But I do urge that you begin practicing now. Your sisters will not be able to defeat Kólasi without you.>>

Who is Kólasi?

<<My brother, the Father of Death. You might know him as Satan, or Lucifer, or the Devil. But really, Satan is Kólasi's son.>>

Marisabel's heart dropped—despite her belief in Gaia, she never dreamt that other gods existed, nor did she ever imagine she'd be the only one who could save humanity from the Devil.

Is he to blame for the rebels surviving?

<<Not completely, but he is to blame for all those human spirits choosing the infinite dark over a rebirth into nature. And for the atrocious metal sprawl covering North America. He thrives on chaos, particularly causing chaos in my worlds. I tried to ruin his edifice during the purge, but I failed. And now, I suspect he is using the portal to stir up more chaos.>>

Are the powers you gave me really strong enough to take on the Devil?

<<That is my hope. I do not wish to intervene further.>>

Perhaps you ought to intervene.

<<It is against my code. I do not like to meddle with the freewill of my creatures.>>

It's not about freewill, it's about survival.

<<If I enter any of my worlds in physical form, the entire ecosystem will instantly combust, leaving a blank canvas from which I must start all over again. That is how it works. And while I have far greater forms of defense than nature, I do not wish to unleash them upon the human race.>>

Why not?

<<Because they too have freewill, and unfortunately, they are also unpredictable. It could end in the unintentional extinction of mankind. I would rather give you the chance to remedy what my brother has begun than unearth a precarious solution to this problem.>>

What if I fail? Marisabel asked, her confidence wavering.

<<You won't.>>

Gaia's ethereal hand comforted Marisabel's spirit. She closed her eyes, her ice-tipped eyelashes long and flowing, and when she opened them again, Gaia's enormous energy was gone.

In its place were thousands of dead snow petrels soaring overhead. Their ghosts flew in beautiful patterns, creating a spiritual shield that blanketed her.

Marisabel lifted her hand and beckoned the birds to come closer. Atop her extended finger landed a single snow bird. It stared at her, seemingly peering into her soul from the afterlife.

"I thought I was alone," she stated. The bird chirped. "But you've been here all along."

The swarm of dead snow birds broke into a harmonious song, one that filled Marisabel with warmth. The small bird on her finger hopped from her arm to her shoulder and then circled her head. Within its tiny whirlwind, it spoke into her mind.

::Our spirits can unite. Through me, you can travel elsewhere.::

Marisabel was shocked. "Like Juniper?" she asked.

::Similar—she can pair with living animals, while you can only tether to the dead.::

"I see."

::There are far more animal spirits roaming about than there are living. The portal into the afterlife became jammed by the humans, and many of us never got a chance to cross over.::

"Can you take me north toward Maine? I need to find the little isle Juniper mentioned."

The bird chirped and flew faster around Marisabel's hair. Her long curls began to levitate as the wind intensified.

::Let go of your body,:: the snow bird instructed.

Marisabel relaxed, releasing control, and her consciousness leapt into the bird.

The cool air tore through their spirits as they flew north. A thin tether kept her bound to her living body, but her soul was now dancing with the dead. It was a freeing feeling; she was weightless—though it felt like a gamble with fate.

::Is my body safe?:: she asked.

::I won't let the tether break.::

::And if it does?::

::Your living life would end.::

Marisabel began flexing the slender tether, hoping to strengthen it. Once it was unbreakable, she'd have nothing to fear.

The snow bird rose and fell, daring the volatile ocean to cover them. Sea spray splashed, passing through them each time. The bird even dove beneath the waves, but the currents could not snag them. They were unreachable.

They flew over Australia, which remained flooded and uninhabited, then east toward North America. The moment the coast of California came into view, Marisabel felt a sickening twist in her stomach—the horizon was blanketed in steel skyscrapers.

Soaring closer, she saw that the entire continent was covered in a grid of metal and asphalt. The stench of tar and fumes filled the sky, and a haze of pollution swathed the sprawling city.

::There is a similar growth in Europe,:: the snow bird informed.

::Do you know if they've recovered the weapons of mass destruction from the past?::

::Of that, I am not sure. I only know what I see from above.::

::If they come for the Champions again, we might be outmatched. And though what they've built is the opposite of Gaia's desires, they

look strong.:: She scanned the never-ending rows of shiny skyscrapers. ::*It goes on forever.*::

::*Just to the coast,*:: the snow bird corrected her.

::*Fly north,*:: she instructed, and the bird obliged.

The metal grid continued, ending near the old border into Canada. The asphalt crumbled, joining the rich soil, and the last of the buildings along the edge appeared vacant—an abrupt stop to the grid. For now, those northern territories were safe from the harmful touch of mankind.

::*Now south,*:: she commanded, and they soared toward the former Mexican border. Again, the steel sprawl ended and the dusty desert began. Marisabel scanned farther south, relived to see that the land between North America and Tier was still untouched by the Lamortes.

::*How do we rid the Earth of this cancerous sore?*::

::*Humans never learn.*::

Marisabel sighed. ::*Let's head to Maine. I have ghosts to deal with first.*::

The snow bird rocketed forward, reaching the northeastern coast in a blink. Marisabel felt her tether tug tighter, but she trusted the gift that Gaia gave her.

Circling the rickety fishing village, Marisabel was shocked to see so many bodies bustling around.

::*Are they all dead?*:: Marisabel asked.

::*All of them,*:: the snow petrel confirmed.

In the distance she could see Kólasi's edifice—the lighthouse glowed despite the dark sky, illuminated by an undefined source. Its haunted energy sent an eerie chill through Marisabel's soul.

She turned her focus back to her current mission.

::*I need to find a ghost named Sergei Lamorte,*:: she stated, unsure where to begin her search, when a blast of purple smoke appeared over the hill past the piers.

They flew toward the mansion on the hill, entering through a broken window, and found the source of the purple smoke in a small courtyard in the back. A young girl was coaching a beleaguered man over a black pot filled with bubbling water. Marisabel spied from a nearby tree.

"You're still doing it wrong," the girl stated, waving away the thick smoke.

"This spell is stupid," the man argued. "I don't want to make rain."

"You have to start small," she countered, then took a deep breath. "Sergei, you must follow my lead. I know what I am doing."

"I want my children to see me!" he screamed, kicking the large pot and spilling the boiling water all over the ground.

The girl lowered her gaze, her energy sinister.

"I will not help you if you act like a child," she warned.

Sergei howled into the sky, throwing a frustrated tantrum for all to hear.

The girl did not react, instead she turned and walked away.

Sergei stopped bellowing the moment she began to depart, groveling as he chased after her.

"No, please stay," he begged. "I need you, Bianca. I cannot learn this magic alone."

"You should have thought of that before."

"I'll do better," he promised, but his pleas did not sway Bianca. She glared over her shoulder, snapped her fingers, and disappeared.

Sergei stood in awe. Dread and self-pity lined his face. He fell to his knees, tears spilling down his face, but after a moment, his expression went blank, as if he had already forgotten the altercation between himself and Bianca. As if his tantrum never happened.

He looked to the tipped pot, then up at the book of spells perched upon a stone podium. With unfocused determination, he flipped through the pages, desperately trying to remember where he was.

Marisabel observed, carefully examining the fragile nature of this man. While he seemed unstable, Bianca surely was not. She was solid and strong—too powerful. It wasn't Sergei they needed to fear, but Bianca's influence over him.

Marisabel waited in the tree, resolved to learn what the ghost girl had planned.

Chapter 26

Quadrant B4, North America

Max took Lucine's hand. "Are you ready?"

She nodded, but she wasn't ready at all. For months, she felt like a prisoner to the mysterious force that was haunting her, and now she was about to seek it out and confront this potential nightmare.

"What do you think we will find?" she asked.

"Answers," Max replied. "If we find nothing, then we can rest easier knowing that you were merely suffering from night terrors. If we find something, then we can assess how to deal with it."

Lucine exhaled deeply—neither option would make the hauntings stop.

"I just want it to end."

"Maybe we will find something beautiful—a gift from another lifetime," he stated. "Perhaps your brother's metal grid is less established there; maybe we will find signs of life under the asphalt."

"I doubt Xavier missed covering a single inch of soil. His fear of nature runs deep."

"Still, I have hope." Max smiled and Lucine let his optimism blanket her anxiety. For a moment, she felt safe. With him, she would be alright.

Bundled up and ready to face the unknown, they jumped into Lucine's government issued Humvee and began the trek north.

"I haven't driven this in forever," Lucine noted as she reacquainted herself with the workings of the large vehicle. The roads in B4 were barren of vehicles and overcrowded with people—she was one of the few with access to a motor vehicle— and the pedestrians accustomed to walking in the middle of the streets were startled as the tanker cruised up behind them. People jumped in surprise, rushing to the sidewalks as Lucine crept slowly behind them, careful not to go too fast and risk hurting anyone.

"We'll never get there at this rate," she groaned.

"Without cars, the streets have become large sidewalks," Max replied with a shrug. "No one is used to seeing trucks drive through."

"I know. I just hope the crowds clear soon."

"There will be less people the farther north we go. We'll move faster soon."

"I bet this is great for my super popular reputation," Lucine remarked sarcastically. "One more thing to make them hate me."

"No one hates you," Max replied, grabbing her free hand and holding it within his. "They just wish you stood up for them."

"My brother scares me too," she confessed. "But I'm trying. And now that I'm with you and part of the revolution, I feel like I can finally take a stand against him. I just need to sort out these terrors I've been experiencing first."

"I will help you. We will figure it out together."

The roads cleared of people once they reached old Albany. There were few highways remaining—Xavier only built three: the Cross Grid interstate running west to east, the Pacific Coast highway that hugged the western coast, and the East Coast highway that ran from old Miami up to the top of Maine. When Lucine reached the East Coast highway, their progress tripled and the trek began to move at a more bearable pace.

The scenery stayed the same: tall steel buildings lined the highway, making it impossible to see beyond the wall of metal. The ocean was to their right, but out of view, and straight ahead all they could see was asphalt and the never-ending rows of empty skyscrapers. There weren't enough surviving people to live in them, but Xavier did not care. He just wanted the land covered in impenetrable steel so that no traces of nature could pop through.

"This is disheartening," Max commented a few hours into their trip. "Xavier was upsettingly thorough in his build."

"I told you. He didn't miss an inch."

"Has he moved into Canada yet?"

"He plans to, but I think this sudden desire to resume my father's hunt for Champions has slowed his expansion north and south. He's consumed by hatred, just like my father was." Lucine paused. "It killed him, this silly hunt for people who chose to live differently than us. It'll likely kill Xavier too."

Max showed no remorse for this possibility, but kept those thoughts to himself. "My fear is that he *will* be more successful than Sergei when he finally strikes. We cannot let him harm Juniper or the others. They are our only hope."

Lucine nodded. "I know. I don't want him to hurt them either. No one wants this war to happen, but he's promising food and shelter to the people he has oppressed, and we can't blame them for taking the bait."

"It's so backwards. He's paying them with the basic rights he has denied them."

"We will find a way to fix everything," Lucine responded with conviction. "Gideon and I have some power too."

"The revolution spans farther than B4. We are everywhere. We just need to unite. We need a plan. We need a leader. We tried to get Gideon to step into that role, but while his presence strengthened the resolve of the movement, he wasn't quite ready to take a true stand against Xavier." Max looked to Lucine, who was staring intently at the road. "So now our hopes land on you."

Her gaze darted to Max for a moment then back to the road. "You want to pit me against him? I thought I was going to try to peacefully sway his focus."

"Do you really think that's possible?"

Lucine sighed. "No."

"Brother versus sister. People will pick a side, and we suspect many will choose yours."

"So you *do* want a war, just one that tears my family apart?"

"How does the rest of your family feel about his plans?"

"No one agrees. We all remember what it did to my father."

"So it won't tear your family apart. It'll just force Xavier to see reason."

"It will only infuriate him. It will make him irrational and unpredictable."

"More so than he is now?"

"Yes," Lucine replied with confidence. "Currently, he is tame. You underestimate his capacity for evil."

"Then we will have to be careful."

"We will need to be calculated and precise in our timing. You cannot associate my face with the revolution until we have a safe plan in place. If Xavier thinks I betrayed him, I can only imagine the horror he'd inflict on everyone." She looked over at Max again. "Are you hearing me? You need to heed my warning."

"I am. I trust you know your brother better than we do. We just cannot wait much longer. He will take his troops south soon, and if we don't act before then, we will lose."

Lucine kept her eyes on the road, deep in thought. The endless rows of buildings began to flicker and then everything went black, causing Lucine to swerve. Max grabbed the steering wheel and jerked them back onto the road.

"What the hell?" he exclaimed.

Lucine shook her head, trying to clear the darkness from her sight. As the light returned, a shadowy silhouette appeared in the middle of the road. She drove straight through it and then looked for it in her rearview mirror.

It was gone.

"We are getting close," she informed Max.

"Are you okay? Should I drive?"

"I'm fine." She ripped her hand from Max's and held onto the steering wheel tightly, ready to reach the end of this nightmare.

They drove to the very end of the East Coast highway, reaching the abrupt edge of Xavier's towering city. Lucine and Max jumped out of the truck and walked to where the asphalt transitioned into dusty soil.

"What now?" Max asked.

Lucine looked to the east. "The mark was off the coast of Maine. We've gone too far north."

"I'll fill the tank," Max stated, heading to the trunk and retrieving one of the canisters filled with spare fuel. This resource was sparse, and only the Lamortes had access to petroleum.

Xavier never built along the coast—the terrain was too soft—so instead, he covered the ground with tar-coated gravel. Hundreds of thousands of pounds of the toxic sediment blanketed the coast, with only a single roadway remaining accessible. Lucine drove along this narrow road, eyes scanning the coast, looking for any sign that she might be close.

The day faded into night, turning the gray sky black, and as her hopes began to deflate, a light appeared in the distance.

"Do you see that?" she asked Max.

He turned his sleepy attention toward the choppy ocean and saw the glowing light.

"Yeah," he replied. "What do you think it is?"

"Our next destination."

"How? We don't have a boat."

"I'm a Lamorte," she reminded him. "I have access to *every* boat." Lucine stopped the car and turned off the engine. "Let's sleep here for the night. I'll reach out to my uncle in the morning."

They climbed into the back of the truck where the seats were folded down and there was room to spread out, and then fell asleep in each other's arms.

A light gray haze and the smell of salty sea water woke them. Lucine sat up first. She rubbed her eyes, looked out the window, and saw nothing where she had seen the glowing light the night before. No land, no boat. Nothing.

The explosive waves crashed against the seawall, spraying foam droplets into the air.

Lucine climbed back into the driver's seat, retrieved her radio from the glove compartment, and turned the dial to the one set for Dante's radio. They communicated frequently when she first left Utah, but they hadn't conversed via radio in years. Lucine prayed he would answer her call. She sent multiple alerts through the receiver, attempting to buzz Dante's radio awake, then waited.

Max rustled in the back of the truck, attempting to steal a few more minutes of sleep.

"Hello?" Dante's voice materialized through the radio.

"Uncle Dante," Lucine greeted. "How are you?"

"I've been better," he replied. "I didn't sleep well."

"Why not?"

"I learned of your brother's plans to resume the hunt for the Champions right before falling asleep. I do hope that is not why you are reaching out to me after so long …"

"I am not aligned with my brother on this matter."

"Good. He's a sneaky devil, that brother of yours."

"I plan to stop him before he sends troops south."

"How will you manage that?"

"I'm not sure yet, but I am going to try."

"If that is why you called, then I would be happy to help."

"That's not why I called, actually, but I will take you up on that offer when the time arrives. Right now, I need your help with a different matter. I need a boat."

"For what?"

"A quick sail off the coast of Maine. I don't imagine I'd need the boat for more than 24-hours. And I'd rather Xavier never find out about it."

"A quick sail? Do you realize how unstable the ocean is? I've lost countless men to the vicious tides. I don't recommend an afternoon frolic."

"It's not for fun—I'm searching for something."

"What?"

"I'm not sure yet … I'll know when I find it."

"You're not making me feel better."

"I promise to tell you all about it if it turns out to be something, but for now I need you to trust me. I need your help."

"Your mother will murder me if I lend you the boat that gets you killed."

"I will be careful."

Dante groaned. "Fine. Where exactly are you?"

Lucine scrolled through the GPS function on her radio until she found her exact coordinates, then sent them to her uncle.

"Did they send?"

"Got 'em. I'll send my best man with a deep vee hull. It'll be your best bet."

"Thank you."

"I expect multiple updates, as well as a follow-through on that promise."

"Understood."

"My guy is stationed a few hours south of you. His name is Larry. I suspect he'll get to you around noon."

"Perfect."

The call ended.

Right on time, Larry's boat soared up to the seawall, crashing into it with force and knocking him off his feet. When he regained his bearings, he tied the boat to the nearest post and launched his body over the railing. He landed on solid ground with a crunch and marched toward Lucine's truck.

"Strange request from the boss," he stated upon arrival. "But I suppose I can scout for fish up this way too."

"Is that what he has you doing these days?" Lucine asked.

"Yeah. Dante has us out on the boats, scouting to see if the fish returned. He wants to feed the masses." Larry sighed. "No luck yet."

"It's a noble task, at least."

Larry nodded. "Maybe the northern seas will hold some signs of life." He glanced at Lucine. "What am I here to help you with?"

"A quick trip off the coast. I saw a light out that way," she said, pointing toward the empty horizon. "I would like to find it."

"We are traversing the volatile sea for a light?"

"I need to know what's out there."

"Do you understand how dangerous the ocean has become? There is no predicting its tides."

"It cannot be far. I promise to let you turn us around at the first sign of trouble."

Larry could not reject orders from a Lamorte, so he shrugged and waved her over.

Lucine stuck her head into the truck. "Wake up," she demanded of Max. "It's time to go."

He rustled where he lay before quickly jumping out of the truck and following Lucine to the boat. Larry helped them board and began the choppy ride into the hazy horizon.

"Which way?" he asked.

"Straight ahead," Lucine replied, looking back at her truck. "I stopped where I saw the light."

They sailed for fifteen minutes in rough conditions when Max broke the silence.

"Whoa," he said, still tired from a restless sleep. "What is that?"

Lucine and Larry turned their attention forward to find an enormous marble-white edifice erected amidst the crashing waves. They had to squint to see it—there was minimal contrast between the white structure and the light gray sky—but it was clearly there.

"Look beyond," Lucine noted. "There's land."

"Is that where you want to go?" Larry asked.

"Yes," Lucine replied, confident that her answers existed on the small, distant isle.

The boat sped forward, lurching precariously over the waves for another half hour before reaching the marble structure.

"I think it's a lighthouse," Max noted with a shiver—the temperature had dropped drastically. "Strange looking one, though."

Lucine leaned into the railing of the boat, staring up and trying to see into the small, intricately carved windows of the edifice. She saw no fire, no lamps, but felt warmth emanating off the rock. A frigid breeze lashed her face, carrying cold water and a shrill whistle. Lucine backed away from the railing and wiped her face.

The unnerving whistle continued, turning into a bereaved wail.

"Where is that noise coming from?" Larry asked, covering his ears.

As the crying grew louder, their attention turned to the cove just beyond the lighthouse.

"Let's get to land," Lucine stated. "I can see structures on the main island ahead."

Larry revved the engine and plowed through the rough waves faster.

Lucine shielded her eyes from the ocean spray that hit her face like sharp daggers. When the boat began to slow down, the stinging lessened and she lowered her arm.

Before her was a little fishing village, ravaged by the purge, but bustling with life. People crowded the docks, carrying on with their lives within their wrecked town. The homes were dilapidated with broken roofs and rotted frames, but no one seemed to care. The people here appeared perfectly content existing amongst the ruins.

"How did they get here?" Max asked.

"Perhaps they rode out the storm," Larry suggested.

"No one survived the ocean's wrath," Max objected.

"Maybe they came here after," Lucine said. "It was a short boat ride."

The boat crept closer, lurching with each wave toward the decayed pier. When the boat hit the wooden dock, an entire plank fell into the ocean.

"Why don't they fix this place?" Max asked, concerned by their lack of initiative. "It's falling apart."

"They probably can't," Lucine replied. "There are no trees to get new wood from."

They exited the boat and didn't get far before another wooden plank broke in two beneath Max's weight. "This isn't safe," he declared as the pieces fell into the ocean below with a splash. He yanked his foot out of the newly created gap in the pier.

"What do you think you're doing?" a short man barked as he stormed toward them. The weathered pier did not appear disturbed by his weight.

"Sorry," Lucine replied. "We will be more careful."

The angry man paused once he was close enough to smell them. His eyes widened with intrigue and his fury melted away. "You stink," he stated.

"Excuse me?" Max replied, offended. "How can you smell anything over the stench of dead fish and mold?"

"Flesh and blood," the man continued, ignoring Max. He then looked up at their flushed faces; their flesh was tinted red. A wicked smile crossed his face. "She will be so delighted."

"Who?" Lucine asked.

The man shook his head, lost in his own thoughts again. "No, no. You're mine. I shouldn't share." His eyebrow lifted. "But I don't know how … I could ask Percival. I could give him the female." He shook his head again. "He'll never agree. It needs to be the girl."

"Have you lost your mind?" Max asked, utterly confused and concerned.

The man glared up at them, his anger returning. "I lost it long ago. Why are you here?"

"To remedy my nightmares," Lucine replied.

He cackled. "You'll only find new nightmares here."

"What is your name," she asked.

"Poe."

"Poe, have you ever seen shadow figures?"

His face scrunched, unenthused. "Like me?"

"No, like a silhouette that appears where light and darkness meet."

"It might've been me, honestly. I do a lot of traveling. I can never remember the places I've been or the people I've seen."

Lucine looked to Max, who rolled his eyes and commented, "We are wasting our time."

A shadow figure flickered ahead, summoning Lucine forward.

"I'll be your friend," Poe stated. "I have dark abilities."

"No thank you," she replied, grabbing Max's hand and pulling him toward the shadow. Larry followed close behind.

"Wait!" Poe shouted after them. "Don't let her see you!"

"What is he talking about?" Lucine whispered to Max.

"She'll steal your body!" Poe hollered.

"He's lost his mind," Max replied, refusing to pay any more attention to Poe.

The bustling pier came to an alarming standstill as Lucine, Max, and Larry walked past.

"This place is unusual," Lucine noted as the clammy air clogged her pores. "Everyone is staring at us like starved wolves."

"They must not get many visitors."

"Where are we going?" Larry asked, his voice filled with dread.

Darkness rippled through the light.

"I am following the shadow," Lucine answered.

"That's comforting," Larry commented with a groan.

No one else bothered them as they charged forward, following Lucine's lead. The shadow came and went, an unsteady image fleeing the light of day. They turned off the main pier, climbed a small hill, and found themselves facing an enormous, rundown mansion.

Lucine announced, "This is it."

"Do we go inside?" Max asked.

Lucine shook her head as the sputtering shadow twirled around the side of the building. She followed it into the back courtyard.

Sitting on the ground was a man, ghostly pale and chanting. He slammed a purple crystal into the ground repeatedly, chipping away at the shimmering rock with each hit.

Though he spoke another language, Lucine recognized his voice.

"Dad?" she asked. Her heart halted.

The man stopped his aggressive hymn immediately and turned to face her.

His dead eyes filled with vapored tears as his grown daughter came into view.

"Lucine," Sergei proclaimed. "You found me!"

Chapter 27

Ouijan Mansion, Nether Isle

"How?" Lucine asked, hardly breathing from fright. Tears filled her eyes—though she wished his survival to be true, her disbelief surpassed her hope. Max and Larry stood behind her, too startled to speak.

"I never entered the light," he explained, standing and walking toward her. She took a step back, too afraid to let him get close. "That wretched lighthouse," he went on. "I came here instead."

"You've been alive all this time?" she asked, voice trembling.

"Oh no," he stammered. "I am very dead."

"Then, how—" Lucine asked, stumbling over her words.

"Do not be afraid," Sergei insisted.

"Are you a ghost?" she asked in a whisper.

"I don't like that word."

"What other word is there to describe it?"

"I still exist," Sergei explained, his tone desperate. Lucine's eyes were aimed at the ground. "Look at me."

Lucine struggled to lift her gaze. "Have you been haunting me?" she asked.

"No!" Sergei proclaimed, moving so close to Lucine she could feel the chill radiating off his dead body. "I was just trying to reach you."

"It terrified me."

"I am sorry."

Lucine took a long pause before lifting her eyes and looking at the ghost of her father. "What do you want?"

Sergei's dead heart contracted. "I wanted to be with you again. I just couldn't figure out how to leave this damned isle and remain visible."

"Why can I see you?"

Sergei shrugged. "That lighthouse, I think. Everyone here is a ghost."

Lucine swallowed the terrified lump in her throat. "But you can only be seen here?"

"Yeah, but I've been learning magic. Bianca was helping me till I made her mad, but I haven't quit. I want to be with you and your brother again."

Lucine was at a loss—this was the last thing she expected to find at the end of her nightmares, and now she wasn't sure how to feel.

"Why?" she asked.

"To help finish what I started."

Max stepped forward, alarmed by this troublesome statement. But Lucine sensed his tense energy and lifted an arm to stop him from intervening.

"Explain to me what that means," she requested of her father.

"Have you forgotten?" Sergei asked, then shook his head. "You were so young. I drilled it into your brother more than you. The Champions," he explained. "They slaughtered millions—they murdered me. We must stop them before they kill more."

"You're dead—how exactly do you plan to do that?"

"With an army of the unliving."

This revelation chilled Lucine to the core. She had to end this horror before it began.

"While I resent them for taking you away from me, they are not a threat," she tried to reason. "Can't you just be happy that you found some sliver of existence in the afterlife? One that allows you to see and communicate with your children?"

"Juniper and her trees killed me!"

"You initiated that fight—"

"You are on *their* side?"

"No, but resentment steals the life from the living. I refuse to live in the past."

"Does your brother know of your disloyalty?" Sergei spat.

Lucine's heart pounded furiously within her chest. "He doesn't care about me. He never has."

"He loves you. I trained him to."

"You were never around," Lucine objected. "Xavier tormented me my entire life."

"I don't believe you."

"He killed Grandpa."

"No."

"Yes. You told Xavier not to follow the traitors who were leaving to join the Tree Champion, and Grandpa caught him. He tried to stop Xavier, so Xavier tried to kill him. He then blamed it on the group that left Utah to join Juniper."

"You're lying."

"Grandpa was trying to stop Xavier from luring you into the jungle, so Xavier put him into the coma that he never woke up from. If you have anyone to blame for *your* death, it's Xavier, not Juniper."

"You were a child."

"Xavier also tried to kill me multiple times. Remember the incident with my stuffed bunny?"

Sergei's expression twisted with confusion—he could not remember.

"No? Well, I remember. Quite clearly. I also remember the countless times he ripped my facemask off and forced me to breathe the ashy air."

"No," Sergei stammered, but struggled to defend the son he hardly got to know.

"I was the only one who saw Xavier for the rotten devil that he was. And now he runs the world, oppressing the masses who adored you." Lucine shook her head. "You were wrong regarding the Champions, but your heart was in the right place for all the other survivors. You'd be so sad to see what Xavier has done to them."

Sergei shook his head. "He is my son. He is my protégé."

"You have a vision of who you wanted him to be, but he never became that. He has failed you."

Sergei's fading mind sparked with a recent memory and his eyes filled with fire. "He listened to me. He is finishing the task that ended my life."

"You saw reason while you were alive, before Grandpa went into that coma—you told Xavier *not* to hunt the Champions. Why can't you see reason now?"

"I did no such thing!"

"Everything spiraled out of control because of Xavier. You are dead because he lied to you about Grandpa and enflamed your rage toward the traitors, and subsequently Juniper. Please believe me."

"I know who I was and what I stood for. You will not turn me into a coward."

Lucine stared at her dead father with contempt, tears welling in her eyes.

"I love you, but you need to go," she said, utterly conflicted between love and fear.

"Go where?" Sergei asked, his own fear rising.

"I don't know," Lucine said, the tears spilling down her cheeks. "Into the light."

"You want to send me away?" he asked, his face lined with hurt. The resentment he felt radiated like electricity. "You don't love me?"

"Of course, I love you, but you are not the same," she tried to explain. "You are different; you are dead."

"I am still me."

"You are empty. I can see you, but I cannot feel the man I once knew as my father. All that's left is cold hollowness."

"You are a rotten brat," Sergei seethed.

Lucine extended her hand behind her, which Max grabbed and held tight.

"Do not visit me anymore," Lucine requested. "I will not help you, and I do not wish to be part of your after life."

"You will regret this!"

Lucine turned without saying anything more.

"Your brother will join me!"

Larry was a few paces ahead of Lucine and Max; attempting to ignore Sergei's enraged shouting. But the farther away she walked, the more his anger turned to desperate sorrow.

"I love you, Lucy!"

Lucine's heart constricted, but she kept her focus forward. Motivated more than ever, all she wanted to do was leave this horrifying place and begin her quest to save Juniper.

Sergei fell to his knees—Lucine was gone and he was alone again. All his efforts to love her were wasted. He wanted to cry, but his eyes could not produce tears. So he stared at the horizon, letting his decayed mind wither into darkness.

"Snap out of it," a familiar voice shouted from the shadows.

Sergei was unable to shake himself free from the nothingness that consumed him.

A hand grabbed his shoulder and shook him violently until the smell of fish and sea water returned. A hard slap to the face brought back the light and Sergei found himself looking up at tiny Bianca.

"You are weak," she spat.

"My daughter rejected my love. All this time, I yearned to find her, only to be told that she wants me gone." His eyes were shiny with grief. "She told me to go through the light."

"You have bigger things to be worrying about."

"Like what?"

"*Our* mission. Have you already forgotten?"

Sergei could not recall. "You left me."

"I am back now and we must resume where we left off."

"I don't remember—"

"Teaching you dark magic," Bianca interjected. "So that we can be alive again."

"What's the point in being alive if my children hate me?"

"Does your son hate you too?"

"I'm not sure. I haven't spoken with him yet."

"Then there is hope. Plus, it seems to me you lived a life far grander than just the approval of your children. Am I wrong?"

"I didn't spend enough time with them," Sergei confessed. "I was too busy building an empire."

"And attempting to avenge the fallen. What if I told you that you could still finish both of those tasks?"

"How? I am dead and cannot be seen by the living elsewhere—I cannot rule a country from this isle."

"If you had a living body, you could."

"They won't believe that it's me. I'd never be able to rise in power without my old face."

"But if the people were possessed by the dead you have avenged, it won't matter which face you're wearing."

Sergei paused to digest her implication. "Give everyone who died in the purge a second chance at life in a new body," he said, making sense of the idea. "Can I do that?"

"If you follow my lead, yes."

"I just wanted to kill the Champions, but this is much better. I can bring all the lost souls back. They deserve life more than those who live amongst the Champions. I can avenge the fallen in ways I never dreamt possible."

"Finally, you are understanding." Bianca smirked. "We will build a ghost army and take back what is rightfully ours."

"I will rule again," Sergei sneered.

"But first, you must learn my magic."

Bianca knelt beside Sergei and began with a simple spell of disappearance. Together, they made a stone vanish and then moved onto a larger task: making it reappear.

Overhead, the ghost of a snow petrel soared out of the dead oak tree and left Nether Isle undetected. Flapping its wings with furious determination, the snow bird returned to Antarctica and released Marisabel's spirit back into her living body.

"I must warn my sisters," she gasped, diving back into the depths of her mind and calling out to her Champion sisters as she raced toward the White Room.

Chapter 28

White Room

"It's much worse than any of us ever dreamt," Marisabel explained, her icy aura glowing brighter than ever. *"There's another ghost helping Sergei, one that knows magic. They are planning to build a ghost army."*

"A what?" Aria asked.

"And they want to take the bodies of the living."

"How do you know all of this?" Eshe asked.

"Gaia visited me. She gave me a gift ... a connection to death."

"How is that a gift?" Sahira asked, horrified.

"I know more about what's going on than the lot of you," Marisabel countered. *"I can see the dead that walk amongst us."*

"They walk amongst us?" Aria asked, her expression alarmed.

"They are everywhere," Marisabel replied. *"People, animals, nature—there is more death walking this planet than life."*

"He'll come for me first," Juniper stated, her tone solemn. *"I killed him, after all."*

"We won't let him," Aria insisted, looking to Marisabel for confirmation. *"Right?"*

"I am going to do all I can, but it's trickier than it seems. This girl, Bianca, who is helping Sergei—she is teaching him magic, and I'm not

sure yet how we will protect ourselves from them when they strike. I don't fully know their strategy."

"Then you must return and learn," Eshe said, clutching her growing belly.

"Of course, I will. But there is more—Gaia suspects their magic might stem from Kólasi."

"Who is Kólasi?" Juniper asked.

"Gaia's brother, father to the Devil," Marisabel replied. Her terror was apparent. *"We know Him as Satan. He has already helped the Debauched rebuild their metal empire. Now he is helping them annihilate us."*

"Why, though?" Aria asked.

"He finds joy in creating mayhem and inspiring anarchy within Gaia's worlds."

"A true devil," Eshe remarked.

"This is ridiculous," Coral stated, jumping into the conversation for the first time. She wore a crown made of pearls and seashells, and her sapphire eyes shimmered like opals. *"Why won't Gaia stop Him Herself?"*

"She says that Earth will combust, killing us all, if She shows up in physical form to defend us."

"Can't She stop him from wherever They exist?" Coral asked. *"The ether, the infinite dark—wherever?"*

"All I know is that She gave me this gift, hoping it would help us."

"A war against the Devil?" Coral spat. "She has led us to a slaughter."

"I won't let that happen," Marisabel insisted, motivated for the first time in years. Her aura was gleaming a radiating blue-silver, and her diamond eyes held no doubt. "I won't let you down."

"Let us know how we can help," Juniper stated, breaking the tense silence the sisters shared. "Or at the least, keep us updated."

"Of course," Marisabel promised. "I will protect us."

"Is there anything we should do in the meantime to prepare?" Aria asked.

"Just keep a close eye on all of your people."

"Should we warn them?" Sahira asked.

Marisabel hesitated. "I suppose that's your call. Warning them might scare them, but leaving them uninformed makes them more vulnerable." She paused again. "I'd tell them. If nothing else, they can try to fight back when the dead attempt to steal their bodies."

"Let's hope it doesn't progress that far," Eshe countered. "I must leave. Zaire is still trying to get to you."

"To me?" Marisabel asked. "How?"

"He left Tier a few months ago," Juniper explained. "Took up residency beneath Cotopaxi—the stratovolcano in the Andes Mountains."

Eshe cut in. *"He has adjusted to the heat within the upper mantle, and now he is digging tunnels, hoping to depressurize the ringwoodite rocks and create water in the process. It's an interesting theory,"* Eshe noted, seemingly impressed. *"Those rocks are made of highly condensed water—pressurized into diamonds from the heat. If Zaire succeeds, the water within the earth would triple the oceans above."*

"Can I help?" Coral asked.

"No," Marisabel objected. *"Don't let him. He cannot love me like this."*

Eshe examined Marisabel with sympathy, but refused to pander to her self-pity. *"You seem to be doing just fine now."*

"I cannot be distracted."

"Fair point," Eshe replied. *"Still, having accessible water beneath the earth serves us all."*

"Is it saline or fresh?" Coral asked.

"Currently, Zaire is only creating steam, and what's left behind is briny mud."

"I can help with that," Coral replied, determined to assist.

"Just keep him far away from me," Marisabel demanded before disappearing. Her aura left behind a bone-rattling chill.

"We would benefit from a fresh water source," Eshe continued. *"We are evolving to a state where our bodies need less water to survive, but we still need to hydrate. I am rooting for Zaire to succeed."*

"I will do what I can to help," Coral promised. *"The water spirits will guide us."*

Eshe nodded with confidence. *"Usual spot?"*

"Yes," Coral replied. *"I'll be there shortly."*

With a splash of sea spray, Coral vanished from the White Room.

"How are the spy tunnels into America coming along?" Juniper asked Eshe.

"Slowly. We are still locating and navigating the seamounts in that region. We have to be careful not to break the barrier between the core and ocean."

"I understand," Juniper said with a nod, overwhelmed by the enormous threats still facing them.

"Shouldn't be long before we break into the western coast," Eshe promised. *"Our first tunnel into North America is aimed at Portland, Oregon."*

"In the meantime, I'll take a falcon into the smog of the American Debauched to see what's going on."

"Good idea," Eshe agreed. *"I must go."*

In a swirl of dark, billowing smoke, she was gone.

Axial Seamount, 300 miles west of Canon Beach, Oregon

Eshe raced through the underground, using her talon-toenails and infallible muscles to launch her body forward. Her speed was great, as was her strength. When the tunnels grew narrower, she was forced to slow down—a temporary hinderance to her evolution, one she had yet to resolve. The tunnels were deep beneath the ocean floor, but when she reached Axial Seamount, she rose into higher elevations and the pressure from the sea lessened.

Up through the center of the underwater mountain, she ran, directing her focus toward the cave where water and fire met.

Light appeared at the end of the tunnel. Shimmering blue shadows danced along the dark walls and decorated Eshe's body as she got closer.

Through the opening she came to an abrupt stop where a pocket of dry land existed beneath the ocean. The wet, volcanic rock terrain slowly dipped into the sea, and above were thousands of blue-hued stalactites hanging from the massive ceiling. The space was enormous. Eshe walked to the edge where the calm salt water lay still against the rock platform. She leaned over and peered into the crystal-clear depths.

Coral wasn't there.

Eshe often arrived quicker than Coral, so she took a step back to wait, when a single air bubble rose to the surface and burst.

Brow furrowed, Eshe crouched to get a closer look. The water was pale blue and the visibility extended for miles, yet she still saw no one lurking below.

Three more bubbles appeared and then disappeared in dramatic fashion.

Aggravation mounting, Eshe turned to the cave wall and found a large, loose boulder. With it raised above her head she walked back to the water's edge.

Gaze focused on the spot where the bubbles last appeared, she hurled the boulder into the water. It hit with a massive splash.

As the ripples settled and the water became still again, a hurtling body came into view. It launched out of the water, shot salty sea spray at Eshe, arched its back, and dove backwards into the water.

Eshe groaned. "The progenies."

The adolescent Coralene children circled like sharks below, blending in and out of the racing currents and disappearing from view.

"Coral," Eshe called out telepathically, uninterested in playing games with the progenies. *"Where are you?"*

"Almost there," Coral replied a moment later.

"Your children beat you here."

Coral clicked her tongue. *"I told them to stay home."*

Eshe returned her focus to the water. "Show yourselves."

Coral's triplets were the first generation of Coralene—ocean people—and their inherent evolution was more advanced than anyone imagined possible.

Eshe crouched by the water, cradling her growing belly, and gently traced her fingertips along the surface. Steam rose where her fire-hot touch seared the chilly water.

Indah emerged in the middle of the pool first.

Eldest of the triplets, she was also the bravest—still, she only let the top of her head crest the water's surface. Her jet-black hair clung to her scalp while the long strands danced freely beneath the water. Her large, opal eyes stared at Eshe with curiosity.

"Why do you play games with me?" Eshe asked.

Indah stared blankly in reply, blinking slowly in contemplation.

"We are family," Eshe reminded the girl.

Indah's beautiful eyes narrowed as she smiled and submerged. Gone from sight with only the rippling of her fast underwater swim visible, she reemerged at the water's edge, gleaming up at Eshe where she crouched.

"Hello, Auntie," Indah greeted. The gills on both sides of her neck contracted as she breathed the oxygen of the cave.

"Why did you hide from me?" Eshe asked, running her hand atop Indah's wet hair.

"We haven't seen you in a while."

"Are your brother and sister down there too?"

Indah nodded.

"You never need to fear me."

"We know. It's just so different up here. Sometimes we forget."

"Perhaps you ought to be spending more time on land," Eshe commented. "Or you might turn into water."

"Oh yes, we can already do that."

"You turn into water?"

"Yup. We become the current."

"So my eyes *weren't* playing tricks on me."

Indah grinned.

A dark blur appeared beneath her, catapulting toward the surface and emerging inches from where Indah clung to the volcanic rock.

"Are you causing trouble?" Coral asked, wiping the sea salt from her eyes. Her blue eyes had flecks of opal-pastels, but unlike her children, her adaptation to the ocean was still developing.

"No, I swear."

Coral looked up at Eshe for confirmation.

Eshe smiled. "Everything is okay. Seems they are still a little frightened by me, though. Annisa and Osbert never surfaced."

A large, dramatic bubble rose from the center of the pool and popped.

Indah chuckled. "Ozy hates when people call him that."

Coral sighed. "The ocean is all consuming. It's hard to explain if you've never experienced it, but it's very easy to forget about the world above while you're down there."

"Maybe you all ought to make trips to the surface more often then. We can't lose you to the sea."

"I will make an effort," Coral promised. "My children must be well adapted." She then looked to Indah and spoke to her daughter in mindspeak. *"Go home. Take your siblings with you. Tell your father I am with Eshe in the caves of Axial."*

"Yes, Mother," Indah replied before diving into the water and leading her brother and sister back to the Anthozoa Kingdom of Coralen.

Coral looked to Eshe, her skin was paler than usual. "I spoke to the ocean. The water spirits will help."

"Wonderful," Eshe replied, her relief apparent. "Saline?"

"Both. Fresh water as well. I suspect it will start with saline rivers, but we can filter them later. Once there are bodies of water underground, I can help also. Having navigable waterways within the core will keep us close."

"I would like that," Eshe said.

"Tell Zaire the news. The water spirits will join him tonight."

"Thank you, Sister."

Coral dove back into the sea without making a splash and Eshe darted back into the darkness of Ahi.

Is this wise? she asked the Core Spirits. *Adding water to my fiery haven?*

<<It is wise to keep Coral close.>>

Eshe nodded, believing this to be true. *It won't hurt my delicately crafted ecosystem? Or the evolution of my people?*

<<Each Element grows stronger together. Isolated you are limited, but together you become a force greater than any individual element. Together, you become Earth.>>

Is that where this is leading?

<<As the fates transpire, it appears so. Nature is not strong enough to rebirth naturally—too many human spirits chose the infinite dark—and there are still humans preventing growth during these fragile days. Their continued presence and resistance against the natural order has halted all the plans Gaia set forth at the start. It is why the sun has not returned. It is why the trees have not grown. It is why the oceans are still violent at the surface.>>

Can't Gaia fix this?

<<She is, by fixing you—Her Champions. You will save Earth by becoming one with it.>>

What about Satan's dad? Whatever His name is.

<<*Kólasi is a constant threat to the sovereignty of Gaia and Her creations.*>>

Why doesn't She stop Him Herself?

<<*A battle between the celestial siblings could destroy everything. All life could cease to exist, on this planet and those that exist beyond.*>>

So we are Her final hope.

<<*You are Her final hope for a peaceful resolution on this planet. Her next move, if you and your sisters fail, will rain fire over Earth.*>>

Will it kill us all?

<<*No, but the consequences of unleashing such a fury could halt forward progress on Earth for centuries.*>>

I see. So we must not fail.

<<*Stop Kólasi and all will be well.*>>

Eshe's mind became silent as the Spirits of the Core vanished.

"Beat the Devil and all will be well," Eshe repeated with a grunt of disbelief as she continued toward the epicenter of her underworld.

Marisabel was the key to their success, for which Eshe felt great hesitation. Being led by the woman who greeted death as a friend was a concerning approach to stay alive.

Chapter 29

Quadrant B4, North America

The trek was as dangerous as Killian predicted—Lamorte devotees were unavoidable in C3 and C4, and they harassed and berated Odette every time she was spotted. Curious to know why she was roaming around without Xavier, accusing her of abandoning her husband, assuming she was a traitor. Odette barely made it to B4, but when she crossed the border, actively avoiding detection by the Palladon twins, the weight she'd been carrying lessened. Lucine was in reach; soon, Odette would be with people who might help her.

The energy was less volatile in B4, though she knew better than to believe she was safe. She kept the map Killian marked close and only went to the hostels he deemed safe.

Three nights spent on dirty floors and Odette was still only halfway to Lucine's skyscraper. She could see it in the distance, though. It stood taller than all the other buildings around it— just like Xavier's home in C2.

She often felt fatigued and nauseous, too weak to carry on, but she could finally see the end of this harrowing journey. The goal was too close to give up now.

On her fourth night in B4, at the fourth stone-cold hostel she was forced to endure, a man stopped her as she aimed for the vacant piece of floor.

"You," he said with a grunt.

"Excuse me?"

"You're the president's whore."

"No," Odette corrected him, using all her energy to contain her anger. "I think the word you meant to say is wife."

"I meant what I said," he spat. "Only a whore could love a monster."

Odette took a deep breath. "Well, if it makes you feel any better, this 'whore' has left the monster." She glared up at him. "Let me pass."

The man did not budge. He continued to stand in her way, staring down at her with a look of deep hatred.

She could feel his anger amplifying; his energy radiated and blanketed her confidence. As he refused to move, she found her conviction wavering. Perhaps Killian marked the map wrong— perhaps she was not safe here.

"What is wrong with you, Frank?" another man shouted, stepping in between them and pushing the large man away.

Frank's laser focus shifted from Odette to the newcomer.

"She doesn't belong here," Frank declared.

The other man looked from Frank to Odette, and upon realizing who she was, his expression shifted from anger to apprehension. Still, he stood his ground.

"It's no excuse to threaten a lady." He stood taller. "And if she's here, surely there is a reason."

Frank growled before storming away.

Odette turned to her unexpected hero. "Thank you."

"Come with me," he stated in a whisper, taking her hand and dragging her toward a back room. The moment they were alone inside, he locked the door and exhaled audibly.

"Am I not safe here?" she asked.

"Why *are* you here?" he inquired.

Odette was tired of being harassed everywhere she went, tired of being questioned and criticized.

"It's strange," she began, "how humans can find illusionary comfort when they imprison themselves in one place. I never left Xavier's home until the day I left him—I never needed to; everything I could possibly need was delivered to me." She paused, her heart racing. "The moment I stepped foot outside, I was stripped bare. Every comfort I'd grown to know in my life with Xavier was gone and I felt exposed." She hesitated. "No, I felt betrayed. And angry at myself for letting his lies blanket the truth—for never lifting the cover to see the ugly horrors he hid from me." Odette shook her head. "And then to be hassled by everyone I met on my journey toward freedom. Whether I was being accused of being a traitor or a monster, both sides of the line hate me because of who I chose to love."

"Can you blame them?" the man asked. "You aligned yourself with a sinister man. If you leave him, you betray those who love him. If you stay, you become the enemy of those who despise him."

"I lose either way."

"Are you truly here to find freedom?" he asked, suspicious gaze narrowed.

"I am not a spy, if that's what you're worried about."

The man narrowed his eyes in contemplation before replying. "You might not have lost yet."

"I suspect I'm surrounded by the rebellion here?"

"I cannot confirm nor deny."

Odette sighed. "If it gives you any comfort, I do not think Xavier knows you exist. Not yet, at least."

"Is that a threat?"

"No," Odette stammered. "It's just that I've been away from him for quite a few weeks, so I cannot promise he hasn't been given word about the rebellion since. But when I was with him, I am confident he did not suspect any insurgence against his reign."

"Would you warn him, if you had the chance?"

"No," Odette swore. "My blind heart was ruthlessly shattered the moment I stepped foot into the nasty world he created." She took a deep breath. "I'm actually here to find Lucine. I need her help."

The man's interest piqued. "With what?"

"I know the woman on those war recruitment flyers," Odette explained. "Juniper isn't a monster. She needs to be protected. I'm hoping I can convince Lucine to help."

The man smirked as he extended his hand.

"My name is Max. Are you ready to join the revolution?"

Shocked by the sudden turn in dynamics, she shook Max's hand, officially choosing to side against Xavier.

"If you betray us," Max went on, squeezing her hand so tight she yelped, "your end will come without mercy." His smile was sincere, but his tone was lethal.

Odette's heart pounded fiercely. "I promise. I won't."

Smile unwavering, Max released her hand and walked toward the door of the broom closet. "Follow me," he instructed.

Light poured into the dark room as the door creaked open and the entire hostel stopped what they were doing to stare at them. Some wore amused expressions, as if they were witnessing the start of juicy gossip; others were still blinded by their hatred for Odette and only saw red at her reappearance. Both energies made Odette feel wildly uncomfortable.

Another man joined them.

"What are you doing?" he demanded of Max in an angry whisper.

"She can help."

"We don't need her help," the man objected. "We can't trust her!"

"Drew," Max stated to his frantic friend, then lowered his voice. "She wants to save Juniper."

Drew hesitated. "Are you certain it's not a ploy?"

"Very." Max swung his arm toward Odette. "Look at her. She's a wreck."

Drew took a cautionary pause before conceding.

"Move!" Drew shouted at a group of angry men blocking the door to the street. Though this small group appeared livid, they obeyed, making way for Max, Drew, and Odette to pass.

Once they were a safe distance from the hostel, Odette broke the silence. "You seem to have a lot of clout amongst the people."

"They know what I am capable of," Drew replied.

As they turned the final corner, the Lamorte building came into view. Max charged through the ornately carved metal doors, and Drew and Odette followed.

Inside the foyer was a desk with a single guardsman. He held a gun in front of his chest and stepped in Max's way as he charged toward the elevator.

"Really, Victor?" Max asked, pausing to address the guard who stood in his way.

"I don't know her."

"Look at her face, you idiot. It's Odette Lamorte—Xavier's wife."

"Xavier recently told his soldiers that she was no longer part of the family."

Odette felt a stinging pang in her chest, but held her tongue.

Max replied on her behalf. "Then call up to Lucine and see for yourself if she'll allow our company."

Victor lingered a moment before stepping away to buzz Lucine.

"You have visitors," he said. "Max, Drew, and Odette." He paused. "Yes, your sister-in-law is here with them." Another long pause and Victor ended the call.

"You may go up," he conceded.

"Gee, thanks," Max replied sarcastically before leading the small group into the elevator. Despite the electricity that now powered the elevator, the old pulley system remained.

"That was how she used to reach the top floor of her penthouse," Drew explained while pointing at the frayed ropes. "She'd lug herself all the way up."

"By herself?"

"Sometimes Victor or another guard would help, but most times she was left unprotected. I guess Xavier figured no one cared enough about her to expend the energy it would take to reach her. She was truly hated, though. I contemplated scaling this skyscraper a few times to teach Xavier a lesson by ending his sister's life."

Odette listened in horror. "You speak quite freely about an incriminating matter."

"Lucine knows how I used to feel about her; now we are aligned."

Odette decided to say no more.

The elevator came to a stop and Max punched in a four-digit code to open the doors.

"A feature added after power was bestowed upon B4," Drew explained, his tone snarky.

The elevator opened to a long hallway with one door at the very end. Emptiness radiated from the floors below.

"Does anyone else live here?" Odette asked.

"Did anyone else live in the luxurious skyscraper with you and Xavier?"

The answer was no.

The familiarity of this strange place set Odette's nerves on edge.

Drew knocked on the door and Lucine's voice answered from the other side.

"Max?" she asked.

"Yep. Me, Drew, and Odette."

Lucine cracked the door open, chain lock still intact while she ensured it was truly Max. Her big eyes scanned her visitors cautiously before unlocking the door and letting them inside.

The moment they stepped foot inside her home, Max relinquished control of the situation and Lucine took over. She wasn't alone—Gideon was also there.

"I never dreamt I'd see you again," Lucine commented, examining Odette's disheveled appearance with pity. "Definitely not like this."

"Neither did I, but here we are."

"Would you like to take a hot shower?" Lucine offered, uninterested in making an enemy out of Odette. "We can discuss why you're here after."

"That would be lovely," Odette replied, her relief apparent.

Lucine gave her a fresh towel and shut the bathroom door, leaving Odette by herself. In solitude she was able to regain her composure and mentally prepare for the drastic life change she was about to embrace. She took her time—this was the first hot shower she'd had since leaving C2. Killian's water was lukewarm, bordering on chilly; this shower was steaming.

When she reemerged, hair still wet, she was greeted by an interrogation.

One chair faced the couch that the three men sat on, and Lucine paced between.

"Take a seat," Lucine stated calmly.

Odette obeyed. Her sense of temporary relief quickly vanished.

"Start from the beginning," Lucine continued. "Tell me everything."

Odette exhaled deeply. "Your brother kicked me out."

"So being here isn't your choice?"

"It is," Odette insisted. "It may not have started that way, but being on the streets has opened my eyes. What Xavier is doing is wrong—both the war on Juniper and the way he has forced the people to live in poverty."

Lucine nodded. "Why did he kick you out?"

"He said I was a traitor."

"What made him think that?"

Odette reached into the pocket of her jacket draped on the back of her chair and retrieved a folded piece of paper. She held it out to Lucine.

"This letter," Odette explained. "Juniper contacted me."

The three men on the couch sat taller and leaned forward.

Lucine unfolded the paper and read the note. Her smile was wide by the end.

"Yes," Lucine stated with a laugh. "I suspect this infuriated my brother."

"I thought he might kill me," Odette replied, no humor in her voice.

Lucine refolded the letter and handed it back to Odette. "You are safe here."

"Until he realizes I'm with you. Or worse—he learns that you're against him."

Lucine shrugged. "He'd be a fool to think I was on his side. He's been nothing but rotten to me."

"I'm sorry for that," Odette expressed. "I pleaded many times that he be kinder to you."

"It's old news. What matters is that his torment ends with me. We must stop him."

"I planned to return to the Amazon after talking with you. Juniper needs to be warned."

"We have far greater problems here. We can save her without her ever knowing."

"Why? Perhaps she could help."

Lucine paused and turned to look at Max. He shook his head.

"It's better, for now, that you don't know all the details," Lucine said. "They are quite horrifying. Just know that we are on the same side and desire the same outcome: dethroning Xavier and protecting Juniper."

Odette did not have the authority to argue with her. "That's all I want."

"Good." She grabbed Max's hand. "We need to check in with my Uncle Dante."

"Wait," Odette continued, desperate to show her value. "He is more alone than he lets on."

"We know," Lucine replied. "No one in my family supports the war he's initiating."

"I mean the men by his side. I saw Killian on my way here."

Lucine's expression shifted. "And?"

"He was forced to help Xavier. He wants to be free too."

"That is great news," Gideon stated from the couch. "Perhaps Xavier's soldiers feel the same. Maybe they just need to be presented with an alternative option."

"We need to secure housing and food for all of them," Drew stated.

"We've solved half of that riddle," Max stated, careful not to reveal too much about his underground greenhouses in front of Odette. "Housing will be much harder."

"I'm working on persuading Xavier to transfer ownership of the buildings in B4 to me," Gideon revealed. "It doesn't solve the issue of housing for everyone in North America, but it does for those who live here. And maybe it'll inspire others to move here."

"He'll never let you," Lucine worried.

"He already has agreed to it," Gideon replied with a smirk and a shrug. "He still trusts that our interests are aligned. He actually seemed quite relieved to have one less responsibility to attend to. His quest for war has dulled his wits. I just need him to sign the papers."

"That's fantastic," Lucine exclaimed. "We are closer to victory than ever."

"We just need to make sure that everything is executed with perfect timing," Max reminded the group. "If he catches onto our schemes too soon, it could ruin everything."

"Exactly," Lucine agreed then looked back to Odette. "How do you feel?"

Odette took a moment to process the onslaught of emotion she was feeling: excitement for the future, guilt for betraying her former love, pride for surviving and choosing the right side of this fight, fear that they might fail.

"Hopeful," she finally replied.

The fate of the surviving world was in their hands.

Chapter 30

Quadrant C2, North America

"Dante sent a single boat north," Oliver Palladon informed Xavier over the radio. "We tracked it, but it stopped in the middle of the ocean for a few hours before turning back around."

"For what purpose?"

"We aren't sure. According to all our maps, old and new, there is no land out there. The boat made two quick pit stops at the coast of Maine before and after. Does anyone live up there?"

"No," Xavier replied. "The city expands through that area, but it's vacant."

"Then I'm not sure what Dante was up to."

"It seems I cannot trust my own family," Xavier seethed.

"You can trust us," Oliver promised. "My brother and I are loyal to the end."

"For that, I am grateful. Thank you for telling me this information. Prepare a small crew to accompany me up the coast. I will be there in a few days to investigate this matter myself."

"Understood," Oliver replied before disconnecting the call.

Xavier sat alone in his penthouse with only his deteriorating thoughts to keep him company. Maddened by the flimsy grip he had over his empire, he couldn't help but imagine how nice it might be if there were no people and he could rule the world in solitude.

Impossible and futile, he knew—he needed hands to build his empire; he needed bodies to fight his wars. Still, he wondered what it might be like to live in his kingdom without the infuriating insolence from the masses.

The lights flickered.

She betrays you.

The voice of his ghost had returned, but Xavier was no longer rattled by its unpredictable visits.

"I already got rid of Odette," he replied.

She betrays you.

Xavier lifted a vase and smashed it against the wall.

Find me.

"Leave me alone!"

Xavier opened the nearest window and pushed the top half of his body into the grimy air. Countless stories high, his false threat to leap scared the voice away. Xavier hung there for a moment, observing the world below. Through the haze, bright lights radiated from all the empty apartments in the neighboring skyscrapers. On the street he could see the silhouettes of countless people, wandering aimlessly, with no place to call home.

"You could join my army!" he shouted, aware no one would hear him.

Aggravated, he reentered his home. The haunting presence had vanished and his focus returned to his hunt for the Champions.

He lifted the receiver of his radio and turned the knob to the frequency where he found Jeffroi Bonaire.

"Jeffroi," Xavier shouted into the handheld in his crude American accent. "I need an update." He waited a moment with no answer. "Jeffroi!"

"What?" Jeffroi finally replied in his rich French accent. He was out of breath from running to his radio.

"I need an update," Xavier answered.

"On what?"

"Your hunt!"

"There is nothing new to report. They remain in the Everest mountains, far from the Capitol le Francais."

"Have you gathered an army?"

"My people are ready to fight."

"When will you strike?"

"We cannot scale Everest to attack. Too many would die on the trek up. It isn't worth it."

"Haven't you recovered any arsenal? Nature left ours untouched—your bombs and nuclear power plants should remain intact as well."

"You want me to bomb a mountain?"

"If you won't climb it, how else do you expect to eliminate the traitors."

Jeffroi paused in thought, choosing his next words carefully. "I am very grateful for all that you have given us. Without your instruction, we'd still be living in ruins. The Capitol le Francais would look nothing like it does today—a metal empire illuminated with light."

"Exactly. You owe me."

"With my sincerest gratitude expressed, I cannot risk the sanctity of what we built for a war I truly do not understand."

"You have used me," Xavier seethed.

"If you find yourself in trouble, we will be ready to defend you, but initiating a war against peaceful people seems unwise."

"They slaughtered the bulk of the human race!" Xavier protested.

"Nature committed that crime. You cannot blame the people who were spared."

Xavier ended the call, fuming with rage, and immediately turned the dial to his connection in Japan.

"Toshiro Higashi," Xavier said into the receiver. "This is North America calling."

"Hai, Mr. Lamorte," Toshiro replied. He spoke enough English for them to communicate effectively.

"What news do you have for me regarding the traitors stationed atop Mount Everest?" Xavier asked.

"Much. They climb a little every day, but they move slowly."

"Can we reach them?"

"Not by foot."

"Are your planes equipped with guns and bombs?"

"No, but I suppose we could work on that."

"You must. We have to stop them."

Toshiro became quiet for a moment before speaking again. "I still mourn for my brother."

"It is appalling what they did to him and his fleet of soldiers."

"He was causing them no harm."

"I told you—they are devils. Touched by the hand of Satan; how else can we rationalize rocks taking down fighter jets? We must eliminate them."

"We are working hard."

"As are we. I hope to move into South America next month."

"Perhaps we will strike at the same time," Toshiro commented. "Have you spoken with the French?"

"Yes. Jeffroi has backed out of our alliance."

"He is weak," Toshiro spat.

"Unlike us, he has no personal ties to this cause, but when they turn against him, his tone will change."

"He dishonors us."

"I agree. I must go. We will talk again soon."

"Sayōnara," Toshiro said before ending the call.

The following day, Xavier traveled to the southern district in C2 to check in on his slow-growing army—which was large, but not large enough. An expansive section of pavement was cleared for training, but none of the soldiers were outside. They all sat in their barracks, playing card games and smoking.

Xavier marched into the main office of the training quarters and sought out Benny Palladon, who he had assigned as the army commander in this region.

"I don't trust you," Xavier spat upon finding Benny hunched over a pile of papers at his desk.

Benny took a deep breath before looking up.

"What have I done to earn your mistrust?"

"Why aren't the soldiers outside training?"

"Because you came during their free period. They've been outside all morning."

"They should have no free time."

"You want to anger the men who have volunteered to join your war?" Benny gave a look of disapproval. "I wouldn't risk losing the few numbers you have."

"Is that a threat?"

"Just the truth," Benny replied confidently.

"I do not trust you," Xavier repeated, pacing in thought.

"Why not?"

"Vinny is your brother."

"He does not control me."

"Do you love him?"

"Yes," Benny stated plainly. "You should too. We grew up together. We are family."

"Not by blood."

"What did he ever do to you?"

"His obsession with helping the weather return goes against everything I stand for."

"Don't you want to feel the warmth of the sun on your skin again?"

"Never. Nor should you."

Benny nodded, wise enough not to argue. "Understood." He swallowed his pride. "I am stationed here to serve you, not my brother."

"Where is he?"

"Vinny? I honestly don't know. He rarely stays in one place long."

"Shifty and conniving. He is surely planning ways to sabotage my war against the Champions."

"He simply wants to study the weather," Benny insisted.

"And nature. He wants to protect the Champions."

"I think you're wrong."

Xavier's fury was growing at an alarming rate.

"Why are there so few volunteers?" Xavier demanded, switching topics.

"I wasn't part of the recruitment initiative."

"Did you not advocate for the nobility of fighting in this war?"

"I did what I could, but I think you also forget that there aren't that many people left in this world. Three-quarters of your city is uninhabited."

"Is this how my army looks in every quadrant?"

Benny nodded.

Xavier stormed out of the room and back to his armored Humvee. Killian sat in the driver's seat, engine running and ready to go.

"Where are the rest?" Xavier asked. "Why is my army so small?"

"These are the only people who signed up," Killian replied as he began to drive north.

"Impossible. The recruitment posters have been up for months. I explained the danger of these traitors. I explained why we need to fight them." Xavier's chest rose and fell with anger. "I promised them food and shelter."

"I suppose it wasn't enough."

"After all I have done for these people," Xavier seethed. "I ask for *one* favor, and they deny me."

"There might be other factors working against you," Killian stated hesitantly.

Xavier's eyes widened with fury. "Dante? Has my uncle intervened?"

"No. As far as I know, he hasn't countered your propaganda."

"Then who?"

Killian hesitated. "You."

"Excuse me?"

"Can I speak frankly?"

"You better."

Killian gulped before unloading the harsh truth. "You are your own worst enemy. You are a polarizing leader—the people either love you or hate you; there is no in between."

"What's wrong with that?"

"The masses come from the 'in between' ... you need those numbers and you don't have them because you ignore that demographic."

"What am I supposed to do to change that?"

"End the poverty."

"How?" Xavier asked, struggling to contain his anger.

"Reduce the taxes—no one can afford them. Create jobs and reinstate the educational system. Turn your empire into a place where people can thrive, where people can be proud to live."

"I cannot strengthen them."

"Why not?"

"Because then they will have the means to rise against me."

Killian bit his tongue, careful not to reveal too much. "They will find a way to rise against you regardless; give them a reason *not* to. Give them what they want, provide their fundamental human needs, and you will never face a revolt."

Xavier's furious gaze softened and darted toward the ground. "I suspect I may be too late to reverse their hatred."

"It's never too late," Killian lied. "They will forgive you."

A frigid chill struck Xavier in the heart, sending a shiver through his veins.

He is wrong, a voice echoed inside his head. *You do not need them.*

Xavier's expression shifted back to rage.

"Stop," he muttered.

"Are you okay?" Killian asked, peering at Xavier through the rearview mirror.

"I'm fine. How far away are we?"

"We should be back to your skyscraper in three hours."

The voice remained, but Xavier managed to suppress its nonsensical ramblings for the remainder of the ride.

When he entered his home, the voice only grew louder.

"Go away," Xavier mumbled.

Find me.

"No," Xavier replied. Killian's eyes widened with alarm as he watched Xavier talk to himself.

Find me!

"No!"

Xavier's vision went black and behind his eyelids flashed a series of images: the coastline of Maine, the volatile sea, a glowing lighthouse, Lucine.

Find me! The voice shouted as Xavier's body was flung by an unseen force into the wall.

Killian raced to where Xavier's crumpled body hit the floor.

"What the hell just happened?" he asked, shaking Xavier till he opened his eyes.

Xavier's expression was vulnerable and scared—an emotion he hadn't expressed openly since the trees took his father's life.

He looked up at Killian, his aging eyes bright with fear. "I need to go to Maine."

Chapter 31

Quadrant A4, North America

The sea could not be tamed. Xavier tried his best to ride the volatile waves, but found himself helpless to its everchanging tides. He wasn't sure where he was going, just that something from beyond the shores of Maine had called to him.

He glanced over his shoulder toward the coast. Killian stood at the edge of the seawall, growing smaller by the minute. Xavier looked forward to the empty horizon. Hazy mist shrouded the horizon, giving no indication that anything existed beyond.

A ferocious squall whipped his small motorized vessel, sending it into an uncontrolled spin. He held on tight, losing sight of his whereabouts, and when the spinning stopped, he could no longer see Killian's silhouette standing at the coast. Xavier scanned the area, but the gray skies camouflaged the horizon.

Eyes squinted, he searched for a sign of life behind the haze—anything to make this trip worthwhile. He was beginning to lose hope, beginning to think he might be losing his mind, when a faint glow radiated beyond the foggy mist.

He revved the engine and turned the wheel, his sights set on the mysterious light. As he got closer, a looming shape took form. The tall structure towered above him and an eerie energy emanated from its stone walls. Xavier felt a slight buzz radiate down his spine, and without warning, the ocean pushed him closer than he ever intended to get. He redirected his boat to avoid crashing into the enigmatic structure, and once he was a safe distance away, he turned back around to examine the strange tower. It was a lighthouse—one that glowed without fire. There were no torches hidden within the small, slit windows, and its light blazed white, not red. Xavier wasn't sure what to make of this foreign lighthouse when his idling motorboat crashed into a wooden beam.

Surroundings still masked by the thick haze, Xavier hadn't seen the intricate maze of piers until they were directly in front of him. He found a ladder, tied his boat to the nearest beam, and climbed.

As he crested the base of the dock, the sight that greeted him came as an infuriating shock—an entire village of people lived here, free from his reign and not paying taxes into his empire. That would change, he determined, as soon as he learned how such an oversight slipped past him. Someone was to blame and he would find the culprit and make them answer for this crime.

Everyone stared at him with wide eyes as he walked by— Xavier supposed seeing strangers was not common in this isolated fishing village. The piers were falling apart, the buildings were in various states of disrepair, and Xavier wasn't sure how these people lived in such conditions. They needed a leader like him, someone who would make their lives better by providing proper shelter and governance.

The first person with enough courage to approach Xavier's menacing charge was a stout, middle-aged man with crazy eyes.

"You smell like wet soil," he said, as if this was a compliment.

"Excuse me?" Xavier replied, taken aback.

"It's deep under the smell of tar and asphalt," the man sniffed the air, his eyes darting around wildly as he tried to recall old memories. "Smoke and garbage, burning coal."

"I am your president. This land falls under my jurisdiction."

The man's eyes narrowed, his gaze ablaze with defiance. "We don't answer to the living."

Xavier furrowed his brow, accepting that this man was mentally unstable. "Who runs this place?"

"I do."

"I don't believe you."

"My name is Poe Lesavage, and I am the president of Nether Isle."

"Then I suppose I ought to kill you," Xavier threatened, "since you are the man who stands in my way."

"You know dark magic?" Poe asked, intrigued.

"Magic? Are you aligned with the Champions?"

"Show me," Poe instigated, but when Xavier continued to stare blankly at him, Poe smirked. "You cannot expect to deliver a second death without an extensive comprehension of dark magic."

"A second death?" Xavier asked, but before the small man could reply, a girl appeared, materializing from thin air. Xavier blinked a few times, fearful that his imagination was on the fritz.

"Who is dying a second time?" she asked. Though she was little, she spoke like she had lived one thousand lives.

"No one," Poe answered, his voice less confident now.

"I can help," she said with a sly smile directed at Poe.

The stout man did not take this insult kindly and charged away in a huff.

She looked back to Xavier, her smile shifting from mischievous to pleasant. "You finally came."

"Who are you?"

"My name is Bianca, but who I am does not matter, not yet anyway."

"Did you call to me in my dreams?"

The girl shook her head, her pale flesh sickly and her eyes cold and dead.

"Then who did?" Xavier asked.

"Your father, of course."

Startled by her quick and unexpected response, Xavier paused, taking a step back.

He examined her, wondering if everyone who lived here was crazy. "My father is dead," he finally replied.

Bianca stepped closer and pointed at his heart. "Aren't we all?"

Xavier stared back blankly.

"Follow me," she commanded while walking away.

The mysterious girl led Xavier inland toward a dilapidated mansion. Half of the windows were broken, shingles were falling off the roof, and the dark siding was covered in mold and overgrown vines.

"Why does everyone here live like this?"

"Like what?" Bianca asked, intrigued.

"In shambles."

She smirked. "None of us here are really living at all."

"I can make it better," he stated, ignoring her relentless morbid commentary. "I can fix these buildings and give you proper shelter."

"You are very good at faking altruism to disguise your selfishness."

"You speak like you know me."

"You are just like your father," she responded. "Except worse. He died when his soul left his body—something inside *you* is already dead. I am very familiar with death, and that hole in your chest is blacker than the infinite dark."

Xavier sighed. "You don't make any sense."

"I wonder if Sergei was as closed-minded as you while alive."

"All he cared about was killing the Champions."

She nodded. "We carry our greatest desires into the afterlife."

They walked through the creaky front door, under the precariously hung candelabra in the foyer, and into a dusty library near the back of the mansion. The windows were tall, dirty, and covered in cracks, but the outside light still crept through.

In the middle of the large room sat a man Xavier knew too well.

"Dad?" he asked, his tone as meek as the little boy who lost his father decades ago.

Sergei sat up straight, his back still facing Xavier, and took his time turning around. When he finally did, his hollow expression was not kind.

"It took you long enough," he said with a grunt.

"How is this possible?" Xavier asked, trying to contain his emotions.

"There are more levels to life than humans realize," Sergei stated, scrutinizing his son's shaken demeanor. "Now is a time to be strong."

"I am," Xavier protested, struggling to mask his elated disbelief.

"Tell me everything," Sergei demanded.

Xavier shuffled through his crisscrossing thoughts. "I've made contact with France and Japan. I shared our rebuilding template with them and it worked just as well. The Japanese regime finished their rebuild in five years. They are expanding west. The Captiol le Francais is almost done with theirs—they had trouble locating the resources needed to build."

He looked to his father, expecting him to be proud, but Sergei's stern expression did not shift.

"Why would you share such valuable information with them?"

"They are our allies."

"How can you be sure of that? They are on the other side of the world."

"They want to eliminate the Champions too."

This forced Sergei to pause, so Xavier continued, "I need their help if I want to eradicate the Champions."

"Don't you have enough able bodies in North America?"

Xavier shook his head. "The people—they aren't loyal."

"They were loyal when I was their leader."

"A lot has changed since then. Without the rebuild to keep everyone occupied and unified, they've grown bored, needy, and resentful. I can only give them so much without making them too strong."

"You are doing the right thing. They must stay oppressed if you wish to rule without opposition."

"But this has led to their loss of faith in me. I tried to build an army, but they'd rather starve to death than fight for me."

"We can make them loyal."

"How?"

Sergei pointed at the lighthouse in the distance. "We take their bodies and replace their minds with those who perished in the purge."

"I don't understand."

Bianca stepped in. "Possession. The spirits of those lost to nature will return through the portal and we will steer them into the bodies of your disloyal subjects."

"What's guaranteeing these ghosts will agree to fight in my war?"

"I will condition their mushy, confused minds as they exit the portal. I will train them. I will mold them. They will do as we command."

Xavier nodded slowly, digesting the strange proposal. "I suppose it could work."

A wicked smile crossed Sergei's face. "And then we can rid the world of the Champions."

Xavier nodded, then looked at his father with eagerness. "When can we start?"

Bianca answered, "Tonight. The full moon will cast enough light onto the portal to open its gates."

Xavier looked at the ghostly girl. "I trust my dad, and if he trusts you, then I trust you too."

"Excellent," Bianca chirped with delight—she had never before experienced such ease while recruiting henchmen. "Mark those who are off-limits for the taking."

"How?"

"Tie something red around their wrists."

Xavier nodded in understanding.

"Go," Bianca insisted. "There is no time to waste."

"Understood." Xavier departed, his mind racing around all the new and unexpected discoveries he made in such a short amount of time. His mind was so flooded he did not have space to consider all the ways this plan could go wrong.

A flock of birds rustled at his departure from the Ouijan mansion and disembarked from the nearby oak tree, amongst them the spirit of a dead snow petrel.

Chapter 32

Hidden within the spirit of the snow petrel, Marisabel listened to Sergei and Bianca groom Xavier for the forthcoming nightmare. Horrified by their intentions, she realized the time to take action was now.

Marisabel left with Xavier, determined to fix the problem before it worsened.

She turned her attention toward the lighthouse. To destroy the edifice was to destroy Kólasi's portal to Earth.

The snow petrel shook with terror.

::*It's the only way,*:: Marisabel expressed.

They soared toward the lighthouse and perched within one of the window cut-outs. Nothing existed there, just chiseled rock from another universe and the portal into the infinite dark.

Thousands of translucent spiders swarmed the lighthouse, crawling in patterns up and down the edifice. Dead, but unflinching in their resolution to remain in the living world, the ethereal glow shone through their tiny bodies.

::*I cannot stay,*:: the snow petrel fretted. ::*The darkness is pulling me in.*::

::*I can feel it too,*:: Marisabel noted. ::*Can you hover above the lighthouse and wait for me there?*::

::*Certainly.*::

Marisabel detached from the snow petrel, becoming a solitary spirit momentarily. In this state she felt vulnerable, but empowered. Supernatural energy charged through her like electricity, and she wondered if it was of her own making or if Gaia was with her now.

Harnessing her mystical gift, she churned up a surge of lightning, guiding it from the pits of her soul and out into the world. The rope of light was ever-moving, snaking itself into loose knots, ready to unravel.

Eyes white as snow, Marisabel lifted the blazing orb above her and focused on her target. With a single swipe of her arms, the cluster of lightning separated and sent thousands of singular bolts at the lighthouse. They struck with ferocity, creating billows of colorful smoke, but as the air cleared, the lack of damage became apparent. Marisabel's fiery strike left no mark — not a single dent, not even a char.

She tried again; the fate of the world depended on her.

With a furious breath of cold air, she summoned the most potent energy she could muster from the depths of her spirit. It emerged as a black fire. Cradling the sphere of glowing darkness, Marisabel circled the lighthouse, deciding where was best to drop her unearthly bomb.

Behind the carved window slots sat a vacant nest. Marisabel pushed her orb through the largest window and let the energy hover back and forth over the curved rock until it came to a stop. As it settled into place over top of the portal, she soared backwards, pressed her hands together, and the black energy imploded. A bruised, purple cloud covered the lighthouse, seeming to consume the edifice, but as it cleared, Marisabel's heart contracted. The lighthouse still stood, pristine as ever, and unharmed. She failed once again.

She looked to the snow petrel who fluttered above, prepared to surrender temporarily, when a familiar, high-pitched and demanding voice echoed from beyond. Marisabel turned to find Bianca soaring toward the lighthouse—too distracted to notice Marisabel rising upward to avoid detection.

Bianca crossed beneath, focused solely on her mumblings and the lighthouse.

This was Marisabel's chance.

Marisabel sent her spirit into one of the many spiders that scaled the lighthouse and clung to the hem of Bianca's nightgown as she crossed through the portal into the infinite dark.

Bianca soared through the black emptiness with ease, confident in her direction, unlike the spirts floating aimlessly around them. She knew the path well and when she found the dark throne, a pair of glowing yellow eyes opened in greeting.

"I finally understand," Bianca confessed.

Kólasi stood from his throne, illuminating his shadowy veil and emerging as a smoky silhouette lined with smoldering liquid gold.

<<*You are doing well, my daughter of darkness.*>>

"*It seems that nothing stands in my way.*"

<<*Do not underestimate my Sister. She's been known to deliver a good trick to save her children.*>>

"*You'll save me if She does, right?*"

The echo of Kólasi's laughter reverberated throughout the infinite abyss.

<<*I gave you a second chance. I owe you nothing more.*>>

Bianca bit her tongue, careful not to push her luck with the only being she feared.

"*I just wanted to update you — I am ready to build my army. I will be back by nightfall to open the gates.*"

<<*The lost humans will be ready.*>>

Bianca nodded and turned to leave, but a forceful surge of air punched her backwards.

<<*Not so fast. You haven't introduced me to your little friend.*>>

"*Who?*"

<<*The spider that clings to the hem of your nightdress.*>>

"*I have no friends,*" Bianca muttered to herself as she snatched the bottom of her dress and frantically looked for her uninvited guest.

Marisabel scurried along the fine stitching, desperate not to be found, but Bianca's cold fingers moved faster than the little spider. As her dead grip seized the spider's leg, Marisabel launched her spirit out of the insect, praying she'd connect with the snow petrel at the portal door, but instead she felt a golden surge of electricity and began spinning out of control as the tether to her body snapped.

Marisabel aimed her attention at Kólasi, who wore a devious smirk as he stared directly at her invisible spirit.

Bianca was focused on the dead spider, which she managed to eviscerate after a few tries. *"It's gone—it died it's second death. Innocent or nefarious, it will not bother me again."*

<<*Good, good,*>> Kólasi cooed. <<*You must get back to your tender-brained humans. They need a strong hand guiding them if we wish to succeed.*>>

"I will not fail."

<<*Be wary of the Champions. They may be more clever than we anticipated.*>>

Bianca narrowed her gaze, unsure how seriously she planned to take this warning, but nodded. *"I will be wary."*

Bianca floated back toward the portal exit and disappeared into the distant light.

Trapped and muted in Kólasi's clutches, Marisabel squirmed futilely.

Kólasi sent another menacing laugh through the endless chambers of his dark abyss.

<<*Dearest Sister,*>> Kólasi boomed. <<*It appears I've captured one of your Champions.*>>

A swell of sorrow pulsated through Marisabel's spirit—she had failed Gaia.

Kólasi soared closer, his divine silhouette blinding. <<*Perhaps I'll bring you home and let you implode upon sight of our glorious true forms.*>> He snatched Marisabel by her hair and dragged her through the weightless space. <<*I'm quite handsome,*>> He gloated. <<*Though you'd be blinded before getting to see for yourself.*>>

Marisabel opened her mouth to speak, but she was rendered mute.

<<*Silly mortal, you cannot talk to me unless I allow you to.*>>

Mouth wide, Marisabel released a silent scream, to which Kólasi chuckled.

<<*You amuse me. I think I'll keep you as my pet.*>>

Defeat washed over her.

<<*Entertain me,*>> Kólasi commanded, and Marisabel felt her invisible muzzle lift.

"Am I dead?"

The constraints of Kólasi's muzzle returned.

<<*Hilarious. You are a good pet, indeed.*>>

Marisabel thought of her vacant body in Antarctica and sorrow spilled from her eyes as vapor—she did not know if her tether to the living world could be repaired.

Not only had she failed Gaia, but also her sisters and the surviving human race. She could not warn her sisters that the true apocalypse was approaching, nor could she stop it. She kept her gaze focused on the direction of the portal, determined not to lose hope, or direction, while imprisoned within the abyss.

Kólasi crafted a golden chain made of magma and tied it to Marisabel's wrist. The burning shackle kept her bound to his throne.

<<*Time to prepare my army for their second chance at life,*>> he declared. <<*Be a good pet while I am gone.*>>

Kólasi vanished, leaving Marisabel alone in the dark. The silence stretched farther than she dared to imagine and she could see nothing. Senses stripped, she feared she might become nothing.

Using all her might, she clung to the direction of the portal and the hope that she might be as clever as Kólasi feared. Her thoughts ran wild, attempting to plan an escape, and though none of her ideas were plausible, as long as she kept trying, she hadn't lost yet.

A grumbling hum accompanied her desperate thoughts, disrupting the infinite silence.

Marisabel quieted her mind in disbelief, but when the foreign noise continued, her hopes fluttered. Even a monster would be welcomed into her crippling isolation.

The sound grew closer and the low grumble turned into a menacing growl—Marisabel suddenly regretted her desire for company. Hope morphed into fear, she lifted the glowing chain that kept her trapped and held it outward. It was her only source of light; her only chance to see what new threat faced her now.

In the dim light she saw a set of sharp, pearly white teeth gritted and bared in her direction.

Marisabel grimaced, horrified that this nightmare had only just begun.

Chapter 33

Tier

"She's gone," Juniper gasped, waking up from a deep slumber. Landon tossed in his hammock above her.

"Who is gone?" he asked.

Juniper's dream slipped from her memory. "Something isn't right."

Landon leaned over the side of his hammock, hanging upside down precariously.

"One of your sisters?" he probed.

"Maybe. I can't remember," Juniper replied.

Landon sighed. "Can I go back to bed?"

"Yes, I'm fine."

He nodded and flipped himself back into his hammock.

Juniper dug for the truth, willing the dream to return, but all she managed to do was increase the worried knot in her stomach.

Coral, she called out to her ocean sister. *Please answer me.*

A few moments later Coral answered with a gurgle. *Juniper, is everything okay?*

I had a horrible nightmare and woke up with an empty feeling in my gut—the same way I felt while Sofyla was dying.

I didn't feel quite right this morning either, Coral noted from the other side of the world.

Do you think it's Marisabel? Juniper asked. *We haven't heard from her since she told us about her connection to death. Maybe something happened while she was trying to find a way to save us.*

Oh, I hope not. I don't know how we're supposed to beat the Devil without her.

Let's call out to her, Juniper suggested, then summoned Marisabel.

They received no reply.

I can feel her body, Coral said. *It's warm and holds a slight vibration, but it feels like no one is home.*

What does that mean?

Perhaps she is in trouble.

Let's go check on her.

Coral swam across the Indian Ocean and Juniper flew with Finian over the South Atlantic Ocean. When they reached Antarctica, they scoured the icy tundra and Juniper eventually found Marisabel's vacant body lying in the middle of a snowfield.

She's over here, she informed Coral and led her toward Marisabel's location. The walk was long, but Coral endured the cold in hopes she might be able to save her sister. As she approached and Marisabel's state of being grew clearer, both Coral and Juniper were forced to assume the worst.

Coral knelt beside Marisabel's snow-covered body and felt for a pulse.

Nothing.

She looked up at Juniper with fearful tears in her large opal eyes.

"She's dead," Coral said aloud.

I thought you said she felt warm in your thoughts, that she had a pulse.

"That's what I thought I felt, but I was wrong. Her body has been vacant for days."

She was all alone, Juniper lamented.

Coral stood and wiped the tears from her eyes. "Now we are alone to deal with the Devil."

If she couldn't defeat him with whatever supernatural gifts she was given by Gaia, how are we expected to?

Coral's scaled shoulders slouched. "We need to warn our people."

There is no time to waste.

Juniper instructed Finian to fly slowly, ensuring Coral reached the ocean safely, then rocketed back to the heart of Tier.

She awoke in her body to sunshine and the imploring faces of her growing children.

"She's back," Jasper said with relief as Juniper blinked a few times to adjust her vision.

"You could warn us next time," Elodie snapped.

"Sorry, I didn't have much time to spare."

"Did you figure out who is missing?" Landon asked.

Juniper nodded, wearing a frown. "Marisabel. She is dead."

"That's horrible," Jasper stated. "How did this happen?"

"I don't know. Coral and I found her lifeless body in the middle of a glacier."

"She's not *really* dead though, right?" Elodie replied, her tone bitter. "None of you *really* die."

Juniper looked at her adolescent daughter with anger. "She *is* dead."

"Which element was she again? She'll surely reappear there."

"Why are you so angry?"

"It isn't natural," Elodie replied.

"It is for us," Landon cut in. "This is our reality. Stop fighting it."

"I don't like it," Elodie insisted.

"Then you really won't like what comes next," Juniper warned, unable to entertain Elodie's disapproval.

"What comes next?" Jasper asked.

"We all die." Juniper took a long breath. "Marisabel was our only hope."

"You aren't making sense …" Jasper coaxed, hoping his mother would divulge a little more.

"Gaia gave Marisabel the ability to become death: to see, to feel, to hear the unliving world that coexists parallel to the living. Kólasi—the God of Death and father to Satan—plans to release the purged human spirits back into the living world so they can take our bodies."

"Possession?" Jasper asked.

"By ghosts?" Landon followed up.

Juniper nodded. "It's strange, I know, but it's the threat we face."

Elodie huffed. "I told you the fine line we straddle between life and death was unnatural. Now, that thin veil will be our end."

"How do we stop this from happening?" Jasper asked his mother.

She shook her head, expression hopeless. "We can't. This task landed on Marisabel."

"Then it's a good thing I've been evolving my connection to Earth," Elodie replied. "Remember when I cast a ward protecting you and Jasper while you left your bodies?"

"Yes," Juniper replied hesitantly.

"Well, I've almost figured out the runes that will keep the dead away. I only intended to protect myself with them, but if they work, maybe we can protect everyone in Tier."

Juniper groaned, both elated and furious. "I'm afraid to ask *who* you were trying to keep away, but I assume it was your father?"

"And the dark phantom that kept chasing him and harassing us. Everything that is dead. I don't want to be haunted."

"Fine. We will talk about this later. For now, go practice. Figure out how to expand the spell to protect more people. The ghosts will swarm us en masse. They will be strong."

Elodie nodded, leading her brothers to her second favorite spot in Tier: the Vale of Night, a secluded valley in the southern region. Impenetrable by light, the dense canopy, deep caves, and bottomless lakes were home to the nocturnal creatures of Juniper's kingdom. After receiving the gift of night vision, Elodie took a new liking to the darkness and discovered her deeper connection to the land. Without light, she bonded with the eternal night and unlocked a terrestrial magic she still struggled to harness.

Elodie, Jasper, and Landon raced off and Juniper was left alone in her hammock. She placed a hand on the tree trunk she hung from.

Roscoe, she said, summoning her love. The energy of the tree radiated beneath her palm—a fierce staccato rhythm, then warmth.

Are you okay? Roscoe asked.

I might be joining you soon.

Why do you say that?

We couldn't stop Sergei Lamorte. He has sided with the Devil and together they killed Marisabel, who was our only hope for survival. The purged spirits will find us and they will take our bodies.

When? What can I do to help?

I don't know when it will happen, just that it is inevitable.

Hide with me in the trees.

My body will still be out here, susceptible to thieves.

Would they want it if it appeared to be dead?

Juniper considered this. *Perhaps.* She paused in thought again. *It's the only option outside Elodie's warding runes.*

Ah, that's the wall I've been feeling.

So it works?

She's managed to keep me away, despite my many attempts to connect with her since we last made contact. I don't know why she hates me. She was so little when I died.

It's my fault. Juniper confessed. *She lost me when we lost you. She resents both of us for that.*

I see.

I've been trying to make it right, but all these threats to our existence have kept me distracted.

You're doing great. Save everyone first, then work on repairing things with Elodie later.

I love you.

I love you more.

Juniper smiled and removed her hand from the tree—she had to warn her people.

The sun was rising over the jungle, shooting rays of orange light through the leaves. She scaled down the tree, bare soles landing in the mossy brush, and headed toward the heart. The short oak tree soaked in the sunlight through the clearing in the canopy. Juniper climbed its many branches until she was perched upon one that faced a large patch of open space below.

The Tierannites slept in their scattered hammocks and tree homes around the heart. She scanned the area, unsure how she'd call them all to her.

Teetering in place atop the thick bough, she closed her eyes and began to hum while the thoughts circling inside her mind revolved around her love for her people. As the melody grew, so did the swell rising within her chest. When it became too much to contain, she raised her hands to her mouth and released a euphonious arpeggio—a raw and harmonious melody for her people.

Sleepy heads lifted from their hammocks, eyes barely open, but hearts awakened. They began climbing down their trees and shuffling toward Juniper. It worked; the call summoned them all—she just hoped it wasn't the last time she'd get to sing their song.

Once everyone was gathered around the heart, Juniper spoke.

"My dear Tierannites, we are in grave danger. A force from my worst nightmares has become a reality and we must prepare." The faces staring up at her shifted from wonder to terror. Juniper continued, "Many of you surely remember Sergei Lamorte, leader of the rebellious legion of Debauched survivors. Well, he found a place where his soul could linger in the living world—he never truly went away. That dark spirit that haunted us for so many months—it was him. He found magic and has been growing stronger every day. I kept this truth from you because my Champion sisters were helping me deal with the matter—Marisabel was leading the charge—but things have changed. Marisabel was killed, by Sergei and the Father of Satan, and now we are on our own."

"The Father of Satan?" Teek asked, his tone incredulous.

"Yes. Just as I am guided by Gaia, Sergei is being guided by Kólasi."

"Are they planning to kill us all?" Noah Wolfe asked.

"Worse. They plan to release the purged spirits from Hell to steal our bodies. They will take control and seize a second chance at life."

"What happens to us?" Liesel Böhme inquired. "Do we die?"

Juniper shook her head. "From my understanding, we will become prisoners within our bodies."

The crowd erupted in a dissenting mumble.

"That is unacceptable," Teek declared. "We cannot let them defeat us without a fight."

"How do you propose we fight off ghosts?" Zoe asked.

"Would you rather roll over?" Teek countered.

"Of course not, I'm just interested to hear your plans, Mr. Ghostbuster."

Infuriated, Teek turned back to Juniper. "I will die before I let anybody steal my body."

"Us too," Misty declared, stepping forward with Brett.

"I'm with them," Noah agreed. His brothers nodded in concurrence.

"Are you suggesting a mass suicide?" Zoe asked. "Because I am not on board with that."

"Of course not," Teek replied, mimicking her sarcastic tone. "I'm imploring that everyone fight back."

"Elodie is working on a shield," Juniper stepped in to dissolve the argument. "Time will tell if it will work, but it's our best option."

"Can we help?" Brett asked.

"I'm sure they could use the extra minds and hands. The more of you who can place the runes, the better."

"Then we will help," Teek jumped in, then looked around. "Where are they?"

"In the Vale of Night. Deep in the darkest recesses of Tier, where the sun does not shine. Elodie says her connection to Earth is strongest amongst the night dwellers."

"Inside the valley's caves?"

"No, no. Amongst the trees, but surely near the caves and bottomless lakes."

"If it's our best chance at survival, we better hurry," Teek advised the others before departing in a brisk jog. Most of the group followed, leaving behind only those too old to run.

Juniper looked down at the weaker portion of her people and her worry returned. She had to save them all.

While Elodie taught the others how to create a supernatural shield, she needed to speak with the trees.

I need you, she professed. *Now more than ever.*

The enormous boughs swayed above.

<<*What is wrong, dear Champion?*>>

Kólasi. The trees trembled at His name. *I need to hide my people from Him.*

<<What are you asking of us?>>

Can you allow my people to enter the trees, temporarily, to save their souls from possession?

<<We cannot.>>

Why not? Juniper demanded.

<<Only your direct descendants can accomplish such a feat.>>

Help them, just this once.

<<We cannot,>> the trees answered in unison. Juniper felt like she was talking to a wall.

Gaia! she shouted. *Command them to help!*

She received no reply.

Have you forsaken us?

Dismissal came in the form of rustling branches and leaves.

Juniper nodded, understanding and accepting the silence.

"We are on our own."

Chapter 34

The Infinite Dark, Kólasi's Abyss

A thundering roar shook Marisabel's spirit and white-hot fire illuminated the dark space. Rendered blind temporarily, she tried to scream, but Kólasi's muzzle was still in place.

Darkness resumed.

::*Hello, friend,*:: a slick, female voice hissed into her ear. The muzzle snapped and fell off.

::*Who are you?*:: Marisabel asked, her guard lowering slightly.

::*My name is Gwyneira.*::

::*Are you an animal? You speak like them.*::

::*Half.*:: Her breath was steamy on Marisabel's neck and smelled like the smoke of a forest fire. ::*Do you want to get out of here?*::

Marisabel perked with hope—perhaps this wasn't a worsening nightmare after all. ::*Yes!*:: she declared.

The undefined creature inhaled deeply then blew directly onto the golden chains that kept Marisabel bound. Her breath came out as ice-fire—freezing then burning the links till they cracked.

Marisabel was free.

She looked down at the broken shackles with amazement. ::*How?*:: she asked.

::*I embody the beauty in death, just like you,*:: Gwyneira replied, her face still disguised by the dark. ::*Gaia sent me.*::

::*How can I thank you?*::

::*Finish what you started.*::

::*How, though? My last attempt left me imprisoned here.*::

::*I will guide you. But your time to depart without detection is running out. You must go.*::

::*Can't I leave with you?*::

::*It's better that your escape remain a secret for as long as possible. I will find you.*::

Marisabel nodded and rubbed her eyes. When she opened them again, she saw a light in the distance. Swimming through the nothingness of the abyss was a challenge, but as she got closer, the souls of thousands being ushered through the portal helped carry her.

Bianca stood at the gateway, chest puffed and expression hard. She stopped the progression after each batch of escapees to address the next set of souls.

"I am your master," she declared. "I am your liberator. You will choose a body and obey only me in your second life. Bodies marked with red wristbands are off-limits. If your allegiance falters, I will send you back into the infinite dark. Do you comply with these conditions?"

The group muttered in agreement, swearing their allegiance to Bianca, and were set free into the living world.

The group Marisabel was sandwiched within was next. Bianca repeated the same statement as before and every soul mumbled their emotionless devotion. Unlike the other spirits, Marisabel had retained her cognizance and saw the manipulation plainly—she was a wolf amongst sheep, but she nodded when Bianca made eye contact with her, ensuring her trip back into the light was fulfilled.

The souls around her dispersed toward North America, and Marisabel followed along until the lighthouse of Nether Isle was out of sight. The moment she could no longer see Bianca, she shifted her direction toward Antarctica.

The farther south she soared, the colder the chill became that seared her soul. When she reached the glacial land mass of Antarctica, she zeroed in on finding her body. The pull she once felt to it was gone, so the search was tiresome. She scoured the lifeless tundra, aimlessly combing every inch with her eyes, terrified that her body might have been covered by a snow drift, when she saw a dark contrast against the blinding white snow.

She lowered her spirit and followed the dark strands of her hair to her iced over body—the thick layer of frost that formed on her dead skin left her camouflaged.

Marisabel rested her spirit atop her lifeless body, hoping to seep into its flesh and reconnect her tether to the living, but it did not work. Her body remained cold and empty.

Desperate, she sat up and reached her hands into her corpse. They passed through all the tangible parts of her body, touching only that which existed in the realm of the dead, and when she found the other end of her broken tether, she yanked it closer. The end was frayed, just like that which had recoiled into her spirit. Marisabel touched the back of her neck, reaching inside to find her end of the broken tether. The moment she touched it a nauseating pain surged through her lifeless gut. She pushed through, tugging the tether until it was long enough to reach her dead body.

With careful precision, she knotted the tether back together. She braided each frayed strand, praying to Gaia that once they were all connected her life would resume. Attempt after attempt, she spent the next few hours rearranging her knots into every combination she could think of, hoping to change the results, but it didn't work.

She was gone, forever, stuck in this realm between the living and the dead.

Marisabel rested her spirit beside her abandoned body.

Alone.

She thought of her Champion sisters and began to miss them terribly. Guilt for failing them wrapped her like a blanket, but her unrelenting sorrow kept her cold. She could not speak to her sisters through the fresh water; her connection to the rivers and lakes was lost.

But to snow and ice, she wondered—perhaps she *could* still reach them. Faith reignited, she traveled to Mount Everest, her spirit coursing through the blizzarding snow. She hoped to warn Aria and Sahira of the forthcoming invasion, but upon arrival, she realized she was too late.

Ghouls swarmed, hijacking the bodies of the living. The air and mountain disciples ran about frantically, trying to escape the invisible threat, but Marisabel could see it all. She saw the mutilated, deranged spirits chasing their chosen hosts and stealing their bodies. She watched as the expressions of the living shifted from terror to calm emptiness as the ghosts took over.

Aria! Marisabel shouted through the snow, hoping her sister might hear, but the scene was too chaotic and she was trapped within the frozen element, unable to help.

She had to destroy Kólasi—it was the only way.

Chapter 35

Vale of Night, Tier

In the shadowed valley amongst the nocturnal creatures of Tier, Elodie practiced her earthly runes. The shields she created were powerful, impenetrable to all of Jasper and Landon's attempts to break through.

"Amazing," Jasper commented as the arrow he shot split into two upon hitting the invisible wall. "Where does this magic come from?"

"Me, I think," Elodie responded. "It's a mindset. If you believe you can, you will."

"Energy?" Landon asked, trying to understand.

"Yes, that is a good way to describe it. Once I totally understand how it works, it'll be easier to teach."

"I think I get it," Landon stated. "Let me try."

Elodie stepped out of the large circle of rocks and Landon took her place. He crouched, toes and fingers dug into the dirt. He memorized the exact locations of each rock in relation to himself, then shut his eyes.

Intentions laser-focused, he envisioned what he desired: a forcefield strong enough to shun the Devil. His chest began to swell, his heart rate quickened, and the rocks began to quiver.

"He's doing it," Jasper whispered in awe.

Elodie was impressed, but unconvinced. "Let's see if it holds."

She started small, lifting a broken tree branch from the ground and lobbing it at her brother. The wooden projectile hit Landon's shield and incinerated upon impact. Only ashes and smoke remained.

Landon opened his eyes, which had taken on the same illuminated shade of green whenever they left their bodies to enter the trees and animals, and he glared up at his siblings with a mischievous smirk.

Elodie's jaw dropped—her runes never produced such power.

"How?" she asked.

"I followed your instructions," he replied. "Seems you weren't really in it to win it," he mocked.

Elodie found a free stone and clutched it in her fist. Fiery desire to pierce Landon's forcefield coursed through her and into the rock. When she felt like her intentions might cause her to combust, she hurtled the stone at her brother. It created a blinding spark upon hitting the wall and sat lodged there. Elodie and Landon made brief eye contact—the battle was on.

Using only his mind, Landon cast the stone from his shield, but Elodie was already fueling another with more intensity. She threw her second rock, which penetrated the shield and hit

Landon in the shoulder. Elodie ran at the wall, thinking she had disarmed his defenses, but the moment she made contact, her body launched backwards through the air.

Jasper quickly dug his fingers into the ground and sprouted a thick bedding of moss for his sister to land on. She hit the soft patch with a thud.

Landon let out a hysteric cackle, and Elodie immediately stood and charged toward him.

"What did you do?" she demanded, ignoring the immense pain already healing in her tailbone.

Landon struggled to stop laughing. "You flew like a salmon jumping up river." He cackled again. "A dead fish."

"It's not funny!" Elodie screeched.

"But if you saw it—"

"You're lucky you're still behind the safety of those runes."

"Enough," Jasper cut in. "Have you both forgotten why we are trying to perfect these shields?" Elodie and Landon quit their squabbling and shamefully went quiet. Jasper continued, "The stronger the better. Good job, Landon. Now it's my turn."

Landon glanced at Elodie before slowly lowering his defenses. The moment he stepped outside the circle of rocks, Elodie chucked the stone she held directly at his head. He ducked just in time, cursing his sister beneath his breath.

Jasper, who was far less aggressive than his siblings, nervously made his way into the circle—the fate of the Tierannites rested upon them.

"I just need to concentrate?" he asked.

"Feel what you want through every fiber of your being," Landon replied, stepping closer to stand next to Elodie.

"Believe you can and you will," Elodie added while shoving Landon away from her.

Jasper nodded and muttered to himself, "Mind over matter."

He ran his hands along the ground, coating them with a layer of soil, then drew an X into the filth. He then stood tall and lifted his marked palms into the sky. Sunlight covered them with warmth. Focused on something greater, something stronger—he thought of Gaia and Her love for them. He thought of how She sacrificed Her beloved but misguided children in order to save the human race and the planet. He thought about how that choice was about to come back to haunt them all.

He had to protect Gaia's will; he had to protect his family.

Distant sunlight pierced his palms, surging through his body and filling him with light. The fire radiated through his flesh and illuminated the shadowed valley. The nocturnal creatures hidden in the dark corners of the vale screeched and hissed in protest, but there was no stopping the heavenly luminosity that poured out of Jasper. Light blazed from his eyes, casting glaring beams wherever he looked.

Elodie and Landon peeked through shielded eyes to observe in amazement.

"Test it," Jasper shouted.

"I'm afraid it might strike back," Elodie countered hesitantly. "This doesn't feel anything like the shields I've made."

"You need to try," Jasper countered. "For all we know, I'm just creating light."

Elodie looked at Landon and shook her head, so he mustered up the courage instead. He found a downed branch and tossed it at his brother. The branch disintegrated into nothing before ever touching the wall of light.

Landon glanced back at Elodie, who wore the same expression of wonder, then back at Jasper.

"Dibs on hiding behind your shield when the ghosts arrive," Landon said.

"So it works?" Jasper asked, unable to see through the light pouring out of his eyes.

"Oh yeah," Landon replied. "I'd say so."

Jasper lowered his hands and the light dimmed. It took a few minutes to release the energy he had channeled, but soon enough, the valley resumed its natural darkness.

Landon ran to Jasper to give him a fist bump, but Elodie remained in a state of frustration.

"How are you *both* better than me at something *I* discovered?"

"You don't take your own advice," Landon replied.

"What do you mean?"

"You told us to believe, and we do, but you still don't. You continue to fight all that Gaia has given us."

"No, I don't!" Elodie objected.

"Then go find Dad and tell him you love him," Landon challenged.

"What does that have to do with this?"

"One day you'll be dead and trapped in the trees—just like Dad, just as Gaia designed. Stop rejecting your fate."

Jasper stepped in, his tone kinder. "If you don't believe in our destiny, you don't truly believe, or trust, in Gaia. It's all connected."

"I'm kind of surprised you discovered this magical connection to the earth at all," Landon noted. "Considering you're the least in tune with it."

Utterly frustrated, and unable to think of a logical defense, Elodie turned away to work on her runes alone. It wasn't that she didn't believe; the implications of such a fate simply scared her. But admitting such a weakness to her older brothers wasn't an option—she'd figure it out on her own.

Clark and Teek led a large group through the trees toward them.

"Thought it might be hard to find you, then an orb of light set fire to the jungle and here we are," Clark explained in greeting.

"Your mother explained what you three were up to and we came to help. To learn, if possible," Teek said.

Jasper considered this. "Best we can do is practice how to let people into our shields while they're up so that everyone can run to safety when the nightmare begins."

Overhearing this plan, Elodie rejoined the group, grateful for the distraction, and they began to practice. Briefly opening small ingresses in the veil was easy for Elodie, as her shield was far less complex than her brothers. For Landon, they had to try many times before a branch passed through without charring. Jasper's was a much harder code to crack—the moment they got too close to the light of his shield, a burning sensation boiled their insides. After three failed attempts, they agreed that his shield might serve better as a weapon.

"But I can't control it," Jasper argued. "And I won't be able to see my targets."

"You better figure it out," Landon replied.

"I could kill so many innocent people," Jasper argued.

"Then practice!"

"No time," Teek grumbled through clenched teeth. The group turned their attention to find Teek fighting off an unseen force. His body moved unnaturally in rigid steps and he struggled to lift his arms.

"Shields up!" Clark ordered, standing next to Elodie as she activated her runes.

They are here, Jasper telecommunicated to Juniper. *We have shields. Hurry with the others.*

"Everyone pick a circle," Elodie instructed as half the group joined her and the other half stood beside Landon and Jasper.

"We need to help Teek," Jasper stated as Landon arranged his circle of runes.

"How?" Landon asked.

Jasper looked to Teek, who was convulsing violently as he tried to shake himself free from their invisible enemy.

"You will not win!" Teek screamed, voice raw from exertion.

His head snapped back and a voice not his own echoed through the dark valley.

"I already have."

"Keep fighting!" Misty screamed from Elodie's circle, tears streaming down her face. She held Brett's hand as they watched their best friend fight a battle no one knew how to win.

Teek trembled, head returning upright and torso jerking. The light behind his eyes came and went—Teek was still in there, fighting to take control. He fought his way toward the nearest tree, stumbling till his body leaned heavily against the thick trunk.

Through forced breath and gritted teeth, Teek declared, "You cannot possess a body that is dead!"

An unearthly shriek resonated from the depths of Teek's being as he began to slam his skull against the tree trunk. Blood poured from the wound, but Teek did not stop. With all his strength, he continued his forceful suicide.

The eerie shriek continued and Teek's body lurched away from the tree—the spirit's attempt to stop this deranged self-attack—but Teek's will was too strong.

"I will die before I let you live," he raged, eyes glassy with fury. A final blow to the head and Teek collapsed. His body seized aggressively before going completely still.

He was gone, but the spirit who forced his fate was surely still there.

Landon's shield was half formed. He summoned his passionate wrath against the Devil and continued building his invisible wall of hellfire.

A sturdy force slammed into Elodie's shield, knocking her to her knees as she held a strong guard. Clark put a hand on her shoulder, wishing he could do more to help.

"Hurry," she shouted to her brother. "It'll come for you next."

Landon kept his focus engaged on his desires and the shield grew taller and stronger. As the impenetrable energy braided together above their heads, the volatile spirit crashed into his shield. Upon impact, an inferno from the pits of Gaia's hell engulfed the ghost, temporarily illuminating its figure—a drowned man with bruised, bloated flesh and dead eyes bright with anger. The quick reveal vanished as the fire swallowed him whole.

The valley became dark again.

"I think he's gone," Landon said, panting from the horror.

"Why is there only one?" Clark asked from the neighboring circle of runes.

"I'm sure more are on their way," Jasper stated, shuddering as he imagined the forthcoming onslaught. "Mom should be here soon ... I hope."

Elodie wiped the tears from her face as she looked at Teek's lifeless body. "I don't think I could be that brave."

Misty let out a sob and Brett buried her in a tight embrace.

"He fought valiantly," Clark said, head hung in sorrow.

"And fearlessly," Landon added. "Maybe his refusal to cave will scare the other ghosts away."

"Doubtful," Elodie quipped.

"Let's just hope the others get here soon," Clark said, and the group became silent. They mourned the loss of Teek without saying a word, and the Vale of Night turned tense with their bereaved, but electric prayers.

Juniper received Jasper's warning and joined her people in a mad dash for the dark valley. Children were carried by those strong enough to do so, and the elderly followed as fast as they could—everyone understood that their lives depended on reaching the Vale of Night.

Juniper could leap into a tree at any time, leaving her body vacant and seemingly dead, so she took her time running, slowing down and speeding up in order to check on everyone in the pack. The Tierannites were so spread out, it was impossible to keep tabs on all of them at once, but Juniper did her best. She was circling the elderly near the back of the group when her cousin Zoe shrieked from the front. Juniper darted ahead.

Knife in hand, Zoe held it against her throat. "I'll do it," she threatened, shaking with terror.

Her body shook violently and a foreign laugh boomed out of her.

"Let me go!" Zoe insisted, afraid but determined.

"*You won't,*" the spirit cackled from inside her.

Zoe looked to Juniper, who stood motionless, unsure how to help.

"I'm sorry," Zoe expressed, holding back brave tears, then plunged the knife into her neck.

Juniper lunged to catch her falling body, and the spirit squealed as it exited the dying vessel. Many stopped to try to help, but Juniper shooed them away. "Keep running or they'll get you too," she demanded.

Zoe gurgled up blood as she stared at Juniper imploringly. She wanted her to keep running, but Juniper stayed by her side.

"Go," Zoe mouthed, unable to speak.

Juniper shook her head. "I'm sorry. You don't deserve this."

Zoe grimaced then mouthed, "I do." Blood poured down her chin.

"I forgive you," Juniper promised.

Zoe's eyes welled with tears. Juniper bent forward to kiss her cousin's forehead, and when she leaned back, Zoe was gone.

Juniper stood, unable to linger any longer, and the back of the group had caught up. She joined the elderly in their brisk jog, praying everyone else could reach her children in the Vale of Night.

A scream echoed from behind and she turned to find her Aunt Mallory sobbing over Zoe's body.

"Get up!" Juniper demanded.

Mallory was too distraught to hear.

"You have to stay alive for your grandchildren," Juniper pleaded, but the same spirit that had tried to steal Zoe's body had regrouped and was sinking its claws into Mallory. She was old and frail, and her brittle bones shook as the possession consumed her.

Mallory stopped crying and became eerily calm. She removed the knife from Zoe's neck, gripped the handle tightly, and narrowed her malicious gaze on Juniper.

"Damnit," Juniper groaned as her elderly aunt ran toward her with unnatural speed. Juniper crouched, dug her fingers into the soil and guided the trees to intervene. A solitary vine lashed from the nearest tree, snagging Mallory's possessed body by the neck and yanking her into the sky.

"If you can hear me, I'm sorry," Juniper grieved, horrified that she needed to take such action against her family.

Mallory's violently wiggling body went still and Juniper was alone. Far behind the others now, she ran to catch up, but the sight she encountered was that of her worst nightmares.

The entire back half of the group was either possessed or actively fighting off a spirit. Birk Wolfe was already possessed and he was holding down his wife Laurel as a different ghost fought to take her body. Russ Hazedelle shook ferociously as he limped toward the nearby river, throwing every rock he could find into his pockets. On the opposite side of the trail was a steep ravine, which his brother Vance Hazedelle dragged his twitching body toward.

There were so many people suffering, Juniper had to keep running. She couldn't stop—she had to reach her children.

Farther down the path, Brett's sisters Chloe, Kallie, and Brynn held hands in a circle while spirits ravaged their bodies. They fought to retain control, but to no avail. The moment Kallie stopped convulsing, possession complete, Brynn shoved her machete into Kallie's gut.

Kallie fell to the ground, shaking as the ghost within her tried to escape before its vessel died.

Brynn glanced at Chloe, who nodded somberly in reply. Trembling, they counted to three and plunged their machetes into each other in unison. They fell, still in an embrace, and died together.

Tears streaked Juniper's cheeks as she charged forward, furious that so many innocent lives were being lost. Outraged that the trees opted for this fate over helping her people take refuge within them. She didn't know how to help them, didn't know how to defeat the dead.

"I cannot save them," Juniper sobbed as she tore through the trees, watching the chaos ensue.

When she reached the Vale of Night, she saw that her children had successfully saved a large portion of the Tierannites, but around their invisible shields skulked a large group of possessed Tierannites, patiently waiting for the magical armor to break.

Juniper looked over her shoulder to see those who lost their fight against the hostile spirits lurking menacingly toward her.

"Mom, hurry!" Elodie pleaded.

"You cannot lower your shield for me," Juniper objected, glancing upward. "Who knows how many more hover above, waiting to strike."

Jasper placed his hand near Landon's shield, careful not to touch, but close enough to send his light through, and with the help of Gaia's earthly magic, he sent a blaring flash through the Vale of Night. His light illumed the darkness temporarily, and its heavenly glow revealed their enemies hidden in the dark. Thousands of resentful spirits surrounded them—some hung in the air, some prowled the forest floor, some sat in the trees. The Tierannites were wildly outnumbered.

Jasper's light faded, concealing their enemy once more. He stared at his mother imploringly.

Juniper shook her head. "It's not worth the risk." A tear rolled down her face. "I will die before I let them take you."

As she prepared to surrender, prepared to sacrifice her life, fire rained over the vale, sending sparks and ashes to the ground.

Juniper stalled in horror, unsure if this new arrival was another nightmare or a potential ally.

The fire rendered the possessed Tierannites nearest the shields immobile, leaving a clear path for Juniper to dart into Elodie's shield. Then she thought of the obscured ghosts all around. Jasper sensed her worry.

I'll illuminate while you open a veil into your shield, Jasper instructed Elodie. Juniper also heard the plan and prepared to run.

With deep concentration, Jasper illuminated the Vale of Night once more.

The ghosts were gone.

How? Juniper asked.

Just run, Jasper replied.

Juniper took her chance and rushed through Elodie's broken shield. The moment she joined them in safety, Elodie resealed their guard.

A blaze reignited the darkness with a scorching inferno. This new light was hot and glowed purple, unlike Jasper's cool, white light. Above, the silhouette of an enormous creature flew overhead. Another fiery discharge and the trees were alight with lavender flames.

The valley of everlasting night had turned into a vale of fire.

Chapter 36

Antarctica

Fiery warmth blanketed Marisabel's spirit as she paced near her vacant body. A glance toward the sunny sky revealed an impossible sight.

A dragon soared above her, lowering slowly in a circling glide. Enormous, pearly white wings with a shimmering purple sheen cast a massive shadow over the land, and the closer it flew, the larger its silhouette became. Marisabel's heart raced, but she had nothing to fear—she was already dead.

::*Hello, dear Champion.*::

Marisabel recognized the slithery voice; it was the same that freed her from Kólasi's abyss.

::*Gwyneira,*:: Marisabel greeted in awe. ::*You found me.*:: She stepped closer to the dragon. It had piercing, diamond eyes and scattered amethyst scales over a stark white body. Enormous in stature, the surrounding glaciers were dwarfed in comparison.

With trepidation, Marisabel extended her hand and placed it onto Gwyneira's slick body. She was colder than death.

::*I thought dragons only existed in fairy tales,*:: Marisabel commented in awe.

::*Technically, I am a drakkina, but there is no time for me to show you my human form. We have work to do.*::

Marisabel was still mesmerized and distracted by the presence of such a fantastical beast. *::Why are you so cold?::*

::I am known as Snow Ghost amongst Gaia and my drakkina sisters. My powers stem from death.::

::Like me,:: Marisabel noted solemnly. *::Until I became death.::*

::Fate has not steered you wrong. In this state, we can become one,:: Gwyneira stated, stepping closer and towering over Marisabel's drastically smaller spirit. *::Do I have your permission?::*

::Permission for what?::

::To bind our spirits.::

Marisabel nodded, nervous to learn how such a task was performed.

Gwyneira leaned downward, opened her monstrous, fanged mouth, and swallowed Marisabel's spirit whole. Instead of landing in the drakkina's belly, her spirit lifted upward into Gwyneira's mind and once settled, Marisabel could see through the drakkina's eyes. Everything was monochrome and lined in silver.

::This is amazing,:: Marisabel reveled.

::We have many souls to save. I helped quite a few of the tree disciples on the way here.:: Connected as one, they scanned the globe, able to detect every living and dead soul through Gwyneira's remarkable sight.

::What's that cluster to the north?:: Marisabel asked.

::Air and mountains.::

::Aria and Sahira,:: Marisabel repeated with more clarity. *::Their situation looks the most dire. Let's help them first.::*

The drakkina released a riotous roar before taking flight toward Mount Everest.

Each beat of Gwyneira's colossal wings matched the steady excitement in Marisabel's heart. Though the physical organ was dead and far away in her vacant body, she could still feel the thrill in her empty chest.

The ride was smooth and fast. When they reached the cloud-covered mountaintops, Marisabel's exhilaration turned to determination. She couldn't help her sisters before, but she hoped to now.

Spirits from the purge flooded the mountain, wreaking havoc everywhere they went.

::Let's find Aria and Sahira first,:: Marisabel expressed, looking for any signs of her sisters. Through Gwyneira's monochrome, metallic vision, each soul looked the same. So Marisabel channeled the White Room and began to see in auras. Everyone on the mountain had a strong aura gifted by nature, but none shone brighter than Aria's or Sahira's.

Countless white tents lined the flat camp between the snow-covered peaks, but only one appeared illuminated from within.

Marisabel directed Gwyneira toward the glowing tent and they tore the fabric off the posts. Within, Erion was huddled in a corner, holding his twin baby girls in his arms. He convulsed violently, refusing to surrender. The tiny girls remained untouched by the ghosts; no spirit wanted a second life constricted by the confines of infancy.

Aria writhed on the ground, attempting to scare off a very determined spirit. The knife she held to her own neck was pressed deep and drawing blood when Gwyneira arrived. Just in time, it seemed, to save Aria from herself.

Gwyneira exhaled an icy chill which froze the living to the bone and paralyzed the dead. Those possessed became immobilized—the twins were trapped tightly in Erion's petrified embrace.

Gwyneira then inhaled, sucking her icy poison from the space. The lingering ghosts were consumed and sent to perish a second time in the drakkina's icy-hot cauldron belly, and the living were stripped of their captors and set free.

The drakkina reversed the freeze, and Aria gasped for air as her demon was eradicated. She began to sob with relief as she chucked the knife as far as she could. Erion slouched in an exhausted heap against a pole, still holding his daughters tightly.

Gwyneira released another icy exhale, but this time it formed a protective dome over the Champion and her family.

::*This will keep them safe until we rid the world of Kólasi's chaos,::* Gwyneira informed Marisabel. ::*Tell her to stay here until we give word otherwise.::*

::*She can't hear me.::*

::*She can't hear me either; only you can speak to her. Send your voice through the ice dome.::*

Marisabel obeyed. *Aria, it's Marisabel. I am inside the dragon.*

Aria sat upright in shock. Her eyes filled with tears. *Marisabel? Juniper said that you died.*

I did. But my spirit lives on, and Gaia sent Gwyneira to me to help save you.

Thank you, Aria expressed, clutching the fresh wound on her neck.

Where will I find Sahira?

I don't know, Aria sobbed. *I lost her. It all happened so fast.*

Don't worry, just stay here. You will be protected under this ice until I make things right again.

Aria nodded and Gwyneira rocketed into the frigid sky.

Marisabel scanned the harrowing scene, searching for an aura as bright as Aria's.

::*Over there,::* she frantically directed Gwyneira toward the mountain's edge. Sahira valiantly fought the spirit that tried to consume her, dragging her body toward death. Wholly distracted by the battle she waged, she did not see the dragon rocketing toward her.

Gwyneira inhaled, insides rattling in preparation to strike. Her wings pounded the air, projecting her massive body forward with incredible speed.

But the Champion of the Mountains remained out of reach.

"You will never win!" Sahira shrieked, frustrated tears pouring from her silver eyes as she greeted death fearlessly.

No! Marisabel shouted, but Sahira could not hear her.

With heroic determination, Sahira found the edge and launched her body over. She fell thousands of feet, ricocheting off of peaks and ledges as she plummeted.

::Chase after her,:: Marisabel instructed, and Gwyneira nose-dived over the edge.

Seconds before hitting a patch of solid ground, Gwyneira caught Sahira between her large talons and redirected her dive upward. She tore through the sky, screeching with adrenaline as she soared.

::Is she alive?:: Marisabel asked.

::It is hard to tell.::

Marisabel understood the grave reality of Sahira's likely condition. *::Keep her safe, but free the others.::*

Gwyneira recharged and expelled a ferocious stream of icy-hot breath over the mountaintop. It froze the living where they stood, immobilizing them in various frenzied positions. As a chill colder than death crept through their paralyzed bodies, the ghosts were forced to flee—they could not withstand Gwyneira's wintry charms; lingering would have killed them within their vessels. As soon as they exited back into the mountain air, Gwyneira sucked every morsel of death into her ice-cauldron belly.

Spirits ripped through the sky, unable to escape the pull of the drakkina magic, and disappeared through her mouth and nostrils. Once every remnant of death was exterminated, Gwyneira blew a heated mouthful of gilded breath onto the frozen people. It warmed them slowly, preventing their bodies from dying of shock.

She then returned to the dome of ice she built over Aria. With a single tap of her talon, the dome shattered.

Gwyneira lowered into the space and gently placed Sahira onto the snowy ground.

Aria ran to her side, sifting through the blood to feel for a pulse. Tears spilled from her eyes as she looked up at the drakkina and silently shook her head.

"She's gone," Aria sobbed.

Are you sure? We have eternal life—maybe she is healing, Marisabel countered, her hope surpassing her doubts.

Aria sat back in wonder. She began examining Sahira's body, looking for signs of a fatal blow. As she scanned her beaten and bruised body, she found nothing, then Gwyneira used her talon to flip Sahira over.

As soon as her dead weight landed face down, reality hit—there was a deep lesion in the back of Sahira's skull. Visceral blood oozed out of the wound.

Aria turned away, nauseated by the horrifying sight.

Erion stepped in to comfort her. "She is gone," he stated aloud for all to hear, then looked up at the dragon. "Sahira is with you now, Marisabel."

Gwyneira nodded her head on behalf of Marisabel.

Another Champion lost.

Will you be okay? Marisabel asked.

Aria nodded, wiping the tears from her face.

Marisabel left with Gwyneira and they turned their focus toward Juniper.

::*We cannot save those who killed themselves to escape possession,*:: Gwyneira explained, ::*but we can help those still fighting.*::

They swooped over the jungle, eradicating every vicious spirit they could. To their dismay, carcasses covered the forest floor. They flew to the place where Juniper and those who took shelter in the earthly domes waited.

Gwyneira cleared the last of the spirits from Tier and then landed with a thud, digging her talons into the soils.

::*Speak to the Champion of Trees,*:: she instructed.

Marisabel obeyed and her voice carried into the soil, through the tree roots, and into Juniper's mind.

You are safe now, she stated, her Brazilian accent thick.

Marisabel? Juniper asked, staring up at Gwyneira in awe.

Yes, I am here. Gaia sent me this drakkina in death, so I could finish my task. We will defeat Kólasi.

I thought the Debauched were the worst of our troubles, Juniper lamented.

The ghosts don't discriminate. The Debauched will be gone soon, taken over by the dead.

It's strange to say I feel sorry for them, but after seeing the horror the dead caused, I wouldn't wish that fate on my worst enemy.

Sahira is gone, Marisabel informed Juniper.

How?

Like many of your Tierannites, she chose death over possession.

Juniper's eyes became glossy with sorrow. *Another sister lost too soon.*

I was so close to saving her. She couldn't hear me coming.

It's not your fault.

Marisabel could not stifle her guilt. *We cannot lose anyone else.*

With dragons on our side, how could we lose?

Marisabel considered this, then spoke internally to Gwyneira.

::We have to destroy Kólasi's edifice.::

::I am strong, but not stronger than Kólasi. My fire will not damage his lighthouse.::

::Then how do we win?::

::Slow and steady, soul by soul.::

Marisabel steadied her intensifying anxiety—they had a long battle ahead.

Chapter 37

Quadrant B4, North America

Odette ran to Lucine's bathroom and vomited violently. The sound woke the others, and Lucine rushed to her side.

"I've been feeling sicker each morning," Odette expressed between heaves.

Lucine's expression turned grave. "Are you pregnant?"

Eyes widened, brow furrowed, Odette considered the possibility before unexpectedly hurling more of her breakfast into the toilet.

"I can't be," she stated, catching her breath and wiping chunks of food off her chin. "I haven't been with Xavier in months."

"I'm afraid you might be."

Tears welled in Odette's eyes. "I can't bring his baby into this world."

Lucine knelt beside her, covering her nose as she flushed the toilet. She examined Odette and spoke sincerely. "You are looking at this wrong. This could be our ticket to reform—a child might be the only way to soften Xavier's hatred and redirect his focus. This child could save everyone."

Odette's panicked breathing slowed as she contemplated this. "Maybe you're right."

"I am going to radio Xavier to tell him the news."

She stood and left the bathroom, leaving Odette to wallow in this unwelcome revelation alone.

Max, Gideon, and Drew waited in the living room.

Lucine nodded.

"I knew it," Max declared. "I had a feeling."

"This is great," Gideon stated. "If a child doesn't soften Xavier, nothing will."

Lucine took the discarded radio out of the bottom drawer of her dining room armoire. She hadn't used it in a while; she gave up trying to communicate with her family weeks ago. Xavier only ever tormented her, her mother was a jaded zombie, and the rest of her extended family remained stubbornly aloof to reality.

With the dials set, she called her brother.

He didn't answer.

Determined to deliver this news, she tried again.

Countless beeps with no answer.

Persistence would prevail—she redialed.

"What?" Xavier shouted from the other end.

"Hello to you too, Brother," Lucine replied, unrattled by his harshness.

"What do you want?"

"How do you feel about being a father?"

"Excuse me?"

"You know, a little, innocent infant that looks just like you and will idolize your every move."

"I am too busy for this nonsense."

"You'll need to learn to make time. Odette is pregnant."

The line went quiet.

After a long, contemplative pause, Xavier spoke again. "Is it mine?"

"Of course it's yours," Lucine ridiculed.

"I haven't seen her in months. It could be anyone's child."

"I am insulted *for* her," Lucine scoffed.

"I am not sure if I believe you."

"Then come to B4 and talk to Odette yourself."

"I don't have time." Xavier panicked—if Lucine was being honest, he had to protect his potential legacy. "Neither do you. Tie something red around Odette's wrist."

"What?" Lucine asked, confused by the strange request. "Why?"

"Just do it."

Xavier ended the call.

Lucine held the receiver in her hand, lost in her perplexed thoughts, when Drew began to shake uncontrollably where he sat.

Everyone's attention turned to him.

"I think he's having a seizure," Max said, cradling Drew's head.

"No," Drew muttered through clenched teeth. "Something … foreign …" His eyes rolled to the back of his head as he convulsed more violently.

Lucine's mind darted to thoughts of her dead father, then back to Xavier's last request—she had to save Odette.

She raced through her apartment and tore through her bedroom collecting everything red. To her dismay, there weren't many options: just a T-shirt, a bandana, and red-lace panties. When she remerged, the lights throughout her home were flickering.

She ran to Odette first, tearing the red T-shirt in half and tying the fabric around her wrist. She then tied the remaining piece around her own wrist.

Looking back at her cousin and boyfriend, her fright amplified—Gideon was now cradling Max's trembling body while kicking Drew away. Drew looked wildly possessed and had his hands around Max's neck.

"Stop!" Lucine screamed as she raced toward them. She reached Drew and punched him hard in the face. The impact hardly slowed him down, so she lifted a chair from her dining room table, swung it with all her might, and connected with Drew's head. He fell to the floor, motionless.

"I hope I didn't kill him," she grieved. Lucine knelt beside Gideon and caressed Max's anguished face. "Keep fighting," she pleaded, tying the red underwear to his wrist.

"What is happening?" Gideon asked, horrified by the nightmarish scene unraveling around them.

"My father—he's trying to take over."

"Your father is dead."

"Exactly."

Gideon's expression remained lined with terrified confusion.

"He died, but he isn't gone. I found the ghost of him in Maine. He warned me that he planned to do something like this." She shook her head and hastily tied the red bandana around Gideon's wrist. "Looks like my brother took the bait."

She then turned her attention back to Max, who continued to shake forcefully. "Why isn't it working?"

Max opened his mouth and a rattling, alien voice emerged. *"You're too late."*

Lucine jumped back in fright and Gideon pushed Max's body off his lap.

"What happened to his voice?" Gideon asked, shuffling away from the stranger wearing his best friend's face.

"I'm too late." Tears streaked Lucine's face. "My father's dead army is here."

Quadrant C2, North America

Xavier paced in his penthouse, aware of the terror unfolding in the streets. It did not bother him that lives were being stolen—his anxiety stemmed from not knowing when the takeover would end.

The only people he warned were Killian and the Palladon twins—Oliver and Dennis—and his sister at the last minute.

His thoughts returned to the possibility of having an heir. He never wanted to be a father—the novelty of such a role was tarnished by his own father years ago—but he did need to bequeath the Lamorte reign to someone, and a blood-relative was certainly preferable. Xavier suddenly found himself hoping that his sister heeded his warning; he wanted Odette to survive.

The voice of his father appeared. *I love you.*

Startled, but grateful, Xavier felt relieved to have his father nearby.

"Thank you for helping me. I am excited to attempt recruitment again."

I love you, Sergei repeated before diving into Xavier's mouth and spreading his spirit throughout his son's body. Xavier fought him, but was unable to wrangle back control.

"Let me go!"

This is the only way.

"No! I plan to do everything you ask of me."

It will be easier this way.

Sergei pounded Xavier's spirt, wailing it deep into the recesses of his being, knocking off chunks until it was small enough to fit into a small pocket of darkness. He then wriggled his soul within Xavier's body, lining up all the right parts: arms, legs, head. Once everything was in place, he found Xavier's eyes and peered through.

"Now," Sergei said through Xavier, "we can defeat the Champions together. With my mind and your body, the Lamorte reign will become more powerful than ever."

Xavier was beat into submission. What remained of him continued to fight against the smothering presence of his father, but he could not break through. He was lost and falling deeper as Sergei grew more comfortable in his new vessel.

"I think we will eliminate the jungle first." Sergei looked around through Xavier's eyes, taking in his new surroundings— he had a lot to catch up on. "I suspect you have missiles by now. Tell me where they are."

Release me! Xavier countered in a small, distant voice.

Sergei huffed. "I will figure it out on my own, then."

His attention turned to the desk with the radio. Around it were piles of confidential folders. Sergei found one labeled "Missiles" and began to read.

A smile crept across his face.

"Looks like a trip to Houston, or as you call it—D2, will lead me to the launching pads." He continued reading before speaking again. "You don't have much liquid fuel, but there appears to be enough to launch a medium-range ballistic missile. 3500 kilometers will surely reach the tree wench."

Sergei resealed the folder, placed it under his arm, and departed.

It was time to seek retribution.

Chapter 38

Savana, Tier

"The lions," Elodie declared, awakening with a jolt. In the morning light, black clouds of billowing smoke became visible over the tree line.

She left her hammock in the southern section of the Savana and raced toward the inferno.

Mom! she shouted. *We're under attack.*

Unable to get any closer, Elodie wept for her lions from afar, praying that some might have been sleeping elsewhere.

Fire rained over Tier, but this time it was not sourced from an ally. The Debauched missile struck the northwestern terrain of the Amazon, what was once Colombia, setting the trees ablaze and killing all the animals within range.

Juniper felt the impact, felt the fire burning her home, and her heart broke as she traveled through the scorched trees to assess the damage—they beat one threat only to be attacked shortly after by another.

She called out to Coral, desperate for reprieve.

The Debauched sent a missile. They massacred a huge section of my jungle.

That's terrible, I am so sorry, Coral replied.

I need your help.

What can I do?

Help me move my continent.

Coral hesitated. *Can we do that?*

I would like to try. The bomb didn't reach the heart of Tier this time, but it might next time. I need to be farther out of their range.

I'm up for the challenge.

Juniper exited the trees and found a sturdy patch of soil near the center of the continent. Once her fingers and toes were dug in, she summoned Coral. *I am ready to begin.*

Juniper lifted as much of the ground as she could while Coral swept massive, deep-water tides into the underside of the continent. She swam to the belly of South America, deeper than any other Coralene could traverse, and learned quickly that Juniper's strength was not enough to dislodge the land mass from its roots.

It won't work, she informed Juniper.

Why not? Juniper asked, exhausted from the exertion, but refusing to give up—she knew no other way to save those who remained in her care.

We need Eshe. If she can shift the tectonic plates, we might be able to move Tier. But would that really help? And what about the climate? If you go too far south, you'll lose warmth.

Juniper sighed. *You're right, I'm just desperate. I feel so vulnerable being this close to the enemy.*

I can flood the other countries that connect North and South America. No one lives there and nature has hardly made a return to those locations.

That would be helpful. Can you also send a fresh stream into Tier? The fire is spreading.

Of course. I will talk to Eshe while you take care of the damage in Tier.

Thank you.

They disconnected and Juniper refocused on her burning home.

The fire was spreading and she had no power to stop its growth. Zaire remained deep within Ahi, digging tunnels toward his deceased love, leaving Juniper with no connection to fresh water. Coral said she'd send fresh water to the strike zone, but it had yet to arrive.

::*Collect all the water you can and meet me where the forest burns,*:: Juniper called out to the animals, praying that with their help, she might be able to extinguish the slow-moving inferno.

The fire raged, flickering maliciously in Juniper's green eyes as she watched her home burn. The sound of wings pounding the air broke her trance—a fleet of sandgrouse pigeons soared overhead, dumping the water stored in their feathers onto the smoldering trees.

Behind them were ten enormous pelicans, beaks brimming with seawater.

While her attention was aimed at the sky, Juniper missed the arrival of the elephants. But as soon as they began spraying water out of their trunks, her focus shifted back to the ground. As the final elephant's spray turned to mist, a flood of murky water cascaded toward them. The loose stream was quick and fierce, carving out a slight canal as it traveled. The elephants reloaded and then blasted the fire with more water.

Juniper breathed easier knowing that between Coral's aid and the elephants, this fire would spread no farther.

::Thank you,:: she expressed, to which the elephants trumpeted and the birds cawed.

She raced back to the Heart, her hands touching the trees as she ran.

You are doing your best, Roscoe stated once he found her.

I have lost so much.

You still have your children.

Juniper stifled a sob, never slowing. *Yes, but we aren't safe.*

Keep fighting. Never give up. You will win—you have nature on your side.

Juniper nodded. *I love you.*

I love you more.

She wiped the tears from her eyes, smearing the layer of dirt collected on her cheeks.

When she reached the Heart, the small group of Tierannite survivors were gathered together, holding hands with their heads down. Jasper stood atop a low hanging branch and led the group in a unifying prayer.

"Like the river, together we flow. Into the darkness, through the unknown. One heart, many lives. Together we live, together we die."

The fresh water disciples repeated Jasper's words in Spanish.

"Como el río, fluimos juntos. Hacia la oscuridad a través de lo desconocido. Un corazón, muchas vidas. Juntos vivimos, juntos morimos."

Juniper looked around, devastated to learn that only six small children from the soil disciples survived—none of which were progenies of Sofyla. Riad was gone, as were all the adults that followed him to the Amazon so many years ago. Sofyla's legacy was nearly obliterated.

Juniper's heart swelled as she looked at her own beautiful children leading their people toward a life of peace and harmony. She was lucky—Juniper reminded herself of her fortune. Her circumstance could be worse.

Jasper repeated his prayer one last time before jumping out of the tree and charging toward Juniper.

"Will we be okay?" he asked.

"Yes. Coral sent us fresh water and the elephants are successfully extinguishing the fire."

Jasper nodded. "How do we prevent this from happening again?"

Landon, Juniper called out telepathically. *Elodie. Follow me.*

They obeyed and followed their mother and older brother to a more secluded section of Tier.

Juniper took a deep breath. "We are going to relocate."

"Where?" Elodie asked. "I can't imagine any place is safer than the jungle."

"I mean, we are going to relocate Tier. I need your help, though. Coral and I tried by ourselves already and we weren't strong enough."

"Let me make sure I am understanding," Landon replied. "You want us to move the entire continent of South America?"

"Yes, a little bit south east."

"How?" Landon asked, expression full of scrutiny.

Juniper knelt, pressed her fingers into the hard dirt, then pulled her arms upward without breaking contact with the ground.

"We lift, Eshe separates, and Coral pushes," Juniper explained.

Her children knelt beside her and mimicked her actions. The weight of the world clung to their fingertips as they did their best to lighten the load for Coral and Eshe.

The weight is lifted, Juniper announced to her sisters.

The tides are on their way, Coral replied.

Scaled feet dug into the sand, Coral stabilized her position and threw powerful surges of water at the massive mound of land. Indah and Annisa swam in circles over their mother, creating a ferocious underwater whirlpool and filtering violent streams from their cyclone into each of Coral's currents. Ozy swam ahead, leading one hundred other Coralene into a collective push against the dense land. Zander swam above, directing their unified direction eastward.

It wasn't enough.

We need the spirits of nature to help, Coral announced to Juniper and Eshe.

<<We are here,>> the ocean replied. <<As are the soil, trees, and core.>>

With a confident smile, Coral pushed harder. They were not alone in this feat, they were never truly alone.

With the extra help from nature's spirits, Coral's efforts began to work and the land started to shift.

Eshe, Coral called out. *It's working. Move the tectonic plates.*

Eshe held one hand on her swollen belly and the other was placed against a rock wall in Ahi. Her eyes turned bright orange as she left her body and traveled through the red rock.

Sparks flew where the heavy rocks grated together beneath the pressure of the push. Eshe found her way to the long tectonic plates lining the western coast of South America. Her spirit darted through the different layers, doing her best to maneuver them and prevent collision as the land mass moved. As the continent moved farther east, Eshe traveled deeper, following the broken flow of lava beneath Cotopaxi. She tore through the massive volcano, pausing only once when she came across Zaire's lifeless body being consumed by lava. Eshe felt a pang of guilt—she stopped helping him dig tunnels to Antarctica when Marisabel died. She had planned to return to the issue of fresh underground water, but her attention was pulled away to deal with more serious matters, and Zaire refused to give up.

His body incinerated as it was swallowed whole.

The only relief Eshe felt was the knowledge that he would now join Marisabel in the afterlife.

She continued onward, grievously aware that the volcano she raced through was about to blow.

Cotopaxi is going to erupt, she warned Juniper.

Can you make it stop?

You'll need to settle the land.

Juniper grimaced, unwilling to surrender just yet. She called out to Coral, *How far have we moved?*

There was a slight pause before Coral replied. *Zander says we've traveled 600 kilometers southeast.*

Is it enough?

The distance is significant.

It was time to submit. *We need to stop. Eshe says Cotopaxi is about to blow.*

Any farther and we'd risk colliding with Africa. This is the best it will get.

I hope it's enough. Thank you.

Juniper disconnected and opened her eyes. Elodie, Landon, and Jasper remained concentrated on lifting the land.

"You can rest now," she stated, lifting her fingers from the soil. "This is as far as we can go."

Elodie looked up at the new patch of sky they sat beneath. "Feels different."

"Hopefully we moved far enough away from the Debauched," Landon added.

"Time will tell. Cotopaxi might explode, so we need to gather everyone at the heart for safety."

Juniper darted toward the heart. Jasper and Landon followed.

Elodie hung behind, lost in thought. So much death surrounded her now, and all the lives lost in Tier were gone forever.

She walked to the nearest Kapok tree and placed her hand on its massive trunk. Watching the swaying branches, she felt the souls of those recently deceased radiating down on her; they chose the trees. Relief coursed through her, followed by a painful surge of guilt—she welcomed their continued presence, yet shunned the one who ought to matter most.

Dad, she cried, hand pressed against the tree. *I'm so sorry.*

The trunk grew warm beneath her palm.

He was already there—he was always there.

It's okay, Roscoe answered. *I love you.*

Mom almost died, and I thought of you in that moment, she sobbed. *I couldn't lose her too. Then I realized, I am beyond lucky—I never really lost you. I just chose to keep you away. And it was awful. I don't know why I did that.*

You were grieving, not only the loss of me, but also the change in your mother. Juniper struggled for a long time after I died, and you and your brothers were forced to be strong. You resented me, and that is okay.

But I don't—and I didn't mean to—I just couldn't make sense of it.

You were a child when my life was taken. You are allowed to grieve however you need to.

Elodie nodded, wiping the tears off her face with her free hand.

Roscoe continued, *I was always here.*

She sniffled. *I know, I could feel you every time I touched a tree.*

I tried to keep my distance.

You did a terrible job, she laughed through the tears. *Thank you for forgiving me.*

There is nothing to forgive. I am grateful you learned to see our fate as a blessing, but even if you hadn't, I would have loved you forever anyway.

I love you too. I'm sorry it took me so long.

I understand. Roscoe paused. *I can feel the group gathering at the Heart. You ought to join them.*

Elodie broke her connection from the tree and raced toward the heart, her constant need to battle Gaia's gifts had finally subsided. She no longer wished to pick a fight with the dead, no longer wrestled with the idea that the dead did not belong alongside the living. Peculiar, considering the army of ghosts they just barely defeated, but her understanding went deeper than their scarce victory. While everyone around her mourned for people they'd never truly connect with again, Elodie was lucky enough to have access to the mind and spirit of her father.

She would never take that for granted again.

Chapter 39

North America

Gwyneira and Marisabel soared over the continent of Debauched rebels, freeing the living street by street.

Iced-fire froze and burned the flesh until the dead were forced to vacate. As they escaped their sweltering vessels, Gwyneira consumed their souls, delivering their second and final deaths. One by one, the world was freed from Kólasi's army. His reign of chaos would be over as quickly as it began.

Delighted by their success, but unable to shake her doubts, Marisabel watched carefully for a counterstrike, but none appeared on the horizon.

::*Would he really just give up like that?*:: she asked the drakkina.

::*He doesn't like to get His hands dirty. Neither does Gaia. They put a plan in motion and let it unfold as it will. His plan was weaker than Gaia's—I am stronger than one thousand armies from the abyss. Gaia will win this round.*::

Marisabel accepted Gwyneira's response and felt comforted by her confidence.

::*We have to find the Lamortes,*:: Marisabel noted, aware that no one would be safe until Sergei was gone for good. ::*He lives somewhere in the middle,*:: Marisabel said, trying to recall the name of the town Juniper mentioned in their meetings.

::We've already cleared the middle regions.::

::Or perhaps he is where the bombs were launched.::

They looked south and saw a swarm of black auras smothering the southern section of Texas.

Gwyneira redirected toward the threat. Another round of missiles were loaded and ready to be launched.

Accompanied by a grievous roar, the drakkina pumped through the polluted sky. Her silhouette grew larger with each thrust of her wings and the possessed below took notice.

"A dragon!" one shouted, sending the whole group into a frenzy. They ran about, struggling to find places to hide.

"Protect me," Sergei demanded through Xavier, and a hoard of his minions gathered around.

Their feeble attempt was futile as Gwyneira easily froze the first layer of vessels and sucked the unliving out of their hosts. She rocketed upward, digesting as she made a large lap, and then dove back toward the trembling group.

The second layer of Sergei's guard was frozen and liberated.

"Kólasi!" Sergei called out to the apathetic devil. "Help me!"

Gwyneira's frost burned the final row of bodies shielding him.

"Bianca!" Sergei shouted as he fell into a fetal position, arms covering Xavier's head.

Gwyneira inhaled deeply, creating thunder with her wings as she hovered menacingly, then released the fatal blow.

Frosty snowflakes waltzed along Xavier's flesh, blanketing his body in ice. Once frozen, the frigid chill of death sunk deeper, reaching Sergei's soul and forcing him to flee.

Vacated, he tried to dash toward freedom, but Gwyneira latched him with her talons. Lifted and hanging directly in front of the dragon's bared teeth, Sergei's ghost flailed violently. Gwyneira licked his spirit with her slithering tongue, tasting his potent afterlife zest, then tossed him into her mouth and bit down. Flavor exploded and the taste of death tickled her tongue.

She savored every ounce of him as he fell to his second death in the frozen cauldron of her belly.

Xavier lay paralyzed on the ground.

::*Kill him,*:: Marisabel instructed, feeling no remorse, and Gwyneira pressed her talon through his heart. Blood crept through the frozen layer covering his flesh. Through the cracks it spilled onto the ground, creating a pool around his lifeless body. As his spirt rose, Marisabel observed.

::*What will you choose?*:: she asked the young president. In death, he was able to hear her telepathic thoughts.

Xavier's spirit was infantile; he did not yet realize he was dead.

"Humans will defeat nature," he stated.

Marisabel shook her head. ::*Nature always wins.*::

Gwyneira swallowed his ghost, guaranteeing that his misguided beliefs did not infect future generations.

The drakkina rocketed into the sky and circled high above North America, observing the immobilized statuettes of the living below.

After five crisscrossing laps, Marisabel broke the silence.

::*Perhaps we shouldn't let any of them live.*::

::*Are you suggesting I kill them all?*::

Marisabel hesitated. ::*I am.*::

::*I am here to serve you. Gaia told me to obey your orders. If that is what you want, I will eliminate your enemies.*::

A long, tense pause lingered between them. Marisabel scanned the immobilized bodies of the innocent mortals below. ::*These people follow the Lamortes,*:: she explained, ::*which makes them my enemy. But perhaps there is good amongst them.*::

::*Then I suggest you do not make any irreversible decisions.*::

::*But if I don't act now, my Champion sisters could be plagued by them for the rest of their lives.*::

::*You cannot undo death.*::

::*What if this decision brings forth the death of my sisters or their progenies? The world would be a better place without the unevolved.*::

::Though we have eradicated Kólasi's army in this section of the world, Earth is still riddled by vengeful ghosts who should not be here, and I yearn to taste their second deaths. If you wish, you have time to consider your choices.::

::You're right. I will think on it.:: Marisabel looked through Gwyneira's eyes and saw countless blackened auras hovering near Africa. *::We ought to check on Eshe.::*

They catapulted toward the land over Ahi and found numerous spirts scouring the continent for bodies to steal. The scene was calm, but desperate, and for the first time, Marisabel did not need to spring into action. She took a moment to observe and found her heart breaking at the sight: half of them were victims of the cyclones and flooding in South America—she could tell by their bloated bodies and fatal placement of lodged debris. Those who were once the people she lived to protect were now her enemies.

::You tried to convince them to follow you,:: Gwyneira stated, sensing the source of Marisabel's dismay. *::They did not listen. Their fate is not your fault.::*

::Easier said than believed.::

Marisabel continued scanning the souls that wished to wreak havoc on Eshe's underground empire.

Burn victims from the super volcanos scorched so badly they barely looked human. Charred flesh covered visible bones; some were walking skeletons.

Victims of the trees walked around with noose bruises on their necks where they were hung by vines. A few had gaping holes in their chests where tree limbs pierced their bodies.

Near the northern coast of Africa were ghosts covered with frost and icicles; victims of the European avalanches. Those with dark veins decorating their flesh were casualties of the Air attack. Marisabel could see where the poison stifled their life — black patches gathered where their veins merged and exploded.

::*I feel sick*,:: Marisabel expressed.

::*They haven't yet figured out where Eshe hides. This will be easy. Close your eyes, I will take care of this on my own.*::

Marisabel obeyed, closing their inner eye, and Gwyneira breathed a fiery blizzard over the scorched land. The ghosts vanished one by one, entering her belly and dying a second time. Blue fire lingered in the wake of every soul she ate, illuminating the dark landscape with majestic light.

She launched into the sky, lapped the globe to assess the success of their mission. Plenty of gray auras of the dead remained, but none of the black that came from Kólasi's army. Gwyneira returned to the supernatural serenity of Africa.

::*We are done here*,:: Gwyneira declared.

Marisabel, the Champion of Death, opened her eyes; a picturesque scene of eerie peace replaced the nightmare. In the midst of the lustrous blue blaze was a patch of pink.

Scorched earth beneath, luscious color above, Marisabel nudged Gwyneira forward to investigate.

With her scaled snout, Gwyneira pushed lightly against the small thicket. Tiny thorns scratched at her impenetrable flesh.

::It's a raspberry bush,:: Marisabel declared once she had a clearer look.

::It smells delicious.::

::Strange that it has grown in the middle of a charred wasteland.::

::I am hungry.:: Gwyneira's voice held a sudden touch of desperation.

::But you just ate all those spirits.::

::I want more,:: she stated plainly, thoughts focused solely on the juicy red fruit glimmering in the blue light.

Unable to sway her conviction, and not terribly driven to, Marisabel tasted the fruit vicariously through Gwyneira as she devoured the bush in one bite.

The drakkina closed her eyes as she chewed the prickly thicket and tiny, juicy explosions popped throughout her massive mouth. After swallowing, she opened her eyes to find that another raspberry bush had grown in place of the other and waited to be ravished by her hunger.

She obliged, making the second bush vanish as quickly as the first.

Marisabel felt nauseous.

::*They taste rotten,*:: she expressed.

::*Are you mad? They taste divine!*::

Marisabel's spirit gagged. ::*I think it's poison.*::

::*Nonsense. This is the best snack ever.*:: She ate the third bush that materialized.

::*It's a trap,*:: Marisabel stated, panicked. ::*Nothing grows that quickly.*::

::*I have to tell my sisters.*::

::*There are more of you?*::

::*We normally feast on adoration, but something in these berries tastes even better. More nourishing, more satisfying. I must share this joy with them.*::

::*What about me?*:: Marisabel asked.

This question forced Gwyneira to pause her gluttonous consumption of the ever-returning fruit.

::*What do you wish for?*::

::*To be alive again.*::

::*But you always wished for death.*::

::*I am changed. I've never wanted to be alive more.*::

::*I see. I must warn you: Life will not feel the same as it did before. You are death now, and you will be forevermore.*::

::I don't care. I want to have my own body again. I want to find my sisters and hug them.::

Gwyneira eyed the fourth raspberry bush before caving. *::Whatever you want, dear Champion.::*

She tore the bush out of the ground and flew to Antarctica, consuming the berries along the way.

They found Marisabel's vacated body under a snow drift.

::This is the end,:: Gwyneira stated.

::Thank you for everything.::

::Anything for a fellow sister of death.:: Gwyneira's massive dragon face twisted with a smile. *::It is time to let go.::*

Marisabel released her hold of Gwyneira, and the drakkina breathed her spirit back into her lifeless body.

She awoke with a start, gasping for air as she came back to life.

"Can you do the same for Sofyla and Sahira?"

Gwyneira shook her head. *::A frozen body I can reanimate, but a severely damaged or decomposed body I cannot. Sofyla's is one with the earth now and I cannot reverse Sahira's head wound.::*

Marisabel nodded in understanding.

::Before I go,:: Gwyneira continued. *::What would you like me to do about the frozen Debauched in North America?::*

Marisabel hesitated, clutching gratefully to the returned sensation of life. If the Debauched felt how she did now upon

370

their resurrections, perhaps swaying them to switch loyalties might not be so tough.

"Let them live," she finally decided.

::As you wish.::

"I will miss you," Marisabel said, finding her voice again.

::We are bonded now; a piece of me will always live inside of you. I will always be with you,:: Gwyneira promised before launching into the icy air, releasing a voracious roar, and disappearing into the sheen of snow clouds.

More connected to death than ever, Marisabel transcended. Eyes stark white and body lifted into the air, she floated, able to travel wherever her deadened heart desired.

Chapter 40

Tier

"We are free," Marisabel announced in a monotone voice as she drifted through the sky, hanging limp as her body floated over the gathered Tierannites. Her dark hair had turned white, and her tan skin was now pale. A layer of ice coated her flesh, and her blue eyes were iced over.

Juniper looked up in horrified awe. "Marisabel … is that you?"

"I am the Champion of Death. Spirits of the fallen have carried me here."

"How are we free if the ghosts remain?" Elodie cut in.

"Kólasi's army is vanquished. I ride with souls lost long ago—long before the purge."

"This is great news," Juniper stated, still unsure how to feel about Marisabel's current condition. "Are *you* okay?"

"I am better than ever," she replied blankly. "I am happy to be alive."

Landon looked at his mother with an expression of disbelief. Juniper ignored his cynicism.

"I am happy you are back too," Juniper expressed. "Without you and the dragon, all would be lost."

"Gwyneira's arrival was a true gift," Marisabel agreed. "You also need not fear the Lamortes anymore—I killed the president."

Juniper's eyes lit up with hope. "Perhaps this is my chance to reverse the damage he caused and recruit his followers."

"I do suspect that is possible."

Juniper's mind spun around the idea.

Marisabel continued, "I must go. I must tell the others of our victory."

She glided higher, limbs dangling lifelessly as her body lifted above the trees and drifted away.

Juniper looked to her people, who wore haunted expressions.

"Are you sure she's alive?" Landon asked.

"She came as our ally," Juniper reminded him. "She's gone through some rough transitions."

"An afterlife spent tree-jumping suddenly seems desirable," Elodie noted. "In comparison."

"She isn't dead," Juniper reminded them. "She saved our lives. Let's not be so quick to cast judgment."

Her children surrendered, but held onto their doubtful thoughts.

Juniper climbed the heart, settling on one of its lower branches, and looked out at the crowd of Tierannites. The fresh water disciples vastly outnumbered those who came from the trees.

"I know that some of you speak English, others are learning, just as we are learning Spanish. One day, we will be able to communicate without complication." The group nodded in understanding. "We have lost much. Let us mourn together."

The group formed a circle around the heart and held hands. Juniper remained on her tree bough pulpit and spoke to her people with empathy and love.

"We have survived great horrors. We have triumphed when the odds were against us. Though we are grieving, we must not lose sight of our blessings. In this new world, good always prevails. Not without suffering, but in the end, the righteous win."

The group murmured in agreement.

Juniper continued, "Never forget this. We must keep our sights set for good, and we must teach our children to do the same." She pointed at the sky. "Gaia will not forsake us if our hearts remain pure."

The Tierannites cheered.

"We will establish a compassionate society with sovereigns who emulate our core beliefs. We will never forget that which has saved us: an unrivaled love for nature."

Elodie began to sing. She sang in a language no one recognized, one that stemmed from the depths of her connection to nature.

Her fellow Tierannites listened in awe.

The melody was enchanting, and the emotion she emitted was felt by the entire group. Tears welled in their eyes as they absorbed every note she sang.

At the crux of the song's climax, Elodie hit a high note, held it, then let her voice trickle down slowly. An older woman from Marisabel's following jumped into the song, singing at a lower octave and creating a lovely harmony. Three more women joined, and the song took on an entirely different energy.

From sorrow to unity, the emotion shifted. Elodie brushed her sandy blonde hair, revealing the rebellious tattoo of small stars she inked onto the rim of her ear, and smiled.

The women sang an enchanted, layered harmony that sounded otherworldly.

Juniper felt immensely grateful; her daughter was beginning to understand how to use her evolutionary gifts for good.

The trees began to sway in time with the song. Juniper placed her hand on the bough and transported into the tree.

Roscoe was there waiting.

Her spirit hugged his and together they enjoyed the music through the heart.

375

"It's beautiful, isn't it?" Roscoe stated.

Juniper listened more closely and realized that from this perspective, she could understand every word Elodie sang.

"I might never see you again,

when the end arrives, take shelter.

In my heart,

I will keep you safe forever.

The wrath of gods may swelter,

bringing fire and thunder together.

But with love,

I will protect you.

I might lose you,

to fates designed against us.

But in my heart,

we will always be together."

"She gets it," Juniper cried.

Roscoe nodded. *"I think she always has. It just took her a little longer to accept it. She finally came to me,"* he expressed with elation.

"She accepts our fated afterlives?"

"It seems so. When she almost lost you, it knocked a little sense into her."

Juniper sighed with relief. *"Let me go back to them."*

Roscoe kissed her bright green aura and then let her go.

Juniper held onto her tether, ready to ricochet back into her body, when the tension snapped.

Juniper's body turned ice cold and fell off the tree bough.

Landing with a thud, Elodie's beautiful song came to an abrupt end.

"Mom," Elodie cried, racing to her side. Jasper and Landon were quick to join her.

"What happened?" Jasper asked.

"She just fell!"

The Tiernan progenies fussed over their mother, feeling for a pulse and using all combinations of science and magic to revive her.

Clark hovered over Landon. "I can try CPR."

Landon moved aside to let Clark in, and when the old man got to his knees, ready to assist, Juniper's eyes shot open.

She sat up with a gasp.

The group stepped back.

"Mom, are you okay?" Jasper asked.

Juniper's head snapped in his direction. A look of confusion crossed her face before a forced smile took its place.

"Yes. Of course." She felt the pain of the fall. "I just lost my balance."

Her voice sounded odd.

"Why do you sound weird?" Landon asked.

Juniper placed a hand to her throat. "What do you mean?"

"You sound different." His face scrunched in contemplation.

"Perhaps the trauma of all the screaming I did in the forest is finally catching up with me. My throat does hurt a bit."

"Let's get her into her hammock so she can rest," Clark stated, breaking up the unexpected interrogation and helping Juniper stand. "You ought to be grateful she's okay," he barked at Landon.

Landon's expression shifted to defiance as he looked at his siblings. "She sounded weird to you too, right?"

"A little," Jasper said with a shrug.

"I'm so happy she's okay," Elodie expressed. "We can't lose her."

Juniper pounded at the walls of the heart.

"That isn't me!" she cried, but no one except Roscoe was listening.

Horrified, she reeled in her tether till she found it's end.

"How?" she fretted, terrified by the foreign dilemma. *"How did this happen?"*

"How is your body up and moving and communicating while your spirit is here?" Roscoe furthered the line of questioning.

"I've been hijacked," Juniper panicked. "Marisabel was wrong — the war isn't over yet."

Chapter 41

A week passed without rescue—Juniper remained a prisoner within the heart.

Roscoe never left her side. Still, she yearned to be set free.

"How is the imposter fooling them all?" she grieved.

"Landon isn't fooled," Roscoe promised. *"He will figure it out."*

"I wish I could talk to him, but he's so busy healing the scorched trees in the Vale of Night—I can't enter the dead trees, and none of them have channeled into a living tree since I fell."

"They will. Give it time."

The Tierannites shared in joyous conversation during breakfast, eating berry-nut stew and drinking mango juice. While everyone's eyes were fixed on each other, Landon's gaze was glued to his mother.

"Aren't you hungry?" he shouted out to her, shoving a fistful of granola in his mouth.

Juniper looked startled. "No, I'm fine."

"I haven't seen you eat since that fall," he said while chewing. "Maybe you're sick."

"No," she reiterated. "I'm fine."

"Leave her alone," Jasper said, nudging his younger brother. He then whispered, "You've been really hard on Mom lately."

"That isn't Mom."

Jasper was exasperated—they had this argument too many times before. "You still think she is possessed?"

Landon nodded, eyes still fixed on Juniper as he shoved another handful of food into his mouth. His gaze was unforgiving.

"How do we test your theory, then?" Jasper asked, drained and ready to squash Landon's obsessive doubts.

Landon's concentration broke as he considered the idea. Without responding, he stood and walked toward her. Jasper followed close behind.

"I haven't heard from Dad in a while. Have you?" he asked Juniper.

"I just saw him the other day," she replied.

"You did? Where?"

"Near the ocean."

"Near the ocean?" Landon asked, his tone scathing. "Did you two go for a swim?"

Juniper hesitated, her expression lost in thought. When she finally replied, her tone was harsh.

"Do you think you're funny?" she spat. "We met in the trees lining the shore."

Landon was forced to halt his interrogation momentarily, but when he resumed, he was onto a new plan of attack.

"Go with me to the Vale of Night," he requested. "We need to check on the aftermath of the fires."

"You want to walk all the way there?" she asked.

"Obviously not," he spat. "I want to tree hop with you."

"No. The trees there are fine. The forest fire was extinguished weeks ago and the regrowth has begun."

Landon grunted in annoyance.

"What is wrong with you?" she asked.

"Nothing," Landon stated before storming away.

Jasper stepped forward. "We lost a lot of people, many of them were his closest friends. I think he's having trouble grieving."

Juniper nodded. "We all handle death in different ways. He will learn to cope."

Though she said the right things, her voice felt empty.

For the first time, Jasper noticed the strange vacancy in her eyes.

"If something was wrong, you'd tell me, right?" he asked.

"Of course, my dear. You are my favorite." Her smile was sincere, but wicked.

Jasper grimaced in return, fully aware that his mother would *never* claim favorites. He left, afraid that she wasn't okay.

"I think she is severely concussed," Jasper announced upon reaching Landon in the Vale of Night.

Landon did not stop working. He lost track of how many trees he had touched, but he placed his palm on another and sent healing energy into the scorched trunk. Once complete, he opened his eyes and stared at Jasper.

"It's not a concussion, it's a possession. And I don't know how to help her."

Elodie came racing into the vale. "She just told the group that she wants greater comforts for us all."

"What does that mean?" Landon asked.

"She wants to build houses, roads—a town. She said tree huts are for monkeys."

Landon shot a knowing glare at Jasper.

"Okay, maybe you're right," Jasper finally conceded.

"How do we save her?" Elodie asked, her desperation apparent.

"We need Marisabel to come back," Landon suggested.

"We don't have access to speak with the other Champions," Elodie reminded him. "Only Mom can do that."

"Then what do you suggest?"

Jasper cut in, "Remember when we made our shields?"

"Yes ... " Landon replied.

"Remember what mine did? Perhaps such power would force the spirit out of Mom."

"What if your light kills her?" Elodie asked. "We saw how it burned Clark."

"I need to practice. If I can control the intensity of the blast, maybe I won't hurt her."

"Then practice," Landon urged. "I'm going to find Dad. He might know what we're up against."

"I'm going with you," Elodie insisted, chasing after Landon's quick leap into the burnt treetops.

They ran for miles to his favorite section of Tier: the Everlands—a cool, coniferous forest in the north. The wolves howled in greeting as they charged through. Landon found the secret nook he crafted years ago—the safe place he often escaped to after his father died—and climbed atop the piled logs. He pressed his bare chest against the evergreen and suddenly felt like a scared little boy again.

Dad, he called out. *I need you.*

I am always here.

Mom is in trouble.

I know, she is here with me.

Landon opened his eyes and waved Elodie over.

His sister climbed the massive arrangement of downed trees and pressed her cheek against the tree.

"Mom is already with Dad," he informed her.

"Is she dead?" Tears welled in Elodie's eyes.

Landon pursed his lips, fear rendering him silent.

Is she okay? he asked his father.

No. Her tether broke and she is trapped here. Whoever has inhabited her body is an imposter.

Yes, we figured that much out. Jasper is learning how to control the light he channels from Gaia so he can use it as a weapon.

Roscoe paused, his energy tense. *We have a tough decision to make.*

What do you mean?

We aren't sure how the tether works. It's broken and she is no longer tied to her body. She might die if her body is vacated.

Where is Mom? Landon asked. *What does she want us to do?*

She is so distraught, she is not thinking properly right now. She wants to eliminate the imposter, no matter the cost.

So we need to make a sound decision, for her, Elodie chimed in.

Yes, Roscoe replied.

We really need to reach Marisabel. She might know what to do.

As they planned to formulate a tactic to summon the Champion of Death, a blaring light illuminated the forest.

Looks like Jasper hasn't quite figured it out yet, Landon commented.

All the more reason to find an alternative, Elodie replied.

Jasper flew backwards into a torched maple tree. The impact knocked the breath out of him and his vision went black for a moment. When the blackout cleared, his mother was standing on the opposite side of the forest, staring at him unkindly.

"What are you doing?" she asked, her tone grave.

"I'm just practicing the magic Elodie taught me."

"Why?" Juniper demanded, stepping closer.

"Wouldn't it be good to have a weapon in case the Debauched attack again?"

"Why are you lying to me?" she screamed, charging toward him at full speed. In a blink, her hand was clutched around his throat and he was pinned to the maple tree.

"I'm not lying!" he insisted, struggling to breathe.

"The other boy got to you, didn't he?"

"Landon?"

The imposter shook Juniper's head. "You were my favorite."

She squeezed harder, choking the life out of Jasper.

Kill her, a voice resonated from the tree.

Mom? Jasper asked, overcome by emotion.

No one is safe while evilness possesses my body. You have to fix this.

I haven't mastered the light yet, he objected. *I might kill you too.*

You won't, she lied. *I am safe within the trees.*

Oxygen running thin and options running out, Jasper had no choice but to believe his mother. With great concentration, he used the last of his energy to muster the power of Gaia and blast Juniper's body with a surge of divine light.

She flew into the air, trembling as she hovered, then fell to the ground in a heap. The Vale of Night remained illuminated, revealing the spirit cast from Juniper's body.

It was a young girl with an ancient spirit. Her long brown curls draped over her shoulders and circles of death rested heavily beneath her eyes. The small ghost of a girl cackled into the dark sky.

"You lose either way!"

"Not if you're gone forever," Jasper growled through gritted teeth as he summoned a second surge and struck the girl where she hovered.

A sinister shriek echoed through the vale as the power of good shook the girl to her empty core. Her sullen eyes widened, and her pasty white skin glowed as she quivered, desperately fighting against her second death.

"How?" she objected. "I was *chosen* by Kólasi Himself."

"Gaia's gifts are stronger—they are rooted in love."

"I am His favorite."

"He loves no one but Himself," Jasper spat. "Be gone!"

He intensified the current streaming through her and cast the demonic child-ghost away.

Deliverance served, Bianca vanished from the realm of life and death.

Chapter 42

You did well, my son. You are a true soldier of light.

Jasper slowly opened his eyes to blurriness. His body rested against the roots of the maple tree, and across the forest, his mother's body lay motionless.

"Mom?" he mumbled.

She did not stir.

His heartrate quickened as he struggled to get to his feet.

One step, and he fell to his knees, weakened from the exertion. He felt helpless while his mother lay in peril mere feet from him.

Help, he shouted repeatedly into his mind.

An eternity in his aching body passed before the sound of running emerged. Jasper peered through heavy eyelids to see his siblings charging to his aid.

Jasper found the energy to cry.

"What happened?" Landon demanded, lifting Jasper's head carefully.

Jasper sobbed.

Elodie cradled Juniper's body in her arms. "She isn't breathing!"

Tears cascaded down Elodie's cheeks. She sang a song of life to her mother, but it did not bring back a pulse. For hours, she tried, singing louder through the tears and willing every bit of earthly charm into Juniper's limp body, but her gifts were not enough. She could not save her mother from this fate.

"She's gone," Elodie stated as the moon began to rise. Her desperation subsided and was replaced by defeat.

"You did all you could," Landon said in comfort.

"How is Jasper?"

"He passed out again, but I think he will be okay. He has bruises around his neck."

"Something terrible happened," Elodie shuddered.

Crunching twigs and rustling leaves came from the east, and when Clark emerged, panting out of breath, the canopy lit up with golden-green light.

"What is happening?" Elodie asked

"Your mother," he panted. "She wants to show you something."

Elodie looked down at her mother's lifeless body sprawled across her lap, then back up at Clark skeptically.

He went on, "I know, I don't get it either. But I learned a long time ago not to ask questions. Juniper is always right." He pointed at the supernatural glow. "C'mon. Let's go!"

Elodie lowered Juniper's body and then kissed her forehead. "We will come back for you," she promised, before following Clark through the woods. Landon lifted his older, yet smaller brother onto his back and carried him toward the heart.

When they arrived, the short oak tree was shrouded by golden light.

"She's in there," Misty stated in wonder as Elodie came to a stop beside her. "Go look."

With a slower pace, Elodie walked toward the golden opening in the tree. Landon and Jasper followed close behind.

Blinded by the glow of her aura, they could not see clearly until they crossed the threshold. Within the tree was a smaller tree—a curly-trunked Juniper tree.

Elodie, Landon, and Jasper stepped closer and placed their hands onto the swirling bark.

Mom? Elodie asked.

I am here, Juniper replied. *I will always be here, until the end of time.*

Her golden aura radiated through Jasper's body and the bruises around his neck disappeared. She had healed his body, but his heart still ached.

I am so sorry, Jasper grieved. *This is all my fault.*

You saved our people.

But I killed you.

You had no other choice, Juniper stated plainly. *I made you.*

Why?

I will always choose my children over myself.

The trio wept, unable to undo what had been done.

Do not cry for me. Be grateful that I am still here.

Elodie nodded. *And you're with Dad.*

An afterlife more perfect than this is impossible to conceive. They could feel her smile as she said this.

What now? Landon asked.

Juniper's energy swelled with pride.

We continue to protect everything we love.

Thank you for reading *Vale of Fire*—I hope you enjoyed the story! If you have a moment, please consider rating and reviewing it on Amazon and sharing your thoughts via social media. All feedback is greatly appreciated!

Amazon Author Account:
www.amazon.com/author/nicolineevans

Facebook:
www.facebook.com/nicoline.eva

Twitter:
www.twitter.com/nicolineevans

Instagram:
www.instagram.com/nicolinenovels

To learn more about my other novels, please visit my official author website:
www.nicolineevans.com

62283926R00230

Made in the USA
Middletown, DE
26 August 2019